Underneath he
starch, Katherine
courageous bundle of beauty.

Even when they clashed, Trey admired her moral fortitude and persistence. She'd triumphed over a scandalous childhood. She was, quite frankly, a woman worthy of his respect.

With the wind snapping tendrils of black hair from her confining hairstyle, she looked like an avenging angel sent to demand his reckoning.

It was always like this between them—volatile, unpredictable, confusing—more so over the last few months.

Alarm spread through him, the reaction shocking him. The corresponding ache in his gut warned him that he'd made a mistake challenging Miss Taylor this time.

"Relent...*Marshal*," she spoke.

The impossible had happened. Trey Scott, defender of justice, protector of women and children, had just suffered defeat. At the hands of a schoolmarm.

RENEE RYAN

Renee Ryan grew up in a small Florida beach town. To entertain herself during countless hours of "laying-out" she read all the classics. It wasn't until the summer between her sophomore and junior years at Florida State University that she read her first romance novel. Hooked from page one, she spent hours consuming one book after another while working on the best (and last!) tan of her life.

Two years later, armed with a degree in Economics and Religion, she explored various career opportunities, including stints at a Florida theme park, a modeling agency and a cosmetic conglomerate. She moved on to teach high school economics, American government and Latin while coaching award-winning cheerleading teams. Several years later, with an eclectic cast of characters swimming around in her head, she began seriously pursuing a writing career.

She lives with her husband, two children and one ornery cat in Georgia.

The MARSHAL TAKES A BRIDE

Renee Ryan

Steeple
Hill®

Published by Steeple Hill Books™

STEEPLE HILL BOOKS

Steeple
Hill®

Recycling programs
for this product may
not exist in your area.

ISBN-13: 978-0-373-82806-7
ISBN-10:   0-373-82806-3

THE MARSHAL TAKES A BRIDE

Copyright © 2009 by Renee Halverson

www.SteepleHill.com

Printed in U.S.A.

Avenge not yourselves, but rather give place unto wrath: for it is written, Vengeance is mine; I will repay, saith the Lord.

—*Romans* 12:19

To my critique partners, Cindy Kirk and Terry Hager. You have no idea how much I appreciate you both. And to my twin, Robin. Thank you for showing endless mercy and forgiveness to a sister who loves you dearly but fails you often. And to my mother, Elsie, who went home to the Lord before she had a chance to read this one. I miss you, Mom!

Chapter One

Denver, Colorado, June 1880

Cornered and nearly out of ideas, U.S. marshal Trey Scott refused to consider retreat. Not while he had a five-year-old little girl counting on him to triumph against the misery that assailed her. What had started as a mere game to the others was a matter of tragic proportions to the child.

Trey would *not* let her down.

Shivering, Molly Taylor pressed her tiny body closer to him. "You gotta save me, Mr. Trey."

Those big round eyes and that trembling lower lip punched through the last remnants of his resolve to remain neutral in this standoff. He would stick by the kid throughout this battle of hers.

Softening his expression, Trey knuckled a long black braid off her shoulder. "I won't let them get you, kitten. Just stay close."

He scooted Molly behind him, mutiny twisting in his gut. No one would stand in his way as he protected the girl from her dreaded fate. The troubled child deserved some peace and joy in her life.

"Leave this child alone." He fixed an uncompromising glare on the leader—a woman of uncompromising valor—and ignored the half dozen or so others crowding closer.

The pale-eyed, persistent female held firm against him in their battle of wills. Apparently, this was no game to her, either.

Trey widened his stance and folded his arms across his chest, settling into the standoff as though he had all the time in the world. He wrestled against the knot of regret tangling inside his anger. At one time, he'd considered this woman beautiful, godly—even fair-minded.

He'd woefully miscalculated.

At least Molly had *him* on her side. A swift glimpse to his left revealed an opening in the hedge that ran along the perimeter of the yard. Mentally, he measured the dimensions and came up victorious. The hole was the perfect size for a forty-pound slip of a girl to glide through to freedom. He'd catch up with her before she made it halfway down Larimer Street and long before she hit the bedlam of horse-drawn taxis on Tabor Block in the business district.

Comfortable with his plan, Trey inched across the grass, tugging Molly along with him.

The *boss* matched him step for step.

Shooting the woman a warning glare, Trey then turned to Molly and cocked his head toward the thicket. "You know what to do," he whispered.

Tears wiggled just below long, sooty lashes. "What if they catch me?"

He lowered his voice. "I'll create a diversion."

"What's that?" Molly asked in a whisper loud enough to be heard two counties over.

"Never mind. When I say run, you run."

But the leader—wrapped in that deceptively feminine package—pulled around to the left, effectively closing off the escape. "Don't even think about it."

At the end of his temper, Trey swallowed back a bitter retort.

As though hearing his unspoken words, inflexible blue eyes cut through the distance between them.

"The game is over…*Marshal,*" the woman said.

Although he had at least a hundred pounds on the stormy-eyed sprite, Trey had to stifle the shocking urge to withdraw. He'd stood up against cannons, gross injustice, crooked judges and vicious criminals, but nothing compared to the disapproval of Katherine Taylor—schoolmarm, official custodian of the Charity House trusts and Molly's overprotective sister.

With that inflexible look on her face, Trey knew he could no longer count on the fact that Miss Taylor would set aside her volatile feelings for him and be reasonable, for Molly's sake.

So be it.

He had to delay. Procrastinate. Postpone the inevitable. But how?

The late afternoon heat pulled sweat onto his brow. He'd lost his hat long before the battle had begun. A light breeze lifted the hair off the back of his neck, the comforting sensation mocking his inability to think straight.

He circled his gaze around the perimeter of the yard, taking note of the snowcapped mountains in the distance. *Too far away.* Growing a little more apprehensive and a lot less confident, he focused on the brick, two-story mansions running shoulder to shoulder for several blocks off to his right. *Too many questions*. As a last resort, Trey shot a quick glance past the manicured lawn and blooming flowers to the large, fancy home behind him. *Too risky*.

His only hope was to take the woman by surprise.

As covertly as possible, he inched toward the hedge, but an irreverent growl wafted on a cloud of threat. A quick look to his right and Trey's gaze connected with two more villains joining the foe's ranks. Shifting to face these newest threats, he snarled at the man he'd once called friend and the woman who co-owned the Charity House orphanage with him. "Marc and Laney Dupree, this is *not* your fight."

A grin slid between the two. "It is now," Marc said for them both.

As one, they glanced to Katherine, then separated, covering the gaps she'd left when she'd moved in front of the hedge.

Blowing out a hiss, Trey lowered his head to Molly's. "Don't worry, kitten. I have everything under control."

Various snorts and snickers cut through his words as more joined the enemy's ranks. Katherine spoke for the group. "Just hand her over, and no one will get hurt."

Wrapping all four feet of trembling little girl in his arms, Trey darted a quick glance to the house in front of him. "Not a chance."

"This is ridiculous. Surrender the child, now." Katherine spoke in a flat, no-nonsense tone that made him bristle.

Marc took two steps closer. "Enough, Trey. Hand her over."

Trey eyed his friend turned traitor. Clean-shaven, dressed

in a fancy vest and matching tie, Marc Dupree didn't look much like the tough, hardened man Trey had once known, a man who had overcome poverty and…worse. In fact, with the sun winking off the dangling watch fob, Marc looked more like a dandy than a threatening opponent.

But Trey knew the man had hidden skills. Came from living with that wily, unpredictable wife of his, the same woman who was now conspiring openly with the enemy in this standoff.

"All right, Molly," Trey whispered in her ear. "We're going to make a run for it."

Another low whimper slipped from her lips. "But, Mr. Trey, I'm not fast."

He folded her deeper into his embrace. "Don't worry. I'll carry you."

She wrapped her spider-thin arms around his neck, nodding her head against his chest.

Shifting her to a more comfortable position, he studied the biggest threat to the child. Her sister.

Just looking at the woman made his throat ache. Underneath all that prim schoolteacher starch, Katherine Taylor was a lovely, courageous bundle of feminine charm and beauty. Even amidst this contest of wills, Trey found a part of him admiring her moral fortitude and persistence. She'd triumphed over a scandalous childhood and the unspeakable violence committed against her. She was, quite frankly, a woman worthy of his respect.

Then again…

With the wind snapping tendrils of black hair free from that hideously confining hairstyle, she looked a lot like an avenging angel sent to demand his reckoning.

It was always like this between them—volatile, unpredictable, confusing—more so over the past few months.

Alarm spread through him, the physical reaction shocking him. The corresponding ache in his gut warned him that he'd made a mistake challenging Miss Taylor on this matter.

Seeking compassion, Trey pivoted to his right. But another glare of disapproval angled back at him. Carrying thirty or so extra pounds and a rounded belly, Laney O'Connor Dupree was just as relentless as Katherine.

"No way out yet, Molly. The flanks are too formidable for a quick escape."

"Don't let them get me," Molly wailed.

"Don't you worry. I'm a United States marshal. They wouldn't dare take me on."

The scoffing and giggles coming from the crowd behind Katherine didn't seem to fill the little girl with confidence. "They don't sound very worried."

"They are. They just don't know it yet."

Balancing on the balls of his feet, Trey tucked Molly firmly in the crook of his arm. Leading with his shoulder, he charged through the front line. With the element of surprise on his side, he knocked his big, overdressed friend back a few yards.

Marc recovered quickly, and while Trey battled with his childhood friend, two pairs of persistent hands worked from behind to wrestle Molly free.

She kicked and squealed. "No, I don't want to go!"

Trey ground his teeth together and dug his heels into the ground.

"Relent…*Marshal*," said Katherine.

Trey pressed Molly tighter against his chest.

"You've taken this too far already," Marc said.

Trey dodged a flying elbow. He spun to his right but slipped, dropping to his knees. Next thing he knew, Molly was wrested out of his grip, and he was lying flat on his back.

The impossible had happened. Trey Scott, defender of justice, protector of women and children, had just suffered defeat. At the hands of a schoolmarm, a dandy and a pregnant woman.

"Attack," yelled the fancy man.

High-pitched squeals lifted into the air.

"And, this time, finish him off."

In a blur, seven children jumped on him, fingers jabbing in his ribs and stomach. Trey clamped his teeth together. "I'm not ticklish."

Undaunted, fourteen miniature hands worked quicker.

Trey finally let out a hoot of laughter. He rose to his knees, just in time to see Molly ushered up the back stairs, caught in the clutches of her relentless big sister. "Mr. Trey," she yelled, "save me."

She reached her thin arms out to him.

Trey hopped to his feet and then darted toward the back porch, but he was held back by the Charity House orphans. One by one, he peeled away hands and feet. A particularly persistent little boy rode on his leg, clutching with the grip of a full-grown man. It took considerable maneuvering to release the kid without hurting him. Trey could use such a man on his side. He nearly considered swearing the boy in as a deputy.

Too bad the brute was only eight years old.

"Mr. Tre-e-e-e-ey…"

Trey raced up the back stairs, then shot in front of the door, barring entrance with his hulking frame.

He looked from one woman to the other. "Laney Dupree and Katherine Taylor, I'll not stand by and watch you degrade this child."

Katherine narrowed her eyes, depositing every bit of the formidable schoolteacher in her expression. "A bath is not degrading."

Trey dropped his gaze to Molly, and his gut twisted. She looked so sad and pitiful with her lower lip trembling. "It can't wait until tomorrow?" he asked.

Katherine pulled her lips into a tight knot of disapproval.

Sensing a stalemate, he appealed to the wisdom of the group. "Laney, do something."

Marc's wife shook her finger at him as though he was the one who'd committed a terrible wrong. "I'm going to have to agree with Katherine. The child needs a bath."

"No," Molly cried. She twisted out of her sister's grip, rushed to Trey and hooked her hand in his. "Mr. Trey says I don't have to if I don't wanna."

Laney chuckled, instantly sobering when Katherine leveled a glare on her.

Sighing, Katherine spun back to look at Molly, the first signs of frustration flushing in her cheeks. With fists planted firmly on her hips, she said, "A bath is not going to kill you, young lady. Just look at you. Not a clean spot to be found."

In a gesture identical to her sister's, Molly jammed her balled fists on her hips. "We was playing marshals and bank robbers with the other Charity House kids."

"And losing, from the sight of you," declared Katherine.

Trey took exception.

"We were just letting them win." He winked at the little girl. "Isn't that right, Molly?"

She favored him with a big gap-toothed grin. "*Right.* We can't never, not ever, let them stinkin' outlaws get the best of us."

Katherine gasped. "Did you teach her that?"

Trey had the presence of mind to cast his gaze to the sky before he responded. "Maybe."

Marc joined them on the porch, turning into the voice of reason. "It's over, Trey."

Trey looked from Katherine to Marc to Laney, then back to Katherine again. Ignoring the satisfied expressions on the faces of the three other adults, he crouched down to the five-year-old little girl's level. Plucking at one of Molly's braids, he said, "Sorry, kitten. Looks like you're taking that bath today."

Her eyelashes fluttered, and one fat tear rolled down her cheek.

Before he gave in to the pleading look, Trey squeezed his eyes shut, rose and shifted out of the way. He opened his lids in time for Katherine to link her disapproving gaze with his. "Stick around…*Marshal.* I'm not through with you."

With that, she spun around and marched inside the house, Molly in tow.

Laney poked him in the chest. "You just made a big mistake, my friend. *Big* mistake."

Chapter Two

With her resolve firmly in place, Katherine marched up the back stairs of the twenty-year-old mansion turned orphanage, tugging a reluctant little girl along with her. The moment her gaze landed on Molly's tear-streaked face, Katherine's determination turned into heart-wrenching guilt.

By engaging in that senseless battle with Marshal Scott, she'd hurt the very person she'd set out to protect.

What kind of big sister did that make her? Usually, she turned to God to help her with the overwhelming task of raising her newfound sister.

Today she'd allowed emotion to get the best of her.

Sighing, she caressed Molly's hair and steered her into the recently refurbished bathroom, where Marc had installed multiple basins for the home's many children to wash up for the evening. On the outside, Charity House looked identical to the rest of the fancy homes on Larimer Street. But inside, the mansion had been perfectly altered to house forty special children and the adults who cared for them.

"Come on, Moll." Katherine clicked the door shut behind them. "Let's get you out of those filthy clothes."

Molly crossed her tiny arms over her chest. "I was having fun, Katherine."

Inhaling a deep, calming breath, Katherine knelt on the floor and cupped the child's cheek. "I know you were. And you can go back outside—"

Molly darted away from the claw-foot tub, but Katherine caught her by the sleeve. "*After* we get you cleaned up."

"But Mr. Trey said playtime was more important than a bath."

"I just bet he did." Frustration speared Katherine's previous remorse into something deeper, darker. Uglier…

Take captive every thought and make it obedient to Christ.

Katherine swallowed back her rising annoyance and forced her voice into an even tone. "Let's leave Marshal Scott out of this for now."

Molly scrunched her face into a frown, her expression reminiscent of one Katherine had seen in her own mirror often enough before she'd made peace with her past, the same one permanently stuck on their mother's face every day before she'd finally succumbed to tuberculosis.

"Don't you like Mr. Trey?" Molly asked.

Katherine's throat tightened. Her feelings for the U.S. marshal could never be classified as something so benign as "like." Explosive, precarious, frightening—those were far better descriptions for the disturbing emotions the man brought out in her.

She closed her eyes and took a deep breath.

Perhaps he'd had good intentions at first. But there was no question in her mind that Marshal Scott was a difficult man, with his own personal demons to battle. Katherine knew, to devastating ends, what such a man was capable of doing when a woman let down her guard. She absently touched the top button of her blouse, made sure it was fastened.

Truth be told, Trey Scott was too dangerous. Too bold. Too *everything* to trust. He simply had to go. Especially now that God had given Katherine the gift of finding the little sister she hadn't known existed until six months ago.

Straightening her shoulders, Katherine turned her attention back to Molly. "Let's get you into the tub, pumpkin."

Molly arranged her face in an expression identical to the one Trey had leveled on her just moments ago on the back porch. "Don't wanna."

Katherine was long past being amused. "Well, sometimes we have to do things we don't want."

"That's not fair to me."

"Life's not fair," Katherine said, with a sigh.

A heart-wrenching sob flew out of Molly. "I wish you'd never come for me. I *hate* you."

Holding back a sob of her own, Katherine prayed for the right words to ease Molly's resentment. The set of the child's jaw was so similar to the look on her face the day Katherine had found her in that bleak mining camp, with only a threadbare blanket on a dirt floor as her bed. The child had been so quiet, so…alone and scared, having been left to fend for herself after her father's fatal accident in the mine.

Katherine pushed a lock of hair off her sister's forehead, praying she could offer her sister a good life here at Charity House. "I know you think you hate me now, but I'll always love you, Molly. You're my sister."

The five-year-old responded with a hiccuping sigh.

To keep from speaking out in anger, Katherine bit

down on her lower lip. The realization that her sister blamed her for what had happened today wounded her far more than the child's hurtful words. Before Trey Scott had entered their lives, Molly had never openly challenged her authority.

As though sensing her misery, Laney chose that moment to duck her head into the room. "Want me to take over?"

Katherine peered at her friend. The sympathy she saw staring back at her clogged the air in her throat, reminding her of the dark night when Laney had wrapped Katherine in her arms and held her until the tears had eventually stopped flowing.

Her friend had made things easier for Katherine then, and she wished she could give in to the offer of help now. "I have to do this myself."

Angling her head to the side, Laney looked at Molly's mutinous expression. "Are you sure?"

Katherine focused on her little sister. The childish rebellion brewing in her gaze warned Katherine the fight wasn't over yet. Perhaps taking a moment to strengthen her resolve would do them both some good.

"Molly, I'm going to step in the hall with Laney for a few minutes. When I return, I want to see you completely undressed and sitting in that tub."

The little girl opened her mouth to protest.

Katherine stopped her with a warning look.

The angry child paused, made a face and then stomped her foot. Hard.

"Molly. Grace. Taylor. That's enough. Get undressed, *now*," ordered Katherine.

Two scrawny shoulders hunched forward, and tears began pouring down the dirt-smudged cheeks. Sniffing loudly between sobs, Molly plopped onto the floor and started tugging off her shoes.

Katherine winced at the pitiful sight her sister made, but she wouldn't give in to the tantrum. Molly needed to learn respect for the new life she had at Charity House. How could Katherine explain to the child just how blessed they were to be living at the orphanage, instead of above some filthy saloon? Or worse.

With unshed tears burning in her own eyes, Katherine motioned Laney into the long hallway that led to five bedrooms and a sitting chamber, then shut the door behind them.

As Katherine turned to look at her ally, her heart swelled with renewed gratitude for Laney's kindness. The woman had virtually saved Katherine from the life that could have been her legacy as the daughter of the most notorious madam in town.

She opened her mouth to speak but Laney beat her to it. "That is one upset little girl in there. Are you sure you don't want me to help you?"

Katherine shook her head. "Molly and I are still trying to get used to one another. I have to put an end to this blatant disobedience, before it goes any further."

"I understand." Laney headed toward the stairs, then stopped and looked back over her shoulder. "If you change your mind, I'll be in the kitchen, helping Mrs. Smythe with supper."

"Laney, wait."

She pivoted around, her eyebrows lifting in inquiry. "Yes?"

While trying to gather her swirling thoughts, Katherine studied her friend. Even at eight months pregnant, her thick mahogany hair and creamy skin glowed with good health. Inside that beautiful exterior, Laney O'Connor Dupree carried a fiercely loyal heart. And Katherine never took that blessing for granted.

"Thanks for—" Katherine cocked her head toward the back of the house "—taking my side out there today."

Laney's amber eyes crinkled at the corners. "Think nothing of it. Trey may be Marc's family, but in all the ways that count you're mine."

Katherine didn't have the words to express her love for this woman, her sister in the faith. She had given Katherine far more than a home on that horrible night two years ago. Her friend had given her an opportunity to start over and had provided a place in the world where Katherine could exist without shame. "I…well, I just want to say thank you for supporting me."

"Always." Laney regarded her with a kind, patient look. "And we both know it goes both ways. I wouldn't have Charity House if it weren't for your help."

Year-old memories pushed to the front of Katherine's mind. Laney had nearly lost Charity House to a shady banker when he'd called in the loan six months earlier than the agreed-upon date.

Yet Katherine had never blamed her friend for her rash actions in trying to save their home. How could she? Laney had given her a safe haven when she'd been attacked by one of her mother's former customers. Even when the townspeople had blamed her, rather than the man who had forced himself on her, Laney had taken Katherine in and had given her a job—one that had allowed her to give back to Charity House.

Katherine might be tainted forever, but God had blessed

her. By being given Laney and the Charity House orphans, Katherine had learned she was not without worth. Thus, it was with a cheerful heart that she had helped her friend raise the money needed to save the orphanage. In the process, the other woman had found the love of her life in Marc, and because of his help, they all still had a home.

"Even if you had lost Charity House, I'd have never blamed you, Laney. You helped save my life, you—"

The sound of hiccuping sobs cut her off.

"This isn't the time to look backward." Her friend slid a glance toward the closed bathroom door. "Right now, you need to focus on your sister."

"You're absolutely correct."

Laney squeezed her shoulder. "Hold firm, Katherine. Remember who's in charge."

"Yes. Yes, I will."

Oh, heavenly Father, please give me the wisdom and strength to face this challenge. Make me a good sister to Molly.

With renewed strength, Katherine turned the doorknob. No matter what else happened today, big sister *would* prevail over little sister. And once she was finished with Molly, she'd turn her attention to a United States marshal who thought he could disrupt her orderly life by pitting one Taylor female against the other.

There was a lesson to be learned here today. And Trey Scott was going to learn it.

Still stinging from his unprecedented defeat, Trey stared out the window of Marc's study, where he'd spent plenty of hours whenever his duties brought him to Denver. The former prairie town had grown since Trey first pinned on

a badge, becoming a city that lured people with its promises of riches and opportunity. Unless, of course, the one
seeking said opportunity was a five-year-old child with a
rigid schoolmarm for a big sister.

Feeling his temper rising, Trey inhaled a slow breath
and slid his glance along the rooftops peppering the nearby
horizon. It struck him as somehow fitting and yet also
ironic that a home for orphans sat in the middle of a
neighborhood designed for the supremely wealthy. A few
of the snobbier neighbors still filed complaints, always unfounded and *always* thrown out of court. In the end Charity
House was here to stay.

Although Marc had always made him welcome here,
Trey's trips had gotten decidedly less restful since Katherine Taylor had taken on the role of zealous protector to her
troubled little sister.

As he watched the Charity House orphans play a game
of tag in the backyard, dark, angry thoughts formed into
one bitter reality. He'd failed little Molly Taylor.

"You through brooding yet?"

Trey spun around and nailed Marc with a hard glare.

"Blast you, your wife and that woman she put in charge
of the Charity House School." He slashed his hand in the
direction of the window, unwilling to dig deeper into the
reasons for his dark mood. "After everything that child's
been through, she should be playing."

Hitching a hip onto his oak desk, Marc considered Trey
for a long moment. "Perhaps. But one bath does not make
an unhappy child. I think she'll survive the disappointment."

Trey paced to the opposite end of the room. Leaning
against the mantel, he dug his toe at the stones in the

hearth. "What possessed that woman to turn a bath into grounds for war?"

Lifting an ironic eyebrow, Marc angled his head. "I think she had some help."

"The poor girl just wanted to stay outside and play with the other children."

"Katherine is pretty rigid about schedules."

Trey made a face. "Boards are more pliant."

Obviously finding some dark humor in the situation, Marc chuckled. "You realize, don't you, that you're in for it now? Katherine won't let this one drop."

Trey was well aware that the prissy schoolmarm was gunning for him. In the cold aftermath of their battle, he actually relished the ensuing confrontation. It was long past time he set the woman straight on a few things, like the value of putting the priorities of a five-year-old child ahead of an unreasonable schedule.

After striding back across the room, Trey sank into a dark blue wing chair opposite his friend. The smell of rich mahogany paneling did nothing to soothe his temper. A vision of Katherine Taylor in the role of avenging big sister scooted frustration deeper. For well over a year now, ever since Marc had married Laney, Trey had found himself on the opposing side of every argument with the schoolmarm. It had only gotten worse with Molly's arrival.

Scrubbing a hand down his face, he said, "I don't understand why that woman treats me like I'm evil incarnate."

"I'd say you give her good reason."

Trey opened his mouth to deny his friend's accusation but shut it without speaking. Looking back, he realized that in his misguided attempt to defend the girl, Molly had ended up hurt.

Guilt gnawed at him, making him jerk out of his chair and start pacing again. Quite frankly, now that the emotion of the moment was gone, he was ashamed of how he'd behaved today.

"Why'd you take it so far, Trey?"

Ah, the real question at hand, and one he couldn't fully explain. "Something about Molly gets to me. Has ever since her sister brought her to live at Charity House with all of you."

"Granted, no child should have to lose both her mother and father at such a young age, or suffer the ridicule of her mother's profession. But there are forty other…*orphans* in this home with similar stories. Why Molly?"

Trey stopped, turned and then dropped slowly into the chair he'd occupied earlier. "I can't explain it."

Marc kept his gaze focused and direct, looking at Trey with a quiet intensity that warned him he wouldn't like what was coming next. "Why do I get the sense that your dedication to Molly has to do with your need to avenge the loss of your wife and child?"

Caught off guard by the unwanted reminder of his dead wife and the baby she'd carried, Trey clenched his fist. "You're wrong."

"Am I? Everything you do is about your quest for vengeance. Let's see. How old would your child be now? About Molly's age?"

Bitterness nearly choked him, the emotion so strong, Trey hadn't realized how deep it ran until this moment. But now that the subject was broached, he couldn't let it pass. "You know I can't stand by passively and allow Ike Hayes to run free. His killing has to stop. No matter what it takes."

Marc leaned forward, a perceptive look blazing in his eyes. "And because he murdered your wife and unborn child, you're now the God-appointed agent for justice, is that it?"

Trey swallowed an angry retort. As far as he was concerned, God had nothing to do with his quest. "I *will* take Ike down."

"It won't bring Laurette or your baby back."

Trey squeezed his eyes shut. "I know that."

How many nights had he lain awake, alone? Always alone, always grieving. Only for a few brief moments, when he was championing little Molly Taylor, had he felt a little less empty. It wasn't something he could put into words. It just…*was.*

As if his friend could read the direction of Trey's thoughts, he said, "Well, singling out Molly won't bring her parents back, either."

Trey struggled to find his breath, his control. His reasoning. "I can't explain how I know this, but Molly needs me more than the others do. And for the first time since I failed Laurette, the fact that another human being requires my protection doesn't scare me half to death."

Leaning back in his chair, his friend steepled his fingers under his chin. "Want to know what I think?"

"No."

Marc continued as though Trey hadn't spoken. "I think it's time you moved past this poisonous need for vengeance. Start over. Begin a family of your own."

Rebellion swept through him, and Trey had to swallow the fresh agony rising out of his grief. He couldn't start over. Not yet. *Not ever.* The memory of his wife and unborn child deserved his total devotion, his complete concentration. And until Ike Hayes was made to pay for murdering Trey's family, there could be no talk of starting over. "It's too soon."

"It's been four years."

Trey grimaced. Had it been that long since he'd held his wife in his arms, since he'd smelled the fresh scent of her hair? Four years since the soft lilt of her laughter filled his home? "I still miss her."

"Me, too." Marc's face softened, and Trey knew his friend was remembering his sister, the one he'd entrusted to Trey's care. The one Trey had failed.

"No one can replace Laurette," Trey said, his voice thick with familiar emotion. "She was sweet, innocent, compassionate. Gentle, through and through."

"Careful, Trey. Don't rewrite history with the prejudice of your guilt. As her big brother, I agree that Laurette was special. But she was human, too, a woman with flaws."

"I don't remember any."

"Maybe you should."

Trey's chest ached too much to respond. Even after four years, he couldn't think of his wife without his mind filling with the image of the last time he'd held her in his arms, pregnant and dying from a bullet that should have found him.

At Laurette's funeral, several members of his church had spoken of God's will. They'd told him Laurette was in a better place, free from the pain and sorrow of this world.

Trey hadn't believed their words for a minute. He would *never* accept that his wife's senseless murder was part of some divine plan for his own life. And with every additional murder he had to investigate, the chasm between him and God widened.

Settling his head into the cushioned softness of the chair, he tried desperately to free his mind of the painful memories. But intense longing for what he could never have again tightened in his throat. The ugly role he'd played in Laurette's death waged a battle inside him, choking the breath out of him. "If only I had been there to protect her and the baby she carried, maybe then—"

He broke off, unable to put into words the self-condemnation that haunted him still.

As though sensing his inability to continue, Marc changed the subject. "How long will you be in Denver this time?"

Thankful for the reprieve, Trey lifted his head and focused his thoughts on the present. "At least a month, maybe two. I don't plan to leave until the trial is over."

"You think you'll get a conviction?"

Uncompromising resolve spread through him. A month ago, Trey had caught Ike's younger brother, Drew, and had brought him in for trial. With one Hayes in custody, it was only a matter of time before Trey captured the other.

"I'll get the conviction *and* I'll find Ike," he said. Laurette deserved nothing less from him. "They don't call me 'Beelzebub's cousin' for nothing."

Marc's lips twitched. "Oh, you're dangerous—except when you're up against a ferocious schoolteacher."

"I can handle Molly's big sister."

"Like you did today?" Marc's expression was too innocent, deceptively so.

Trey ground his teeth together and dug his heels into the rug. "Yeah, well, she got lucky."

As if she'd planned her entrance for effect, the object of their discussion marched into the room, arms wrapped around her waist. Her glare pinned Trey in his chair.

Well, now. If that's the way she wanted to play it. His earlier feelings of shame at sparring with this woman instantly disappeared. Perhaps it was time to put Miss Rigid-Rule-Setter on the defensive for a change.

With deliberate slowness, he took in her appearance, concentrating on the streaks of dirt on her cheek, the smudges on her once-crisp white blouse.

So Molly had fought to the end.

Good girl.

As he linked his gaze with Katherine's again, he noted the sudden flicker of uncertainty flashing in her eyes before she covered it with her usual prissy determination.

Interesting.

She squared her shoulders. "I'd like that word with you, Marshal Scott. *Now.*"

Trey didn't like her attitude, nor was he overly fond of the riot of emotion spinning in his gut. "I'm not in the mood for a discussion."

"Perfect, because I plan to do all the talking."

Marc rose and slapped Trey on the knee. "Go get her, *Beelzebub's cousin.*"

Chapter Three

By the time Marc left the study, Katherine's frustration threatened to steal the remaining scraps of her composure. Trey Scott, with his challenging stare and unyielding presence, didn't help matters. He looked too masculine, too intimidating for someone who had just championed a five-year-old over a bath.

With the arrogance only a lawman could pull off, he lifted a single eyebrow, relaxed back into his chair then propped a foot on his knee. "So talk."

His attitude made Katherine forget all the reasons why this big, hard man alarmed her. "Marshal Scott, you are a disreputable, ill-mannered disturber of the peace."

There. Very pleasant under the circumstances.

He returned his foot to the floor, then leaned forward to rest his elbows on his knees. "Don't hold back, Miss Taylor. Tell me how you really feel."

His gray eyes regarded her without a sliver of amusement, while the rich Southern drawl rumbled across her tight nerves.

"Oh, I've only just begun," she said, allowing her growing resentment to take hold. She found it much easier to deal with the large, dangerous lawman when she thought of him as nothing more than a disruptive troublemaker.

Unraveling his hulking frame from the chair, he rose and began striding toward her. "By all means, go ahead and give it to me."

Guard what has been entrusted to your care....

The Scripture from 1 Timothy gave her the courage to hold her ground as he approached. For Molly's sake, she had to stand firm. "Stay away from my sister."

Thankfully, her words stopped his pursuit, and two matching black brows slammed together. "Why? What is it you have against me?"

Katherine ignored the twist of unease in her stomach and concentrated on an image of Molly's tearstained cheeks. "Must you ask after your behavior this afternoon?"

"I didn't work alone out there." He pulled his lips into a sarcastic grin. "Or don't you remember that part?"

Swamped with regret over her own role in Molly's distress, Katherine slapped her hands onto her hips. "Molly has been through too much trauma already. When our mother became ill, instead of contacting me, she sent the poor child to live with her father in a remote mining camp. From all accounts, he did his best, but he still died in an accident, which left Molly all alone."

A wave of regret pressed inside her chest. Katherine hadn't even known of Molly's existence until the letter from the mine's foreman had arrived at Charity House. Why her mother hadn't told her about her baby sister was a mystery that would never be solved. And by the time

Katherine had rescued Molly from the mining camp, the little girl had been on her own for two weeks.

After all her losses, will the child ever believe I'm here to stay?

Katherine shoved the worry aside. If Marshal Scott kept undermining her efforts, it would only destroy the fragile bond she had with Molly. "I don't want my sister hurt further."

Genuine shock rippled across his features. "You think I'd intentionally harm that child?"

Surprised by his vehemence, Katherine shook her head. "Not intentionally, no. But singling her out from the rest of the children will only make her feel different from the group."

"Don't you think you're being a bit overprotective?" He crossed his arms over his chest. "Molly is too timid, too closed off from the others for a normal five-year-old. The child needs shaking up."

Katherine didn't like how he summed up her sister's problem so accurately, nor did she trust the look of genuine distress she saw in his eyes. Finding common ground with this man, especially where her sister was concerned, brought matters to a dangerously personal level. And that simply would not do.

She had to remember he was her adversary. "And you're the man to do the shaking up, is that it?"

He lifted a shoulder. "Why not me?"

Oh, she could give him several reasons, but she focused on the main one. "You treat her like a toy you can play with whenever the mood strikes, and then off you go, back to your…*marshaling*."

"You mean off I go, *pursuing* men who kill innocent women and children."

And therein lay the real issue between them. Trey Scott's drive for vengeance was in direct conflict with Katherine's need to forgive, even—no, especially—the unforgivable.

"Your actions send the wrong message," she said. "They teach her that it's acceptable to trust in her own power instead of relying on God's."

He gave her a mutinous expression. "Maybe that wouldn't be such a bad lesson."

"I don't want her to think revenge is the answer. Because of her circumstances, it would be too easy for her to hate. I want her to learn God's healing power of forgiveness." Katherine knew better than most just how hard that lesson was to learn, but she also knew the peace that came with offering absolution where it wasn't deserved.

"There is *no* forgiveness for senseless murder and violence," he said. His expression hardened as he spoke, but not before Katherine caught a glimpse of real pain just below the surface.

In that moment, she realized he would never understand her point, not with his own grief still so raw. Overwhelmed with emotion and consumed with compassion for his terrible loss, Katherine reached out and touched his arm. "What happened to your wife was horrendous. If only you could learn to let God—"

He jerked away from her and strode to the window. "This isn't about me."

"Yes, it is. At least, partly."

He paced to the desk on the opposite end of the room but didn't meet her gaze. "How do you figure that?"

"Ever since Marc married Laney, you've been coming around here a lot." She lifted her chin at him. "Of course, you would. In fact, I think you should. You're Marc's brother-in-law. Nevertheless, I won't stand by and watch you give my sister the wrong message every time you go after another outlaw for your own personal reasons."

He clenched his hand into a fist. "You know nothing about what drives me."

"Oh, but I do."

He locked his gaze with hers and studied her with his hawklike eyes. The day-old growth of stubble on his jaw added a sinister look to his already hardened expression.

Katherine swallowed her own trepidation and dropped her gaze to the tin star pinned to his shirt. "Try to understand, I don't want Molly to suffer another loss. Even if I were able to put aside the reasons *why* you hunt those criminals, one day you will leave and never come back. And the fonder she is of you, the more it will hurt."

His eyes turned sad, haunted. "One day we all leave and never come back."

She knew he was still thinking of his wife. "That's not what I meant."

His expression cleared into a blank, unreadable glare. "You certainly seem to know a lot about what you *don't* mean."

Struggling for control, Katherine whirled away. How could she explain the pain she had suffered as a child and subsequently as an adult without baring her soul? He wasn't the only one who'd known suffering.

When she was Molly's age, her own father had died a dedicated lawman, killed by an outlaw's bullet. He'd left his family penniless, and as a result, Katherine's mother had looked to a life of prostitution for her answers. Even after Sadie Taylor's death, men still came looking for the infamous madam. Two years ago, one mean-spirited ranch hand had found Katherine instead.

In a rational moment, she knew linking her attack back to her father's murder was defective thinking at best. However, she couldn't deny that her father's death had been the first in a long line of other tragedies in her life.

"Men who wear badges die. That is—" She broke off, swallowed. "Just stay away from Molly."

He pushed away from the desk, his gaze dark and serious.

She fought the urge to turn tail and run. "I'm warning you…"

He halted several feet in front of her and waited for her to finish her threat.

As the silence grew heavy between them, Katherine's heartbeat picked up speed, and she dropped her gaze to her toes. "Please, Marshal Scott, don't champion my sister anymore."

She hated the desperation in her voice. But now that she had Molly with her, all Katherine wanted for them both was a safe, orderly life that honored God.

Why was that so hard for him to understand?

He closed the distance between them until he was towering over her. "Look at me, Miss Taylor."

Katherine jerked her gaze back to his. The sight of his inky-black hair, day-old growth of beard and fierce gray eyes sent a wave of fear through her.

"You're standing too close," she whispered.

"Is this really about Molly?" he asked as his hard, callused hand closed over hers.

His touch was surprisingly gentle. And…and…*terrifying.* She yanked her hand free, flinched two full steps back when he tried to touch her again.

"Of course it's about Molly," she said.

"You don't think it's about you? Me? Us?" He took a slow, careful step in her direction. "And the antagonism you have toward me?"

"Please." A shudder shot through her. "D-d-don't come any closer." She had to squeeze her hands together to keep them from trembling.

He froze in midstep, dropped his gaze to her clasped fingers and then quickly moved away from her. "I'm sorry, Miss Taylor. I wasn't thinking. I didn't mean to frighten you. That was never my intention."

Why was it always like this between them? Why couldn't she simply talk to Marshal Scott like a reasonable, well-adjusted woman spoke with a friend? Why did she have to be such a coward around him?

Frustration at him, fury at her own fears, and disappointment at them *both* made her voice come out harsher than usual. "I…I know you didn't mean any harm," she said.

He pulled a deep, audible breath into his lungs. "Regardless, I only wanted to—"

"Mr. Trey, Mr. Trey, you gotta come see." Molly chose that moment to skip into the room. "Laney's talking bird said my name. Twice. He—"

As though sensing the tension in the room, she broke off and shifted her large, rounded gaze from Trey to Katherine and back to Trey again. "You wanna come see?"

Molly's devoted expression reminded Katherine just why this man was so dangerous. He held too much power over them both. In a purely protective gesture, Katherine gently pulled her sister against her. "No, Moll, Marshal Scott was just leaving."

"You are?" asked Molly.

As though the past five minutes had never happened, he slid Katherine a challenging look before smiling down at Molly. "Of course not, kitten. I wouldn't disappoint my favorite five-year-old."

Several hours after his confrontation with the prissy schoolmarm, Trey left the orphanage and headed back to his room at Miss Martha's boardinghouse. Out of habit, he surveyed his surroundings, hunting for potential danger hidden in the shadows. All he found was a kaleidoscope of yellows and gold that spilled from the streetlamps and mansion windows into a patchwork of sporadic light along the lane.

Taking a deep breath of the crisp night air, he crammed his hat onto his head and increased his pace. Various wagon-wheel tracks pointed the way toward the center of town. After passing several mansions nearly identical to Charity House, Trey eventually turned onto Sixteenth Street. A few blocks later the two-story homes became three- and four-story businesses, and Trey found his mind returning to the events of the night.

He knew he shouldn't have stayed at Charity House as long as he had, but Molly's eager devotion had torn at his heart, making him set aside his own conflicting emotions concerning her sister. The child made him want to right the wrongs done to her.

He tried to tell himself his present restlessness was due to his concern for the kid, but Trey knew Molly wasn't the real source of his agitation.

It was her sister.

He'd known there was going to be trouble the moment Miss Taylor had sauntered into Marc's study, with her self-righteousness wrapped around her like a winter cloak. She'd spoken of forgiveness. Then flinched from his touch.

The woman had genuinely been afraid of him. The shock of it still sat heavy in his chest. Once he'd recognized her terror—terror of *him*—all he'd wanted to do was ease her worry.

Trey knew her past; Marc had told him what she'd endured. Hot anger rose inside him. Considering her terrible trauma, she had every right to be afraid of men.

Yet, beneath her fear, there was a real innocence about her. She truly believed there was healing after unspeakable pain and violence. With such a naive view of life, Miss Taylor could never understand what drove Trey.

How could she? In his experience, people who spoke of forgiveness had already done their forgiving. Well, he would *never* forgive Ike Hayes. He couldn't allow Laurette's killer off that easily.

Laurette.

At the thought of his wife a swift, unrelenting wave of guilt whipped through him. He'd nearly betrayed the memory of her tonight, all because he'd wanted to ease another woman's fears.

Ripping off his hat, Trey slammed it against his thigh. He'd like to think he'd been drawn to Katherine tonight because he'd wanted to show her that all men weren't like the one who had attacked her, but he knew better. Something about the woman dug past his well-built defenses and made him want to be a better man.

A man worthy of trust.

It must have been all that talk of "moving on" he'd had with Marc prior to their confrontation over Molly. He'd been missing Laurette so much, he'd ached inside.

Still shaken from the encounter, Trey desperately tried to call forth memories of the only woman he'd allowed in his heart since childhood. Instead, images of a beautiful, spitting-mad schoolteacher defeated his efforts.

Laurette's memory deserved his total devotion. He *had* to get Katherine Taylor out of his head.

But how?

What he needed was a diversion, something that would put his mind back on important issues.

Like the whereabouts of Ike Hayes.

Changing course, he crossed over to Fifteenth Street and headed toward the jail where Ike's brother, Drew, awaited trial. It was time to focus on serving justice the only way Trey knew how.

By his own hands.

Chapter Four

Drew Hayes's rotund body lay sprawled haphazardly across the lone bed in the back of the jail cell. With his jowls slack from sleep and his face full of belligerent beard, the outlaw looked like the animal Trey knew him to be.

A jolt of anger came fast and hard, filling Trey with such hatred, his throat burned from it. This man, *this outlaw,* had played a leading role in the murder of Trey's wife and child. The reminder brought a driving need to lash out, to end the life of the man who had stolen what was so precious to Trey. He had to brace himself against a nearby wall to keep from taking action.

Breathing hard and trying urgently to gain control over his turbulent emotions, Trey forced his attention to the window above Drew's bed. The rising moon glittered through the rusty metal bars, casting a thin ray of light that led from the cell door to the foot of Drew's bed.

Trey wanted to follow that path, and end the battle with a single bullet. But as he struggled inside the blinding haze of his hate, he knew he wouldn't do it. Drew Hayes didn't deserve such an easy out.

Motioning to the deputy on duty to join him, Trey lifted the keys off the hook and then turned to enter Hayes's cell. Once inside, he tossed the keys and a warning look at the other lawman.

"Stay close," he said. "And keep your ears open. I may need your testimony, if he talks."

The deputy nodded.

Forcing aside all emotion except uncompromising resolve, Trey moved deeper into the cell, kicked the leg of the bed. "Wake up."

The body stirred under the blanket.

Trey waited, watched, gauged.

Although the man had fifty pounds on him, without his brother, Ike, by his side, Drew Hayes was a coward. He'd proven that well enough when Trey had found him in Mattie Silks's brothel on Market Street. A few threats and a cocked pistol were all it had taken to bring the man into custody without a fight.

The easy arrest hadn't been the only surprise. Trey had expected a simple admission of guilt and a full disclosure of his brother's whereabouts. Drew hadn't talked.

"I want a word with you." Trey yanked the blanket to the ground. "Now."

The outlaw lifted his head. "I ain't talkin' to no law dog."

Leaning against the wall, Trey folded his arms across his chest and clung to the last scraps of his humanity. He forced all thought of Laurette out of his mind and focused only on the most recent murders, the ones he could pin on Drew with or without an admission. "About the night of the twenty-third, on the McCaulley ranch…"

"I ain't answering none of your questions," Drew snarled, then launched into a string of obscenities.

Trey ignored the foul language and continued. "Was it only you and your brother that day?"

Snorting, Drew sat up, swung his beefy feet to the ground. "What do you care? It was just a woman and some snot-nosed kids."

A dark rage swept over Trey, one he hadn't felt since that night in Colorado Springs when he'd found the twisted bodies of Mrs. McCaulley and her boys. The unforgettable images of blood and brutal death were still clean and sharp in his mind. The fact that the Hayes brothers had done the same thing to Trey's wife and child added fuel to his fury.

In that moment, Trey knew that Marc was dead wrong. Trey didn't seek vengeance only for his own behalf. He sought justice for all the innocent victims murdered by the Hayes brothers.

"I'm gonna see you hang for what you've done," Trey said.

"I ain't afraid of you."

"You should be."

Drew vaulted off the bed.

In a heartbeat, Trey drew his gun and pressed it against the man's temple. Death was gunning for Drew Hayes. And in that moment it didn't matter to Trey how it came about, just that it came swiftly.

"All I need is a reason." His finger itched to pull the trigger. "Just one."

Palms facing forward, Drew inched two paces back toward the bed. "I don't want no trouble."

"Then start talking."

The outlaw's small, deep-set eyes narrowed into calculating slits. "I know your kind, Marshal. You ain't no better than me."

"We're nothing alike," Trey said, holstering his gun to punctuate his point.

"You enjoy killing, Marshal." Drew dropped to the bed, and a sinister grin glinted behind the dirty beard. "Same as me."

Black crept across his vision as Trey yanked Drew off the bed and wrapped his fingers around the outlaw's throat. "You and I aren't anything alike."

"Turn him loose, Marshal. You…"

Trey couldn't hear the rest of the deputy's plea over the sound of his own pulse drumming loudly in his ears. Nor did he pay much attention to the metal click of a key turning in the lock.

"Marshal Scott."

Trey squeezed tighter, and Drew's eyes began to bulge.

"Marshal. Stop."

The urgent yank on his arm finally got through to Trey. Slowly, deliberately, he loosened his grip from around Drew's neck, then launched the outlaw to the floor.

Drew flopped around like a dying fish, clutching his throat and wheezing in between coughs.

"Don't you ever compare yourself to me again." Trey turned his attention to the deputy. "I'll be back tomorrow. Make sure he's in a more talkative mood by then."

The deputy flattened his lips into a grim line. "You can count on it, Marshal."

Without looking back, Trey walked out of the jail. Once he was on the street, a burst of cold mountain air punched through his black mood.

He felt dirty. Contemptible.

Vile.

Was Drew Hayes right? Was Trey more like the outlaw than he wanted to admit?

No. The need to protect, especially women and children, was deeply ingrained in him—as much a part of the reason why he'd accepted President Grant's appointment to the U.S. marshal post as to avenge Laurette's death.

All Trey had to do was think back over the events earlier in the day with five-year-old Molly Taylor. No matter how silly and foolish, he'd set out to defend a little girl who'd simply wanted a few more hours of play.

Didn't that make him better than the Hayes brothers?

Perhaps. But now, with the distance of time, Trey's reasoning told him that he'd chosen the wrong path to demonstrate his loyalty to the child.

Marc's accusations suddenly shot through his mind. Had Trey silently made a promise to champion Molly Taylor for his own purposes, even knowing he couldn't give false guarantees where the future was concerned?

At least he could right that particular wrong. First thing in the morning, he would set matters straight with Molly and Miss Taylor. Perhaps with the schoolmarm's forgiveness, Trey could erase some of the ugliness from his recent encounter with Drew Hayes.

Once she'd helped settle the other children and said all their evening prayers, Katherine returned to her sister's bed for a final good-night kiss. Pulling the blanket up to the child's chin, she tucked the corners underneath her tiny shoulders. "Pleasant dreams, sweetheart."

Big round eyes filled with childlike worry looked up at her. "You still angry at me, Katherine?"

Katherine dragged her sister into a fierce hug. "I was never angry *at* you, Molly. I was only upset with your behavior. I didn't set out to ruin your fun, but rules are rules."

The little girl rubbed a wet cheek into her shoulder. "I don't really hate you, you know."

Tightening her hold, Katherine dropped a kiss onto her sister's forehead. "I know."

Oh, Lord, make me worthy of raising this child. Help me to show her Your unconditional love so she'll turn to You when times get tough, or when I fail her.

With gentle movements, Katherine lowered Molly back to the bed. "No more worries, pumpkin. All's forgotten."

Molly swiped the back of her hand across her cheek. "Really?"

"*Really.* We're family. And now that God has brought us together, I won't ever leave you or let you go."

As Molly grinned through her tears, devotion brimmed in her eyes. "You're the best sister ever."

Katherine reached out and tweaked the upturned nose. "So are you, Molly."

"Night, Katherine."

Smiling, she leaned over and blew out the bedside lantern. "Night, Molly. I love you."

"Me, too."

Katherine quietly edged out of the room, then shut the door behind her. Tiptoeing toward the back staircase that led to the kitchen below, she offered up a silent prayer of gratitude to God. She and Molly had stumbled today, but they'd avoided any permanent rift.

No thanks to Trey Scott.

The U.S. marshal had gotten in the middle of a situation where he quite simply hadn't belonged. Perhaps his intentions had been honorable, but in the end he'd caused far more harm than good.

And not just in Molly's case.

Katherine stifled a shudder as unwanted memories of their latest encounter crept into her thoughts. If only he'd agreed to leave her sister alone, Katherine might have been able to keep her precarious emotions under control during their argument.

But he'd pushed and demanded explanations that weren't easily voiced. Then he'd stood too close. And she'd become unreasonably terrified.

During a moment of clarity, Katherine knew the man would never hurt her. Not in the way her attacker had. Then why was she so afraid of him? Why did she always feel the need to run whenever Marshal Scott got too close?

Even now, hours later, the humiliation of her panicky reaction dug deep.

Collapsing against the wall, Katherine shut her eyes against the shame that still burned in her. *No.* She wouldn't take the blame this time. Her uncomfortable reaction to Trey's nearness wasn't her fault. It was the legacy of her past. Nothing more.

In fact, her fear of Marc's friend was a small annoyance compared to the importance of maintaining stability in her life. Especially now that she had Molly's welfare to consider.

With renewed determination, Katherine marched down the stairs, then pushed through the door leading into the kitchen.

The sight of Mrs. Smythe washing dishes at the sink improved Katherine's mood considerably. Tall, broad-shouldered and gray-haired, Mrs. Smythe was the perfect adopted grandmother for forty orphans—and one grown woman in need of a friendly face. Arranging a smile on her lips, Katherine greeted the other woman. "Good evening, Mrs. Smythe."

The older woman turned, her smoke-gray eyes sparkling with pleasure. "Hello, dear."

The housekeeper's affectionate reception warmed Katherine's heart, but after the events of the day, she found she wasn't in the mood for company, after all. "Why don't you go on home? I can finish the washing."

Mrs. Smythe's face cracked into a wide smile. "Are you sure? I certainly don't mind staying until I'm through."

Katherine nodded. "I feel like cleaning tonight."

Wiping her hands on the front of her skirt, the older woman let out a hearty chuckle. "Well, then, I won't ask again."

Mrs. Smythe hurried around the chopping block in the center of the kitchen, then gathered her belongings out of the supply closet. "I'll see you first thing in the morning."

"Night," Katherine said.

Just as the door shut with a bang, Laney waddled into the kitchen, carrying an armload of dishes. Avoiding her friend's eyes, Katherine took the stack of plates and set them in the soapy water. "I sent Mrs. Smythe home."

"I see that."

"Why don't you go rest, enjoy some time alone with Marc?"

Laney blew out a sigh of gratitude. "My feet *are* hurting, and I certainly won't turn down a quiet moment with my husband. I'll just bring in the rest of the dishes before I head upstairs."

"You don't have to do that."

"I want to."

All argued out, Katherine relented. "That would be a great help, thank you."

As Laney trudged back to the dining room, Katherine picked up a plate from the soapy water, grabbed a rag and began scrubbing. She tried to empty her mind of all thought, but images of Trey's stricken expression when he'd realized how frightened she was of him kept flashing through her mind.

Just thinking of the genuine remorse flickering in his eyes made her feel so…so…guilty.

Why did she feel as though *she'd* hurt *him* when she'd flinched from his touch?

"You're going to wipe the pattern right off that china."

Katherine jerked at the sound of Laney's voice. Looking over her shoulder, she let her gaze unite with her friend's worried expression.

"Are you all right?" Laney asked.

Sniffing, Katherine flicked the water off her fingers. "Perfect."

"You don't look perfect," Laney said, her gaze sharp and assessing.

Katherine took the stack of dirty dishes, then set them on the counter next to the sink, with a thud. "I've never been better."

Returning to work, she yanked another dish out of the water, spraying soapsuds into the air.

Laney wiped a bubble off Katherine's cheek, then laid a hand on her arm. "Did you argue with Trey again?"

Katherine increased the vigor of her scrubbing, her erratic movements sloshing water and bubbles onto the floor. "Trey and I always argue."

"Over Molly?"

"I told him to stay away from her."

Sliding a look from beneath her lashes, Laney fiddled with the dishes, stacking them largest to smallest. "He's good with her, you know. And with the rest of the children, for that matter."

Perhaps. Maybe. Okay, yes, he was good with the orphans.

It changed nothing. "Ever since he started hanging around here, he's disrupted my, I mean, *our* lives. Molly never defied me before today."

"It was bound to happen sooner or later. She's a child, after all."

Katherine knew Laney was right—to a point—but she also knew that her concerns over Trey's impact on her sister's well-being were valid as well. "He's too bitter. And his anger at God is tangible. I don't want the man's influence to result in Molly's unbelief."

Laney abandoned all pretense of helping and turned her full attention to Katherine. "I'll admit Trey can seem hard on the surface, but deep down he's a good man. And none of his anger shows when he's with the children."

Katherine swung around to glare at her friend. "Are you defending him?"

Throwing a palm in the air between them, Laney shook her head. "No. No. It's just that he's—"

"A U.S. marshal."

"Yes, that's right. And although he's not exactly godly, he is a man of high morals, sworn to protect the citizens of this country. All things considered, he's an acceptable example for the children, including Molly."

Katherine dismissed the notion with a flick of her wrist. "You know what I mean."

"Yes, I'm afraid I do." Laney lowered her hand, sighed. "It's his job to hunt down criminals, Katherine, including the men who murdered his wife and child. Maybe instead of condemning him, you could try understanding him better."

Clenching tense fingers around a plate, Katherine set her jaw. "Let's say I do find compassion for his lethal quest. What if he's killed in the process?"

"Oh, honey." Laney's eyes softened. "Not every lawman dies."

Katherine shook her head, refusing to let her mind go in that direction. "Trey Scott is the embodiment of instability. I don't want Molly getting attached to him."

"In case you hadn't noticed, she already is."

Katherine cringed over the statement, seriously concerned Molly wasn't the only one growing attached to the man. "Well, it's not too late to prevent any further harm. As long as he stays away from her, everything will be fine."

"Aren't you being a bit overprotective?"

Trey had used similar words against her. The accusation hadn't sat well with Katherine then, and it didn't sit well with her now. "Isn't that the role of a big sister?"

Laney gently pried the plate out of Katherine's grip. Steering her to a stool, she forced her to sit. "I'm worried about you. You've been on edge a lot lately, and I think it has more to do with a certain U.S. marshal than your struggle to find your way as Molly's guardian."

Katherine tried to rise, but Laney placed a restraining hand on her shoulder. "It's time we talked about what's really bothering you."

"*Nothing's* bothering me except my concern over Marshal Scott's damaging influence over Molly's life."

Laney pressed her nose inches from Katherine's. "Why don't we get to the real problem? Shall we?"

"And here I thought we had."

A shrewd look filled Laney's gaze. "I think you should admit you have strong feelings for Trey Scott, ones that have nothing to do with your little sister."

Katherine shot off the stool. "That's ridiculous."

"Correction." Laney pointed a finger at her. "*Very* strong feelings."

Chapter Five

The next morning, Katherine exited Charity House with the notion of using work to alleviate her restlessness from the night before. Unfortunately, the crisp mountain air did nothing to shake her melancholy. Perched on the top step of the wraparound porch, she looked to the heavens and sighed. Large puffs of cottony white clouds drifted aimlessly against the deep blue sky.

If only she could be that carefree. But Laney's accusation about her feelings toward Marshal Scott had put dangerous thoughts into Katherine's head, making her want to cast off the chains of her past. To start a new life free of fear.

If only I deserved a second chance.

More agitated than before, Katherine trudged down the steps and started along the sidewalk that led from the orphanage to the Charity House School two doors away. The faint whinny of a horse in the distance had her looking up.

Realizing she wasn't alone on the path, Katherine immediately stopped in her tracks. Two ladies slowly approached from the opposite direction. They were dressed in beautiful tight-waisted dresses in identical shades of pink satin. With each graceful step, their skirts billowed over their dainty feet. They shimmered in the morning light, looking like purity personified.

In spite of her best efforts to remain calm, instant trepidation sprang to life. Katherine knew these women. She had seen the two sitting together with their families in church. They were either sisters or very good friends, but Katherine had failed to find out which because no matter how often she smiled at them, they never acknowledged her in return.

The reflex to rush back into Charity House came fast, nearly too powerful to resist. But Katherine was no coward. Thus, she held her ground and took courage in the last line from Psalm 31. *Be strong and take heart, all you who hope in the Lord.*

As the two drew nearer, Katherine lifted her chin a little higher. They studied her from under the brim of their feathered hats. Their gazes were unreadable but not overly antagonistic. Pleased the women hadn't snubbed her right away, Katherine smiled.

"Good morning," she said.

The taller woman grabbed the elbow of the smaller and pulled her closer, as though she were saving her from stepping in a cow pie. A snarled lip confirmed her disgust.

Katherine swallowed down the bile rising in her throat. A shiver slithered up her spine, and her hands started to shake.

Oh, please, Lord, not again.

Her prayer went unanswered. As one, the ladies lifted their regal noses in the air, snorted—they actually snorted!—and all but scrambled across the street in their haste to get to the other side.

Stunned, Katherine's eyes began to sting, and she had to fight a wave of hysteria as their pointed whispers lifted in the air.

"Tramp," one said to the other, menace dripping in her voice. "She's just like her mother."

"I heard she led that man on," came the harsh reply.

At that comment the women turned back and stared at Katherine from over their shoulders. From the measuring glint in their eyes, it was obvious they thought very little of her.

Katherine had experienced this sort of shunning often enough before, but the pain and humiliation were still sharp, like burning shards stabbing into her heart. For several heartbeats, Katherine stood with her head high and her breath stuck in her throat.

On her left, the Charity House School stood like a sentinel, offering sanctuary. Giving in to her humiliation, Katherine rushed up the steps and quickly fit the key into the lock.

Once inside the safety of the building, she leaned back against the shut door and gulped for air. Blinking away the tears in her eyes, she swallowed hard, again and again and again, until she had her emotions under control. Katherine would not allow those cruel women's barbs to hit their mark. Not today. Not ever.

At last her breathing evened out, and she wandered aimlessly through the rooms of the school. Unfortunately, and against her best efforts, Katherine's thoughts kept circling back to what the women had said on the street.

She'd led that man on....

No. It wasn't true. Katherine hadn't asked to be forced like that. All her life she'd kept her distance from men.

They'd always scared her, a legacy from the ugly side of their nature, which she'd witnessed often enough in her mother's brothel.

And no matter what people claimed about her, Katherine would never have relations with a man, not willingly. Which made Laney's accusations about her feelings for Trey Scott all the more absurd. The man was too intense, too dangerous, and…and… Katherine had worked too hard to achieve normalcy in her life to give any man— especially a lawman with a death wish—the power to hurt her again.

With her head thick and heavy from her troubling thoughts, Katherine prayed for focus. *O Lord, be not silent. Do not be far from me.*

She looked around her and studied the safe world she'd created out of an incomplete education and necessity.

No man could hurt her here.

This was *her* territory. Her home. The one place where she had complete control. Each desk, book and writing tablet had been chosen with care. She and Laney had turned the two-story brick building into a reputable school for the children banished from all the others in town.

She and the orphans might be outcasts in the community, but they had a place of belonging here.

Katherine crossed to her desk and straightened a stack of papers that didn't need straightening. The fresh smell of soap and furniture polish told her Mrs. Smythe had indulged in some deep cleaning earlier this morning.

Strolling through her domain, Katherine released a sigh. Every detail reflected her taste for precision and order.

Admit you have strong feelings for Trey Scott…

Laney's words from the night before echoed through

Katherine's thoughts. Taunting her. Mocking her. Far worse than any whispered attempts at hurting her with untrue accusations.

Frantic for some relief, she wove her way between the desks and trekked toward the supply closet in the back of the building. After lighting a lantern, she carried it with her into the dark, tiny room.

Katherine's trademark military-style order was reflected here as well. Inkwells, writing tablets and fresh sticks of chalk marched in straight rows along the lower two shelves on her left. More writing tablets were stacked on the upper shelves, along with rulers and other miscellaneous supplies.

Katherine set down the lantern and breathed in the comforting scent of books and paper. She ran her fingertip across the cold inkwells, and then along the smooth book spines. But even here, in her favorite refuge, thoughts of Trey Scott threatened her peace of mind.

What if she hadn't flinched from his touch? Would such a man ever be able to give her the genuine caring and devotion she secretly craved, in spite of what others thought of her?

She was only kidding herself with dreams of the impossible. No man would give her the love and respect that another, untainted woman deserved. Her attacker, and the subsequent response from the townspeople, had shown Katherine exactly what her value was in this world.

Anyone who trusts God will never be put to shame.

The verse from Romans swept through her mind, giving her the reassurance she sought. Ever since that dark night, Katherine had turned to God as her salvation. And she'd always found peace in His shelter.

His opinion was all that mattered. Today would be no exception. Instead of feeling sorry for herself, she would take a quick inventory of her supplies.

She focused her attention of the rows of *Michel's Geography* and *The Pilgrim's Progress* on her right. Looking forward to the mind-numbing task, she dropped to the floor and began counting the books on the bottom shelves first. She had to bend all the way over in order to reach the books nudged in the farthest back corner.

"Ten, eleven, twelve." She jabbed at the last one. "That makes thirteen. I'll definitely have to order more this week."

"Well, now." The familiar drawl dropped through the stuffy air and skidded down the back of Katherine's neck. "This is by far the most interesting sight I've seen all morning."

Katherine jerked upward and promptly thumped her head against the shelf above her. "Don't you know how to knock?"

A masculine chuckle was Trey's only response.

She tried twisting around but only managed to bang her head on the shelf again.

"Careful now."

She quickly flipped over, sat up and hugged her knees against her chest. Huddled in a tight ball, she had to look up—and up farther still—in order to bestow her indignation upon the man.

"Ma'am." He whipped off his hat and bowed. "Always a pleasure."

From her vantage point, the brute appeared more mountain than man. "Isn't there a rule or code or something against sneaking up on unsuspecting women?"

He lifted a shoulder. "Probably. But I think I skipped that day at lawman's school."

"You are a mule-headed—"

"Stubborn pig." A touch of mischief danced in his eyes. "Or so I've been told a time or two."

In this lighthearted mood, with his face clean-shaven and his hair damp on the ends, Trey Scott was far more dangerous than he had been the day before.

This time, however, she would not give in to her fear of him. She would *not*. The neighbor ladies had caught her at a weak moment this morning. Trey Scott would not be given the same chance. "You've only heard that once or twice?"

He laughed, the gesture swiping ten years off his features. She didn't like the way her stomach twisted in response. But from dread, or something else entirely? Disturbed by the direction of her thoughts, she dropped her gaze and instantly noticed he hadn't worn his guns.

Come to think of it, he never wore the six-shooters when he came around the children. The consideration for their safety made him infinitely more likable.

The big, heartless brute.

It was so much easier to control her emotions around him when he acted like the mule-headed, stubborn pig he claimed to be. But Trey Scott had hidden depths that Katherine was only beginning to notice after their yearlong, precarious acquaintance.

Oh, Lord, what now?

"Are you going to sit down there all day?" he asked.

"Are you going to prove yourself a gentleman and help me up?"

The aggravating grin on his face widened as he flipped his hat onto one of the desks behind him. "Ask nicely."

What gave Trey Scott the right to look so vital and handsome, like he was a hero out of a ridiculous dime novel? "Would you stop staring at me like…like…*that?*"

He rubbed his chin between his thumb and forefinger. "Are you taking a tone with me, Miss Taylor?"

His outrageous remark pushed her to stand on her own, but her foot tangled in her skirts, and she fell back down. "Oh, now look at what you've done."

He angled his head at her. "For a good Christian woman, you have a pretty mean temper."

"How absurd. Christian women get angry, too."

"Obviously."

She didn't like this teasing side of him. What had happened to the Trey Scott who couldn't go three sentences without arguing with her? *That* man she could handle.

"You can save the snide remarks, Marshal. And. Help. Me. Up."

The light from the lantern flickered off the watch fob dangling from one of his vest buttons, blinding her for a moment.

"I wish you'd turn around again." He drew out a long, dramatic sigh. "The other end didn't bite."

A seed of rebellion took hold of her. "Don't forget, a bee keeps her stinger in her behind."

His lips twitched. "Miss Taylor, I'm shocked!"

Panicked he might start laughing, and then get her started as well, she gave him her let's-get-down-to-business look. "Marshal Scott—"

"Right, right. Help you up."

Pushing from the wall, he reached out to her. Palm met palm, and…nothing. No fear. No terror. Just a pleasant warmth.

Then, when he shifted his hold slightly, all she felt in response was…

Contentment?

At that odd thought, a riot of confusion shot through her already addled brain, and she pulled on her hand. "Either help me up or let go."

"Right." With a flick of his wrist, he yanked her to her feet.

Quickly dropping her hand to her side, she took a careful step back and then straightened to her full height. Feeling remarkably out of her depth, she resorted to the one tactic that kept her on an even footing with the man. Antagonism.

"I don't know why you're here, but I refuse to continue trading insults with you today," she said.

He had the nerve to look shocked by her words. "Is that what we're doing? I thought we were getting on rather well. For us."

She took a deep breath. "Step back please. So I can pass."

His expression turned serious, concerned even, and he quickly did as she asked. "Of course."

Right. Now he had to be heroic and honor her fears, like he had the day before in Marc's study. Did he know that when he acted like this, with such careful consideration of her feelings, his closeness didn't frighten her so much?

But, if that were truly the case, why were her hands shaking?

In an effort to hide her trembling fingers, she busied herself with brushing off her skirt.

"I'd be happy to assist." He peered around the side of her. "Unless, of course, you brought your stinger with you."

"You, sir, are outrageous." And the more he talked with that smooth Southern drawl, the more her uncertainty increased. "Maybe you should be on your way now."

"Don't you want to know why I searched you out?"

"Not particularly." But curiosity poked through her wish to be rid of him. "How did you know I was here?"

"I stopped at Charity House first. Laney told me where to find you."

She couldn't stop a small jolt of surprise from spreading into something more tangible, more pleasant. But reality set in just as quickly. Had the two ladies from her earlier encounter seen Trey enter the building? Would they think Katherine had set up a secret rendezvous?

No, she was being oversensitive because of their rudeness. Surely they'd been long gone by the time Trey had arrived. "You came looking for me?" she asked at last, suspicion digging deep. "Why?"

"I want to talk to you about Molly." As he spoke, everything about him turned serious—his expression, his body language, even his tone.

Surprised by the change in him, and her intrigued reaction in response, she focused on ending their discussion as quickly as possible. "There's nothing more to discuss. In fact, it's all very simple—"

"Is it? I was under the impression it was—" he blew out a slow breath "—*complicated.*"

She started to push around him, but he evened out his weight, barring the exit. He seemed to fill every available space.

He looked too big, too casual, and for a brief moment, she feared he would attack. But instead of making her shake, or even tremble, the notion made her temper flare.

Finally, an emotion she understood. "Get out of my way."

A troubled look pooled in his gaze, and he scrubbed a hand through his hair. He shifted to one side, leaving a small opening for her, but he didn't move completely away. "Not until I've said my piece."

After his earlier consideration of her fears, she knew she owed him that much. "Go ahead then. Say what you came to say."

He nodded. "I was wrong to get between you and your sister yesterday."

"You admit it?" Katherine could hardly believe her ears.

"Yes."

Blinking at this newest change in him, she didn't know what to think. Trey Scott had just given her what she wanted.

So why didn't she feel any satisfaction?

"It's not personal, you know," she said, the truth finally hitting her. "It's simply that you can't offer Molly the stability she needs, especially now."

"You're correct. I can't make promises."

She suddenly wished he would. Because she sensed, all the way down to the last hair on her head, that if Trey Scott made a promise, he would keep it.

"I won't come around the orphanage anymore," he said.

Her stomach bounced to her toes. Now that he'd given her exactly what she wanted, she realized she wasn't sure she wanted it anymore.

In truth, she couldn't bear the thought of never seeing him again. "What about Marc?"

"I can visit with him during school hours."

He looked so sad, troubled, and she found herself no longer concerned about her own fears.

She reached to him and touched his sleeve.

It was his turn to shrug her off.

"Molly's your sister. Your word stands. I won't interfere anymore. However—" he commanded her gaze with a hard, unrelenting look "—you should know that I will not stop hunting Ike Hayes until I find him and bring him to justice."

Katherine sighed, realizing he'd missed the crucial point in all her arguments. Didn't he understand that it wasn't the hunt she feared, but rather Trey's motivation? "Seeking vengeance won't—"

"*That* is not up for discussion." His closed-off expression couldn't hide his pain.

Katherine shook her head, feeling as though she'd failed him and unsure why that thought hurt so much.

She didn't want him to walk away. Not like this. With nothing really settled between them.

But before she could plead with him to hear her out, he said, "You were right all along."

"I…I was?"

His eyes clouded over. "Men with badges die."

Chapter Six

Unable to sort through his chaotic thoughts, Trey shoved his own turmoil aside and studied the myriad of emotions that swept across Katherine's face at his declaration. Dread. Pain. Sorrow.

He wanted to offer her words of reassurance, to promise her they'd figure everything out for Molly's sake, as well their own.

But he couldn't lie to her now that they were starting to have an honest conversation.

"That's all I had to say." He reached for his hat.

"Stay." She gripped his arm. "Please. This isn't right. Can't we find another way?"

He shook his head at her. "You want me to forgive murderers, while I never can."

"Maybe not on your own." She dropped her hand and sighed. "But with God's help…"

"Don't you understand, Katherine? I don't believe in turning the other cheek. I'm Old Testament. An eye for an eye."

"Seeking revenge only hurts you, Trey, not—"

"Tell that to my wife, and all the others Ike Hayes has killed. Good, decent people."

Katherine lowered her gaze to her toes. "I'm…sorry. I didn't mean to make light of your loss."

"I know."

Now was the time he should walk away, but the unmistakable sadness in Katherine's eyes—sadness for *him*—touched the part of his soul he'd thought he'd buried with Laurette. Vengeance still burned in his gut, probably always would until he captured Ike, yet Trey didn't want to walk away without attempting to assure Katherine his anger wasn't directed at her.

With unsteady fingers, he touched her cheek, dropped his hand at her flinch. Why couldn't she trust him, even a little? "I know I argued the point yesterday, but like you, I don't want to put Molly through another loss."

She blinked at him but didn't respond.

He took a step closer, determined to set aside his own bitterness for a moment so he could help her understand. Katherine was courageous and good. She deserved a future free of the fear that still gripped her, the same fear that still held her captive after two years of living in the safety of Charity House.

With slow, careful movements he shifted the long black braid off her shoulder and sent it tumbling down her back. He couldn't help but notice how her skin stood pale against the slash of her arched eyebrows. "I don't want to hurt Molly any more than you do. In spite of what my actions might have said yesterday, I only want what's best for her."

An emotion he couldn't read wavered in her eyes before

she covered it with a scowl. "Then we're in agreement. Now, if you'll excuse me, I have work to do."

"Not yet. It's time we had the rest of it out between us." He shifted his weight. "*All* of it."

Her clenched fists spoke of inflexible resolve. "Now is not a good time for me."

"Nevertheless, we're going to settle this. Not only for your sister's sake, but for yours as well."

And maybe even for his own.

Here, now, in the confines of the school's supply closet, Trey finally admitted to himself that he'd been moved by this woman and her painful past long before she'd brought Molly to live with her.

The discovery sat heavy on his heart. How could he have feelings for this woman when his hate and anger drove him so hard? How could he be drawn to Katherine when his only goal should be to avenge his wife's senseless murder?

How could he betray Laurette like this, even in the secret corners of his mind?

"Please." Her trapped gaze darted to the exit. "Can't we do this later?"

He nearly relented at the sight of her unconcealed dismay, at the wave of guilt that had begun to spread through him, but it was time they addressed the real problem standing between them. Without the issue of Molly or the little girl's future as a buffer. Without his mind consumed with his wife.

He reached to Katherine, brushing aside a strand of hair that had freed itself from the braid. "We have to work through this, before our antagonism explodes in some unforeseen way, and we do something *you'll* regret."

"Me? What about you?"

"I'm long past regrets."

Trey had told himself the only reason he'd sought out Katherine today was to tell her he would honor her wishes concerning Molly.

He'd been lying to himself.

Katherine Taylor awakened tender emotions in him he'd thought dead. She gave him a glimpse of who he used to be before anger and hatred had taken root. He wanted to teach her how to trust him, as a *friend* would trust another, and that all men didn't want to use her for their own selfish desires.

"I won't hurt you, Katherine. Ever."

He meant every word, but she stiffened anyway, and then shifted away from him.

Feeling helpless, foolish, he stepped back. Focusing on her fears helped him remember why they needed to work through this awkwardness between them. He tried another topic. "I know you and Molly shared the same mother, but you had different fathers. I also know how your sister's father died. But, tell me, Katherine, what happened to yours?"

Her closed, stony expression made him fear she wouldn't answer his question, but she surprised him. "He was a town sheriff, shot in the line of duty."

His stomach dropped, and he felt like he'd been gut-punched. Why hadn't Marc warned him? Now her worries for her little sister made more sense. "How old were you when he died?"

"About Molly's age. He left us with less than nothing."

"Us?"

"Me and my mother. It's why she turned to her scandalous profession." The look in her eyes explained more than her words. "Momma didn't have any skills. When the last of our money ran out, she did what she thought she had to do. Eventually, she started her own business and, well, you know the rest."

"You admired her."

Katherine started trembling, her eyes clouding over as though she was lost inside painful memories. "No. I wept for her. She was a strong woman, capable and resourceful. But because of the choices she made, she lived a bitter and lonely life."

He reached to her again.

She shrugged him off. Again.

"You escaped her legacy."

"Yes." Her face took on a faraway look. "I guess she knew what would happen if I grew up in her brothel, so she sent me to school back East. But I had to leave right before graduation and care for her during her illness. It was an honor and a blessing to share those final days with her, and to see her come to know the Lord."

He had to swallow back his own anger at the thought of Katherine leaving the safety of school, only to have a man violate her in the most vile way possible. "You truly believe returning home was a blessing, after what happened to you?"

"Oh, Trey." She gave him a serene smile, the one he'd seen her use on the smaller children when they were confused. "Despite all the tragedy, I eventually found my real home. Here at Charity House."

Her naive response swelled a primitive need to lash out. "Good doesn't always come out of evil. Look at Molly. Tell me, what good has come out of her loss?"

Katherine sighed. "God never promised us a life without adversity. But He gave us the strength we need to bear up under it. Molly may have lost both her mother and father, as I did, but she's not alone. She has me. We have each other, and we have our heavenly Father."

"How can you speak of God as though He cares?" Trey demanded, no longer thinking of Molly now, but of his wife.

She'd been a woman of faith, too, just like Katherine. However, God hadn't given Laurette the strength to face Ike Hayes and his rotten brother, Drew. Her faith had been grossly rewarded with unspeakable violence. "Look around you. God abandons those who care for Him most."

Katherine winced, but she didn't challenge him. Instead, she reached out and placed her hand on his shoulder. "If you give it a chance, healing will come with time."

She was wrong. Time healed nothing. At least not for him. Not until he caught Ike Hayes.

But maybe, *maybe,* the future could be different for Molly. She was just an innocent child, one who deserved peace in her life. And she'd get it, too. If he walked away now.

"I've been reckless with your sister." He placed his fingertips against his temples, his heartbeat coming fast and hard under his touch. "I'm sorry, Katherine."

"Do you know, until yesterday you never used my given name?" She wrapped her fingers around his wrist. "Say it again."

Foggy memories screamed at him to stop before it was too late. He ignored the good sense that told him to pull away; instead, he touched her cheek with a gentleness he didn't know he still possessed. "Katherine."

She tilted her head at him, smiled.

All thoughts escaped him. All but one. "Am I scaring you?"

"I…" She pressed her hand over his. "No."

She sounded shocked. Puzzled.

Amazed.

"Ah, Katherine." Slowly, he lowered his hands to her shoulders. "Do you know what's happening between us?"

"No."

"Neither do I." He started to pull her closer. "But I—"

"*Mr. Trey!* Whatcha doin' to my sister?"

At the sound of Molly's voice, resignation filled Katherine. She let out a choppy breath, drew in another, and then glanced into Trey's eyes.

He dropped his hands immediately from her shoulders. His expression gave away nothing of his emotions. In fact, his face was stark, fathomless, his gray-eyed gaze guarded.

Katherine gave him an exasperated look.

He sent her a small shrug.

"*Mr. Trey!* I was talkin' to you."

Trey gently pushed Katherine farther away from him, but he kept his gaze locked with hers as he answered Molly.

"I heard you, kitten." His lips curved into a slow, sardonic smile. "We were just talking."

Molly scooted around the back of Trey and then shoved between them. "Huh?"

Trey flashed Katherine a fearless grin and then lowered his attention to Molly. "What are you doing here, kid?"

Furrowing her brows, the little girl looked from Trey to Katherine and back again. "Laney told us to come get Katherine for lunch."

Katherine's breath caught in her lungs. *"Us?"*

Molly pointed to a spot just behind Trey. "Me, Megan and Johnny."

Leaning to her right, Katherine groaned at the sight of the older children shifting from foot to foot. Both were looking intently at the ceiling, but their smirks told her that they knew exactly what they'd just interrupted.

Perfect. Two fifteen-year-old *witnesses.*

Trey's shoulders stiffened as he pivoted completely around. "Johnny, Megan, please take Molly back to Charity House. Kath—that is, *Miss* Taylor—and I will be right behind you."

Molly marched around Trey and parked two balled fists on her hips. "We can't leave 'less Katherine comes, too."

"Go on, Molly," Katherine said, squelching her sister's mutiny with a firm voice and firmer frown. "I need to talk to Marshal Scott. Alone."

The little girl stomped her foot. "But I wanna stay."

Trey stooped to Molly's height and then plucked at one of her braids. "We'll be right behind you."

Molly cocked her head. "Really?"

"Promise. And after lunch we'll finish our game of marshals versus the big bad bank robbers," said Trey.

Molly cocked her head at him. "Do I get to be the marshal this time?"

Trey nodded. "Of course."

"Well, okay." Molly skipped over to Megan, clutched the girl's hand and then looked at Katherine over her shoulder. "Bye, Katherine."

Katherine gave both girls a shaky smile. "Bye."

With a knowing grin, Johnny addressed Trey directly. "See you in a few...*minutes,* Marshal." He wiggled his eyebrows but followed the girls out of the room without commenting further.

"Perfect. Just perfect," Katherine said once they were alone again. "Everyone at Charity House is sure to hear about this."

She's just like her mother. The woman's words from her earlier encounter echoed through her head.

Trey turned to face her then, his gaze impossible to read. Katherine didn't much care for the tug of unease that sped up her spine. Even before he opened his mouth to speak, she knew she wasn't going to like what he had to say.

"I guess this means we're getting married," he said, with a heavy dose of resignation in his voice.

Married? Katherine couldn't breathe under the weight of her confusion. How on earth had the man come to that conclusion? It took several seconds for her pounding heart-beat to settle enough for her to speak. "Pardon me?"

In the silence that followed, their gazes met and held. And held. And *held.*

Trey blinked first. "I didn't mean to put you into this predicament." He sighed. "Not only did three children catch us alone, but a passing neighbor or deliveryman could have seen me come in here."

"Maybe not," she said, a little too desperate, a little too shrill.

"Ugly talk, even unfounded, could bring trouble to the school. Or worse, yet another complaint against the entire Charity House venture." He darted his gaze around the room, speared his fingers through his hair, then gave a quick nod. "Under the circumstances, marriage is our best option."

Tears of indignation pricked in Katherine's eyes, but her

pride refused to allow a single drop to fall. Her only defense was to drop a cold chill into her words. "Stop talking nonsense. Even if someone saw us and filed a complaint, it…"

She trailed off, realizing the trouble that could come to Marc and Laney. To Charity House.

No. They were speculating now. Nothing more. There hadn't been a formal complaint against the orphanage in well over a year. The probability of a renewed grievance was ridiculous. "Let me pass."

As though he'd forgotten where they were, his gaze flicked around. "Katherine, you must realize how sor—"

"Don't apologize."

He clamped his lips shut, but his unspoken remorse hung between them.

As the silence grew, a burning throb of shame knotted in her throat. For one blinding moment, Katherine had actually wanted him to hold her. Was she leading him on?

Why hadn't she tried to stop him?

As though hearing her silent chagrin, Trey looked deep into her eyes, winced. "Let me make this right for you."

She fought the disparaging echo in her head. Too late. Too late. Too, *too* late. A blast of sunlight chose that moment to spill into the room, blinding Katherine as it chased away the dark.

She started forward, but Trey's voice, melodious and smooth, stopped her. "Marry me."

Let your conversation be always full of grace, seasoned with salt, so that you may know how to answer everyone. Even as Paul's words to the Colossians echoed through her head, Katherine could only stare at Trey, a blank, lifeless sense of doom fisting around her heart. "No."

For the first time that day, he actually looked angry, as though she'd finally pushed him past his limit. "Why not?"

Refusing to allow his bad manners to intimidate her, she stepped back, stopping his approach by shoving her palms hard against his chest. "I shouldn't have to explain myself after everything we've discussed. I won't marry a man—"

"Who wears a badge?"

She let her hands drift to her sides. "That's only part of it."

He raked a tender gaze across her face, but he didn't come any closer. "I'm not like the man who attacked you, Katherine. I *won't* hurt you."

As a slice of yearning clung to the edges of her resolve, her heart hammered out her words. "I know that."

"Do you?" he asked, gripping her shoulders again.

She slapped his hands away. "I don't think I'll let you paw at me anymore today."

He stepped back and waited until her eyes locked with his. "Marriage is the only way out of this. If we go to Charity House and tell the children we're engaged, word will get out quickly. If I was seen coming here, alone, all will be forgotten with the news of our impending marriage."

At the sight of the turbulent emotions in his eyes, a spasm of longing threatened her resolve. But nothing had changed between them, and although his argument had some merit, she wouldn't marry a man simply to stave off the mere possibility of trouble.

"We did nothing wrong," she said. "But you're right about one thing. We don't need any additional talk. If we're seen leaving together, the neighbors might not be kind in their estimation of the situation. You go first, out the back door, and I'll follow out the front after a considerable amount of time has passed."

His expression turned into stone. "I won't allow you to walk into Charity House with rumors flying among the children. You suffer enough of that in town."

"So this is some sort of misguided sense of gallantry? U.S. marshal Trey Scott saves the day?"

"No." He paused, hissed. "Yes. Maybe. I don't know. I hear how they speak about you and Molly."

"They?"

"You know who I mean. The gossipmongers." His gaze softened. "You and Molly deserve better than inaccurate rumors and nasty hearsay."

"They're words without substance. Anyone who knows me will know the truth of who I am and what I stand for."

"Some claim you're Molly's mother."

For a dreadful moment, Katherine's heart skipped a beat, and another. She'd suspected this but hadn't known for sure until now. Although Trey meant well, his desire to protect her through marriage was misguided at best. It wouldn't change the reality of what others chose to say about her or her connection to her sister.

"I've never worried about talk before. I won't start now. A marriage license would change nothing. I'm still the daughter of the most notorious madam in Denver next to Mattie Silks, and I'll always be a ruined woman in the eyes of the town."

He stiffened at her blunt words. "What about Molly? Do you want to teach her that cavorting in supply closets is acceptable behavior for an unmarried woman?"

His point hit its mark. For a moment, Katherine wavered on the edge of relenting, but then reality burst through the shield of her other emotions. "I'll simply explain the truth to her."

He speared his fingers through his hair. "You're being unreasonable."

"And you're suddenly the voice of logic here? You're offering marriage on the off chance someone sees us leaving together and will ultimately file a complaint with nothing more than conjecture to base it on. I won't stand here and hypothesize about a situation that may never happen." She shoved at him again. "Now let me pass."

His expression dropped into a frown as he shifted to his left and waved her forward. Tilting her nose at a regal angle, she sailed past him. But he caught her by the sleeve.

"Let me go."

"Not yet. You throw around words like *off chance* and *conjecture,* but you know I have a point. Give me one good reason why you won't marry me." Turning her to face him, he added, "Other than my profession, and I'll leave this alone until we know for sure if there will be any consequences over this meeting of ours."

Although his words were spoken in a firm tone, the masculine confusion that blazed out of Trey touched a hidden corner of her soul.

Katherine had a sudden urge to ignore her own fears and take a crazy chance with this man. But she had someone to consider besides herself. And Molly deserved to know that a woman never had to settle for being second best, not even one with a ruined reputation.

"I can't marry you, Trey." Katherine swallowed hard.

"Because…?" he prompted.

She met his gaze without wavering. "*Because* you're still in love with your wife."

Chapter Seven

Later that afternoon, Trey decided to use work to rid himself of the painful emotions Katherine had awakened in him. How could she speak so boldly of forgiveness given the tragedies she'd suffered?

Where did that strength of faith come from?

And why did he admire her for it?

Disturbed by his train of thoughts, he charged up the steps of the newly completed Arapahoe County Courthouse. The smell of fresh varnish hit him as he entered the building. Italian marble floors reminiscent of the Capitol in Washington gleamed white and pristine in the late morning light.

The three-story building, by its regal existence alone, changed the look of Denver from a prairie town to an up-and-coming city. Important business occurred in this building, carried out by important people. The same important people Trey didn't especially want to see at the moment.

Increasing his pace to a significant clip, Trey avoided eye contact with the various politicians, lawyers and other civil servants he passed along the wood-paneled corridors. At last, he entered his makeshift office at the back of the building and slammed the door shut with a bang.

Thin rays of light slipped through the seams of the windows, creating little pockets of warmth in the otherwise austere room. One desk, one chair, countless stacks of papers and a thick layer of dust spoke of the respect Trey had given to his administrative duties of late.

Determined to keep his mind on business, he gathered the nearest pile of papers. But as he glanced down at the writing, the black script drifted into one unreadable blur.

Accepting defeat, he tossed the stack aside and gave his chaotic thoughts full rein. What had possessed him to confront Katherine Taylor this morning, alone, in the school's supply closet no less? It was bad enough two impressionable teenagers had witnessed their impromptu meeting. Anyone could have seen him enter the building alone and then exit after Katherine.

If they were looking.

Trey knew that some of Charity House's neighbors weren't exactly overjoyed at the notion of the unique orphanage in their high-class neighborhood. Several had filed complaints about excessive noise and other ridiculous offensives.

What would they do with a meaty scandal, unfounded or not?

He'd acted without a thought to the consequences. But there had been repercussions, in the form of two fifteen-year-olds who thought they'd seen more than they had. And nosy neighbors or not, if word got past those Charity House children, the town gossips would have more ammunition in their battle to destroy Katherine's already tenuous reputation. Would they go so far as to try to shut down the school?

What would happen to Katherine then?

Why hadn't Trey forced the issue of marriage, instead of allowing the mule-headed woman to walk away with nothing resolved between them?

You're still in love with your wife…

Trey's heart weighed heavy in his chest. Even after Katherine had brought up Laurette, Trey had been more concerned over the stricken expression on the schoolmarm's face than the momentary betrayal of his wife's memory.

Given the opportunity again, would he attempt to offer comfort to Katherine and alleviate her fears?

Yes. Yes, he would, because what had happened between them in that supply closet had nothing to do with Laurette or Trey's search for Ike Hayes. For a brief moment, and he assured himself it had been brief, Trey had allowed himself to forget his hate. He'd wanted to give Katherine a reason to trust again, and to help free her from the dark legacy of her attack.

His motives had started out pure enough, yet he'd hurt Kathcrine anyway. He probably always would. She needed a man unsullied of heart, less broken and certainly not consumed with hate. A man who loved and trusted God as much as she did. Trey, on the other hand, hadn't stepped inside a church since Laurette's funeral.

With that thought, he circled around his desk and dropped into the lone chair in the room. The leather and wood protested under his weight in the form of a succession of creaks and groans.

He tried to call forth memories of his wife, but his mind kept straying back to a prissy, frightened schoolmarm who hadn't been quite so afraid this morning.

A jolt of satisfaction passed through him. For once, Katherine Taylor hadn't flinched from his touch.

As soon as the thought came, guilt and regret lashed into one another. Katherine's reputation could be irreparably damaged. If the neighbors had seen them, had put two and two together, there could be more trouble for her than a damaged reputation. Why wasn't she more concerned?

For one dark, dangerous moment, Trey considered charging back to the orphanage and shaking some sense into the woman. Of course, he still had the obstacle of a three-inch tin star to overcome.

Yes, he wore a badge. Yes, he could be killed in the line of duty, just like Katherine's father. But his usual, day-to-day duties were far from dangerous. The biggest problem besetting him this week was the accounting of monies he'd used in the past six months to run the courts.

He would much rather be out on the trail, pursuing bank robbers and other outlaws—men like Ike Hayes—but a small army of accountants at the Justice Department had started auditing his every expenditure. They'd gone so far as to deny his last request for additional funds to run his trials properly. Hence Drew Hayes's far too lengthy stay in the Denver jail.

So here he sat, keeping track of the money used by the court, instead of enforcing the law of the land. The biggest threat to him right now was a paper cut.

Loud, insistent knocking at the door ripped Trey out of his thoughts. "Go away."

Ignoring the command, Logan Mitchell pushed into the room, hat in hand, a wary look on his face. Trey scowled at his deputy. With his blond hair matted to his head, the man looked more like a greenhorn rancher than a seasoned lawman. Trey knew better than to believe the deception. Logan was fast and accurate with a pistol. He was also smart, discerning and mean as a snake when it came to serving justice. The younger man reminded Trey of… himself.

"What do you want?" Trey asked.

"You got a visitor over at the jail, Marshal."

Trey picked up a random piece of paper and studied it intently. "I'm busy."

With his lips curling in distaste, Logan shifted his gaze to the papers scattered on the desk. "The audit?"

Trey bared his teeth in response.

Logan lifted a shoulder. "All right, I get the hint. I'm leaving. But I think you'll want to see this particular visitor."

Trey placed the paper on the desk, picked up a ledger and flipped open the front cover. Running his finger down one of the columns, he pretended grave interest in the declining numbers. "I doubt it."

"She asked to see *Mr. Trey.*"

The ledger crashed to the floor as Trey hurled himself out of his chair. He was around the desk in the same amount of time it took his heart to take a single beat. "You left her alone? With Drew Hayes in there?"

Logan took a step back, palms in the air, his eyes wary. "I'm not stupid. She's playing checkers with Sheriff Lassiter."

Nursing his anger at the thought of Drew Hayes within fifty feet of Molly, even if thick bars did separate them, he growled. "She's inside the jailhouse?"

"They're on the covered walkway out front. The sheriff set up two chairs with a crate in between."

Regardless of this new information, Trey's temper prowled like a hungry lion seeking to devour anything in its path. Right now, that meant Logan Mitchell. To keep from taking out the other man for the sheer pleasure of it, Trey clenched his jaw until his teeth started to ache. "She say what she wanted?"

"Nope."

Shoving his hat on his head, Trey headed toward the hallway.

Logan dropped a weary look onto the open ledger. "I guess this means you'll want me to stay here and work on balancing those numbers for you."

Already out the door, Trey looked back over his shoulder. "The bean counters in Washington can wait until I get around to it."

Logan grinned as he fell into step beside him, and the two wound their way through the maze of hallways. "I like the way you think, Marshal."

Deciding his temper needed an outlet after all, Trey sliced a glare at the other man. "Where are you going?"

"With you."

"You're not coming with me."

"I'm not?"

Trey held the pause for effect, then pulled his lips into a sarcastic grin. "You're going over to Mattie Silks's place to question her again about the night we found Drew Hayes in her brothel."

Logan's expression darkened. "We both know it's a waste of time."

Trey shrugged in response, increasing his speed once they were outside the courthouse and heading toward the jail. When Logan continued to walk alongside him, he pointed to his left. "Market Street is that way."

"I know where it is."

"Then why are you still following me?"

For the first time since he'd sworn the man in, Logan looked uncertain. "Come on, Marshal. That woman won't tell me any more than she has the past fifteen times we've questioned her. She'll probably start talking in circles again." He tipped his hat back and rubbed his forehead. "It makes my head hurt just thinking about it."

"Eventually, she's going to talk herself into a corner and reveal what we want to know. And one of us is going to be the man to get her there. Why not you?"

"Are you forgetting that Mattie hates me almost as much as she hates you?"

The frustration in Logan's voice was exactly the reaction Trey had expected, but he refused to relent now that the idea had taken hold.

"She likes you just fine." Trey slapped the younger man on the back. "Except when you're asking her questions about the Hayes brothers."

A defeated hiss whipped out of Logan. "You know, Marshal, what they say about you is true. You really are Beelzebub's cousin."

Trey's grin turned into a genuine smile. "Just be glad we're on the same side."

"Yeah, well, I have my doubts about that."

* * *

Ignoring the activity around him, Trey strode purposely down the busy streets of Denver's business district, en route to the jail. A steady stream of people meandered alongside him, their murmurs indistinguishable from one another. Determined to make good time, Trey clenched his jaw and bit into some of the grit kicked up from a passing carriage. A few unsavory types made an especially wide berth for him to pass. Sometimes a badge had its advantages, he thought, with a smile.

Still grinning, he swung around to his left and crossed the street. A group of well-dressed ladies stopped in conversation and simply stared at him in a gesture just short of rude. Undaunted, he tipped his hat as he drew near. They quickly looked away, whispered among themselves and then hurried off in the opposite direction.

Although Trey thought their behavior odd, his mind was too focused on other, more important matters to be overly concerned with the particulars of the brief encounter. Logan had assured him Molly was safely outside the jail; nevertheless, Trey increased his pace. Relief speared through him the moment he turned the last corner and caught sight of two heads bent over a checkerboard.

Slowing, he focused on the little girl in the crisp green dress. Her pitch-black hair gleamed almost blue in the sun, and one long braid hung down her back. She looked too young, too innocent, for the harsh setting of the jailhouse behind her.

Trey couldn't deny the truth any longer. Molly Taylor deserved every bit of the stability her sister wanted for her.

The sudden craving to be the man to make that happen nearly brought him to his knees.

He wondered when he'd gotten in so deep. In his none-too-subtle way, Marc had recently claimed that Trey's affection for the kid was directly connected to his loss of Laurette and their unborn child. Granted, his friend might have been on the right track, but Trey's paternal feelings for Molly Taylor had grown separate and distinct in the past few weeks. A reprieve, of sorts, from his feelings of hate and anger.

Unable to catch a decent breath, he continued to watch as Molly considered her next move. She chewed on her lower lip, then picked up a black checker. Grinning up at the sheriff, she slammed her wooden playing chip on an empty square in front of him. "King me."

The grizzled old man shook his head and lifted his palms in the air. "I'm all out. Looks like you win again."

"Well, 'course I did. It's 'cause I's good."

"Won't argue with that." A twinkle danced in the sheriff's eyes. "Molly Taylor, you play a mean game of checkers."

Trey could only marvel at the change in Sheriff Lassiter. What had happened to the nasty curmudgeon, known throughout the West for his lack of tolerance of anything frivolous? Right now, his hard eyes actually looked…kind.

Closing the distance, Trey called out. "Molly? You wanted to see me?"

At the sound of her name, the little girl lifted her head. The moment her gaze connected with Trey's, her face broke into her hallmark gap-toothed grin.

"Mr. Trey!" She vaulted off her chair and, with a leap, launched herself into his arms.

Unable to deny the momentary pleasure he got from her childish devotion, Trey shoved aside the ugly emotions that usually resided in him and allowed the kid's glee to fill his heart. He wrapped her tightly in his embrace and breathed in her goodness. She smelled of soap and little girl and everything innocent. A swell of protective instincts, abrupt and violent, rose inside him.

She giggled, then pulled back. "Hi."

He smiled in return, wanting very much to be the man he saw shining in her eyes. "Hello, kitten."

Giggling again, she kissed him on the cheek, then squirmed out of his arms.

"I hurted my finger." Standing tall, she thrust her hand toward him. "See?"

Trey squinted. Taking her small hand, he arranged his face into a look of genuine concern and examined the tiny slit. "Looks like it hurts real bad."

"It don't really hurt no more."

Trey kept his expression serious, intent. "Well, that's a relief."

Little worry lines dug between her arched brows as she toed the wooden slats beneath her feet. "I have a loose tooth, too."

Trey had seen his share of stalling tactics to know when he was in the midst of some of the best. He stamped down his impatience and continued to play her game. "No kidding?"

She wiggled one of her remaining two front teeth with her thumb. "See?"

"I do, indeed."

Suddenly realizing there weren't any other Charity House children in the general area, he took a quick, covert glance down the street. "Are you alone, Molly?"

Skinny shoulders hunched forward. "Maybe."

Trey's gut flipped inside itself. If her trembling lips were anything to go by, trouble lay ahead. And there was going to be one ornery schoolmarm at the other end of it. "Does your sister know where you are?"

"No." She gave him a pleading look that tore at his defenses.

"But I gotta talk to you, Mr. Trey. Really, really bad. Katherine said I couldn't come see you." Molly sighed, then puffed out her chest. "But I came anyway."

A wisp of regret expanded into soul-deep guilt. Because of him, Molly had defied her sister. *Again.* He had to put a stop to it. Now. "Let's get you back to Charity House."

"But I came to—"

"You can tell me why you're here on the way back to the orphanage."

She looked ready to argue, but Lassiter chose that moment to break into the conversation. Clearing his throat, he cocked his head toward the jail and said, "Well, I'm heading back inside."

Molly shoved her hand forward. "Good game."

The grown-up, manly gesture had the older man's lip twitching. Taking her hand in his, he pumped it up and down. "It was. But next time you won't be so lucky."

"Yes, I will."

Lassiter patted her head. "I like your conviction, kid." He glanced to Trey. "Are we gonna finalize that date on Hayes's trial soon?"

Trey shared a look with the sheriff as he spun Molly

toward the direction of her home. "I'll be back in an hour. We'll discuss it then."

"Right."

Molly slipped a wave over her shoulder. "Bye, Sheriff, see ya."

"See ya, kid."

Once Trey had Molly heading reluctantly down the street, he nudged her onto the planked sidewalk and pointed her in the direction of Charity House.

She scuffed her feet, digging the tips of her shoes into a wooden seam every third plank. "Mr. Trey?" she said, keeping her gaze focused on her feet.

He ignored the foreboding skipping along the base of his spine. "Yes?"

"Will you—" She broke off and sighed. "Will you…"

"Will I what?"

Throwing back her shoulders, she jutted her chin toward the sky and turned to look at him straight in the eye. "Will you be my daddy?"

Trey's heart lifted, then dropped. Swallowing the lump in his throat, he stopped walking and turned to look at her.

She shifted from foot to foot but held his stare, with a hopeful plea in her eyes. For a long moment, a cloak of silence enveloped them, broken only by the sounds of the people and horses milling about.

For one glorious second, he wanted to tell her that of course he would be her daddy, but he hadn't settled the particulars with Katherine yet. He still had to make the woman understand that this was more than a mere discussion of stability versus her reputation.

He was afraid talk had already begun. If an unsavory

scandal was brewing, Trey knew it could affect far more than himself and Katherine.

Something had to be done. Soon.

"Ah, Molly," he said. "I'd like nothing better than—"

"Good." She threaded her fingers with his and grinned up at him. "'Cause I need two parents. And I want you most of all."

Her look of absolute hero worship frightened him more than her request. What if he let this child down? What if she came to harm because of him?

And what if he hurt Katherine in the process as well?

He hadn't been able to protect Laurette. What made him think it would be any different with Molly and her sister? "You have Katherine as your big sister. That's almost like a parent."

"No." She stamped her foot. "That's not good enough. She can be my momma. And you get to be my daddy."

"Kitten…"

Mutiny swept across her features. "Well, if you don't wanna, then I'll get Dr. Shane to do it. He likes Katherine. I know, 'cause he's always around the house and he smiles at her a lot and he said so when I asked."

Trey's heart rebelled at the notion of the good doctor marrying Katherine, sharing her smiles, her future. Her life.

The rush of sickening jealousy took root, the sheer power of it dragging air out of his lungs in an unpleasant wheeze. Dr. Shane Bartlett was a perfect match for Katherine, and completely, totally wrong for her. Trey suspected Molly might have continued speaking, but his own turbulent thoughts smothered her chatter.

Panic rushed blood through his veins, pounding one thought through his head. Although he wasn't sure he wanted to explore the subject too deeply, he couldn't let Katherine marry Shane Bartlett.

Eventually, Molly's words jolted him back to the immediate disaster at hand. "So whattaya say?"

Their gazes met, hers hopeful, his unable to focus. How could he become a husband and a father with Ike Hayes still alive? Could he live within one set of parameters, for Molly and Katherine's sake, and still pursue the most important goal of his life?

"You haven't been listening," she accused.

He shook his head. "Sure I have. You want me to... to..."

"Marry my sister. Then you can be my daddy."

"I think we better slow down here."

She gave him a look that made him feel like the five-year-old instead of the adult. "We aren't walking, Mr. Trey."

"That's not what I meant. We need to think this through."

"What's to think about? Just ask Katherine to marry you."

"Let's say I agree to this."

The air around her crackled with pleasure. "You'll do it?"

"Now wait a minute. Aren't you forgetting that Katherine doesn't like me very much? *She* might not want to marry *me*." The thought made him unreasonably anxious.

Jamming her fists on her hips, she gave him another pitying look that had five-year-old tenacity clinging to the edges of it. "Well, then, you change her mind."

Doomed. He was doomed. He knew it with a lawman's

instincts. The same innate reaction that had kept him alive in deadly situations told him it was too late to stop the inevitable now. No matter his drive for vengeance on Laurette's behalf, no matter how ugly his own life had become, Trey could not find it in his heart to let this child down.

Acting as though he still held a portion of the control, he carefully said, "If I agree to this—"

Molly's flushed words cut him off. "I knew you'd say yes."

"Now let me finish. *If* I agree, I'm gonna need your full cooperation."

Her eyes lit up. "I'll do anything you say. *Anything*. As long as you'll be my daddy."

She punctuated each word with a little swish of her shoulders, each movement solidifying his resolve.

"The first thing you'll have to do is stop disobeying your sister."

"Well…" She went perfectly still. "Okay. I guess."

"I want a solid answer out of you."

"Yes. I'll do it."

"And you're gonna have to let me do all the talking."

Her face scrunched into a scowl. "You think that's a good idea, Mr. Trey? She gets kinda, I don't know…upset when you talk to her."

Ah, there it was. The truth spoken so bluntly by the five-year-old had him second-guessing himself. Talking sense, logic—or even reason, for that matter—into Katherine Taylor might prove impossible.

Then again, perhaps it was time to stop thinking in terms of logic and reason. Perhaps it was time to consider alternative weapons.

Perhaps it was time to stop playing by the rules.

As he stared into Molly's eager face, Trey realized he still held a portion of the control. No matter her arguments to the contrary, Katherine Taylor would marry him. For all the right reasons, and maybe even for a few of the wrong ones.

"Just leave it all to me, kitten. I'll convince your sister she needs to become my wife."

"Really? How?"

"I have a plan." And this time, Katherine Taylor would not get the chance to walk away from him.

Chapter Eight

Once back in the safety of her room, Katherine changed clothes and then washed her face, never once allowing her mind to think beyond one task at a time. It was only after lacing up her boots that the shock finally set in. She sank slowly to the bed and then simply sat motionless, in a state of disbelief.

Holding back a sob, she buried her face in her hands, taking only mild comfort from the black solitude she found there.

She'd been caught in a compromising position, in front of Molly, no less. And although innocent enough on the surface, she and Trey had been caught alone—*alone!*—inside the school's supply closet. Katherine had always tried to remain above reproach, and not just for Molly's sake. In spite of the whispers, and the public shunning, Katherine held herself to a high moral standard for the benefit of Charity House and the school.

Which made the whole situation so much worse. In fact, if she and Trey hadn't been interrupted, Katherine could only wonder how far things would have gone.

What must Megan and Johnny think of her? Katherine was supposed to be an example to the children. She was not supposed to be some reckless woman who allowed herself to be caught up in the moment.

She pounded her fists into the bed, stood up and trudged toward the mirror hanging over her dresser. Studying her image for a long, breathless moment, she wondered why she didn't look any different than she had before she'd met up with Trey at the schoolhouse.

Where was the remorse? The humiliation?

The fear?

Pressing her palms against her temples, she prayed for sanity to return.

On that terrible night two years ago, her attacker had claimed she'd led him to believe she was a willing partner, simply because she hadn't told him to stop. And now, another man had nearly kissed her because she hadn't told him to stop.

She closed her eyes against the sting of tears.

Was she like her mother, as her attacker had viciously claimed in front of all the townspeople, a woman with carnal appetites that made a man force himself on her?

Her heart clenched.

No. She would not torture herself with such flawed thinking. No matter what her attacker had claimed, and what others said now, she'd been the victim that night.

Swallowing, she forced all doubt to the back of her mind and went to the Bible for solace. After flipping to 1 Corinthians, she quickly found the verse she was looking for in chapter ten. "God is faithful." She read aloud, "He will not suffer you to be tempted above that ye are able; but will with the temptation also make a way to escape, that ye may be able to bear it."

Unfortunately, God's Word only brought more trepidation. Just how much temptation could she stand around Trey Scott? How long before she…before he…before they…

No.

Appalled at her own worries, she set the Bible down and took to pacing. After what had nearly happened between Trey and her, she should be staying far, far away from him, and yet she didn't want to stay far, far away. Against all signs otherwise, she was beginning to trust the man.

And wasn't that ridiculous? Nothing was resolved between them. Trey was still a lawman. He was still in love with his wife. And he was still set on seeking vengeance by his own hands. If talk began… Well, they would deal with that when and if it happened. Katherine wouldn't worry about something that had yet to occur.

At least Trey had let her walk away from him this morning, even after he'd lectured her on her reputation and the consequences of their time alone together. Unfortunately, she'd recognized the look of unyielding determination in his eyes. He wasn't through with her yet.

If only he would…

Her breathing picked up speed.

If only he would what? What did she want from him?

Determined to get her answers, one way or another, Katherine took a deep breath and pivoted toward the door. She was a grown woman. A Christian. It was time she started acting like one.

My flesh and my heart faileth: but God is the strength of my heart, and my portion forever.

Fortified once again, she sailed into the hallway,

marched down the stairs and out of the house. But the moment she turned toward town, her gaze connected with Trey and Molly laughing in tandem as they made their way down the lane, toward her. With the manicured lawns and perfectly sculpted hedges lining their path, the two looked like a real father and daughter journeying home from a day of play in town.

Katherine didn't have time to wonder why they were together before a swift jolt of pleasure took hold of her.

If only Trey wasn't as driven as he was to seek vengeance. If only he wasn't so bitter toward God. As things stood, he would never be able to provide the stability Molly needed—or the security that Katherine secretly wanted for herself.

Miserable and heavyhearted, Katherine shifted out of sight and watched the two interact. Molly stumbled, but Trey caught her before she fell and scooped her up into his arms. Raising her high in the air, he spun her around in fast, dizzying circles. The little girl's childish giggles united with Trey's deep, masculine chuckles.

Katherine's knees nearly gave way, and she reached for the railing to steady herself. Trey Scott brought out the child in Molly, the one Katherine had once feared didn't exist.

In those first few weeks after retrieving Molly from the mining camp, Katherine had fretted that the little girl was lost forever inside the frightening silence she'd wrapped around herself after her father's death.

How could Katherine have forgotten the role Trey had played in bringing Molly out of that dark world? He'd been the first person to make the child laugh. It had happened several months ago, during one of the infamous

Charity House baseball games. Trey had just hit a home run, but instead of running the bases alone, he'd rushed to the porch, whisked Molly into his arms and taken her with him. From that day forth, Trey had found ways to include the little girl in other games, until she had taken to joining on her own.

Oh, how Katherine wanted to believe in Trey Scott. But she was honest enough with herself to admit that her own fears and her concern for Molly's future chased away any hope. The reality of his badge and what drove him to wear it wouldn't go away.

Molly couldn't handle another loss, and Katherine couldn't bear to watch the little girl close herself off from the world again. No matter how happy Molly and Trey looked right now, Katherine wasn't going to allow the man to stand in her way of protecting her little sister.

Trey chose that moment to look up. As though he sensed her confusion, his piercing gray eyes turned serious and intent, silently demanding of her the one thing she couldn't fully give him. Her trust. As he continued to hold her stare, her head started to pound. She wanted to run, to flee.

To him or *away* from him, she couldn't say.

Maintaining eye contact, he started advancing on her, his eyes communicating his resolve. Desperate to free herself from the power he suddenly held over her, she searched for a flaw in him. Just one. But she found only masculine beauty in his fiercely handsome features, arrogant scowl and bold swagger.

Katherine couldn't remember ever having been so aware of a man before. Was she more like her mother than she thought, after all? Was she a "tramp," like the ladies had claimed earlier today? Was there something deep inside her that wanted to explore the temptation Trey Scott presented?

Ridiculous. Absurd.

Shocking.

Determined to regain control over her emotions, Katherine forced her gaze to Molly. The look of guilt in the little girl's eyes put Katherine instantly on alert.

"Where have you been, Molly?" she asked.

Shifting her gaze to Trey, Molly drew her bottom lip between her teeth. "Um...with Mr. Trey?"

Katherine angled her head and waited for more, but neither man nor child felt the need to explain further. "I see."

Trey's lips pushed into a lopsided grin. "No, you don't."

Katherine bristled, ready to do battle, until she noted the hint of worry in his gaze and the twinge of some other, deeper emotion she didn't dare name.

"Run inside, kitten. I want to talk to your sister." Trey paused and looked meaningfully at the little girl. *"Alone."*

To Katherine's utter surprise, Molly instantly obeyed. "Okay, Mr. Trey. See ya later."

Trey tugged on her braid. "Bye, kid."

He waited until the door banged shut behind Molly before joining Katherine on the porch.

"I'm not sure I have anything to say to you right now," she said.

He removed his hat and gave her a grin that had her thinking about...well, things better left alone.

"Good," he said. "Because I'm not sure I want to hear what you have to say."

Astoundingly enough, fear of his touch wasn't her first concern at the moment. No, no, it was the possibility of future happiness with the man—or rather the *impossibility*—that frightened her now.

"What do you want from me, *Marshal?*" She made sure she put special emphasis on his job title, as much for her own benefit as for his.

He inched closer. "You're looking very lovely this fine afternoon, Miss Taylor."

She took offense at his far too late attempt to soften her with pretty words. "Charm won't work on me at this point in our relationship."

His boot heels clicked on the wooden slats as he edged around her, circling her like a dog with a particularly meaty bone. "Pity."

Feeling more than a little unbalanced, she decided not to argue the point. Yet.

He stopped behind her. "What? No clever reply this time?"

"I'm working on it."

He paced to the front of her. "I see you changed your dress."

She pursed her lips into what she hoped was a mixture of boredom and prim scolding. "I felt it necessary after you pestered me earlier."

"Are you claiming I acted against your will?" His words were barely above a whisper.

Katherine shut her eyes against the implication of his question, trying desperately to keep her thoughts in the present. But slowly, oh so slowly, her mind slid back in time to a place where a man *had* forced her.

The muscles in Katherine's heart tightened from the effort to stop the memories from overwhelming her. The effort left her breathless.

Panicky.

The other man had made her feel so dirty, while Trey never, never ever, did. She shouldn't have let him believe otherwise, not even for a moment.

Feeling remorseful, she lifted her eyes back to Trey's. His stricken expression sent fresh guilt through her.

"Against my will? No. No, of course not," she rushed to say. "I didn't mean to imply otherwise."

He nodded, relief filling his gaze. "Then let's settle down and talk this through."

"Oh, Trey, the past few times we tried to talk, we didn't do so well."

He slid her an amused grin and then waved her toward one of the chairs. "So we get back on the horse and try again."

"I don't ride horses."

"Well, then." He tapped her lightly on the nose. "That makes it more likely you'll learn something here."

She bit back a flippant retort, annoyed as much by her shaky reaction to his nearness as by the arrogance of his tone. He had the insolence to smile at her again, and everything in her softened. "Don't, Trey."

"Don't what?"

"This is hard enough as it is." Resignation tripped along her spine. "Don't make me like you on top of everything else."

He touched her cheek. "Would that be such a bad thing?"

"The worst."

He dropped his hand and clenched his jaw so hard, a muscle jumped.

Realizing she'd insulted him, she shook her head. "I'm not making myself clear. Perhaps this isn't the best time to talk."

She started to turn, but he caught her by the arm.

"No, it's the perfect time. We… Let's start again, shall we?"

"Can we do that?" She had her doubts, for very good reasons.

He steered her toward one of the rockers. "We can try."

She scooted out of his reach and perched against the railing. "How do you propose we start again when we can't have a single conversation without arguing?"

"I'm confident we can do this. I'll start. By apologizing."

He took her hand gently into his.

"I don't think this is a good idea," she said.

"The apology or—" he dropped his gaze to their joined hands "—this?"

She quickly pulled her hand free. "*This* is the sort of behavior that got us into trouble earlier. Aren't you rather forgetting yourself?"

He made a deep sound in his throat. "Seems I always do when I'm around you."

"Well, in my estimation, that makes you *very* unpredictable."

His smile never faltered. "I certainly hope so."

Resisting the urge to smile back at him, she swallowed. *Slowly.* "Your charm isn't working on me."

"So you said already."

"Keep it up and I might say it again."

"You know, Miss Taylor, there is nothing worse than when a man is trying to be sincere and the woman is not."

"This is your attempt at sincere?" she asked.

"I'm trying, Katherine." He let out a slow breath, his eyes slightly less haunted than usual. "I'm really trying."

She shut her own eyes against the intensity in his gaze, wishing she knew how to shut out the tender emotions trying to break free from her heart. "I won't marry you." She hissed, "I *won't.*"

"I didn't ask."

Shocked, she whipped open her eyes and gaped at him. He winked at her.

"You're a skunk, Trey Scott."

"Make no mistake, Miss Taylor. I'll ask." Masculine triumph narrowed his eyes. "When I'm ready."

With that pithy remark, he placed his hat on his head, turned and sauntered down the steps, never once looking back at her.

Although Katherine would have liked nothing more than to follow after the beast and kick him in the shins, a part of her was thrilled at the way he'd once again caught her off guard with his outrageous conceit.

And that frightened her far more than his touch.

Chapter Nine

Trey met up again with Sheriff Lassiter exactly one hour after leaving Katherine on the Charity House porch. The traffic was dying down on the street, but Trey hardly noticed. A stream of tobacco juice arced through the air and landed inches from Trey's feet.

"Nice shot, Sheriff."

Lassiter ignored him.

Dropping into the empty chair that Molly had occupied earlier, Trey tried to focus his thoughts on anything other than the stubborn schoolteacher who made his blood boil with irritation.

With a shake of his head, he banished the disturbing woman from his thoughts and turned his attention to Denver's notorious sheriff. Lassiter had pulled the wide hat brim over his weather-beaten face, the relaxed posture making him appear asleep.

Trey propped his feet against the rail in a gesture identical to the sheriff's and inhaled the sharp, spicy fragrance of a coming rain. "Surveying your domain, Lassiter?"

With two fingers, the sheriff pushed his hat back, leaned forward and spat another rivulet of tobacco juice to the ground. "You get Molly home safe?"

"Yeah, she's back at the orphanage, probably causing trouble already." His tone reflected all the admiration he felt for the little girl, and all the frustration he felt toward the older sister.

"No doubt." After a moment of shuffling around in his chair, the sheriff leveled a measuring look at Trey. "So what did our little Molly want from you that couldn't wait until later?"

Trey lifted his gaze to the heavens. As the warmth of the day skidded behind threatening rain clouds, his mood turned the same dreary gray as the sky. "She just wanted to talk."

He didn't feel the need to add the particulars of their disturbing conversation, or to reveal the resulting clash he'd had with Katherine.

Lassiter dropped his feet to the ground, then leaned forward. "She came all that way, by herself, just to talk?"

"That's what I said."

Rubbing his chin between his thumb and forefinger, the sheriff slid a shrewd look at Trey from below his hat. "Molly's a pretty little thing. Already a charmer."

Why deny the truth? "I'd say."

Lassiter shifted the wad of tobacco around in his mouth. "She's a lot like her sister. Don't you think?"

Trey knew where the sheriff was heading, knew he should put a stop to it, but he didn't have the strength to fend off the attack. *"A lot."*

Even as he spoke the admission, Trey accepted the complexity of the task that lay before him. Katherine Taylor was proving far more difficult than he'd expected. All he wanted was to secure her good reputation and protect Charity House from a potential scandal.

Or so he told himself.

But, even now, as frustrated as he was with Katherine, he could feel the pull of attraction between them growing stronger by the day. He was drawn to the way she made him feel less anger. His need to strike out dimmed when he was around her. But Trey knew the feeling was only temporary. The hate was still in him, bubbling just under the surface, festering and spreading like a cancer. Driving him to hunt down Ike Hayes and make him pay.

"Do you want to talk about the big sister?"

"No."

Trey didn't even want to *think* about Katherine Taylor until he figured out what marriage to her would mean to Laurette's legacy.

One thing he knew for certain. When he focused on vengeance, he honored his wife's memory. So Trey would focus on finding Ike Hayes. He would concern himself with the schoolmarm later. "I'm setting Drew's trial for two weeks from next Monday."

Lassiter nodded, taking up the new topic with ease. "You got the okay for the money?"

Trey snorted. "I'm through waiting for the Justice Department to approve my request. I want this trial over, even if that means using my own money to make it happen."

"Too bad it ain't a double trial. Ike is the real brains of the operation. Drew's too stupid to have planned that raid in Colorado Springs all on his own."

Trey couldn't argue with the truth. Unfortunately, after his numerous conversations with Drew Hayes, he'd decided it wasn't family loyalty keeping the man's mouth shut. The outlaw didn't know where his brother was hiding.

"At least we have one of them in custody. That's gonna have to do, for now," Lassiter said.

Trey nodded. "It's something."

Out of the corner of his eye, Trey caught sight of his deputy trudging down the street. The man's shoulders were slumped in defeat.

Scuffing his heels as he walked, Logan wended his way around a horse and rider, a carriage, a mother and her small posse of children. With his head hung low, the twenty-year-old deputy looked like one of the Charity House children after a good scolding.

"Talking to that woman was a complete waste of my time," Logan said on a wave of disgust.

Trey held back a sigh of resignation. "So Mattie won this round, too."

"I'd have had better luck getting information out of a dead mule."

As Trey listened to Logan expound on the worst of Mattie's qualities, his mind sorted through various possibilities to get the tight-lipped madam speaking.

Rising in the middle of Logan's tirade, Trey slapped his hat against his thigh and turned in the direction of Market Street. The thriving red-light district between Eighteenth and Twentieth Street had been the source of great frustration in Trey's early days of marshaling. For weeks he'd fought a losing battle in his attempt to clean up the area. The community's tolerance, coupled with the politicians' blind eye to prostitution, had been too powerful an alliance to overcome.

Today, however, Trey was not on a moral errand. This one was far more personal. He'd had enough of women running him around in circles. At least one of them was going to cooperate this afternoon.

"Hey," Logan called after him. "Where are you going?"

"Mattie's. It's time I explained to that ornery madam the value of female compliance."

A clap of thunder punctuated his words with an ominous clash.

Resolved to get his answers, Trey stood outside Mattie's brothel and considered the heavy double doors that led into the unremarkable two-story brick building. As though to mock him, the rain began falling in heavy sheets, making him impatient to be done with this filthy business. Without waiting for a response to his knock, he twisted the knob and pushed into the gaudy foyer.

Barely taking note of the decor, Trey continued forward, bypassing several pieces of furniture, including a red velvet divan.

Although it was still early afternoon, Mattie's brothel was full of customers. Trey ignored the men, warned off Mattie's infamous bouncer with a look and then trudged deeper into the activity around him.

The magnificence of this parlor house had always struck him as off-kilter with the rest of the world. The prostitution business did a solid trade in Denver, making madams like Mattie Silks among the wealthiest in town. As he continued to study the room and its occupants, Trey took special note of the women's painted faces and their expensive dresses, designed in the latest Parisian fashion.

Circling his gaze to the back of the room, he found

Mattie in deep conversation with a notable banker in town. The woman, in all her theatrical glory, was his link to Ike.

Today she would talk.

Trey moved in between the woman and her customer, not caring that he was interrupting. "I want a word with you, Mattie. *Alone.*"

She didn't respond but instead chose to continue her conversation with her customer.

Trey took the opportunity to measure his small, blond adversary. Just like her brothel, everything about Mattie Silks was overdone. Her hair was too blond, her eyes were too large, and her mouth was too red. Born to live in the sensational, moment by moment, she struck a pose after every sentence she spoke.

Apparently, Ike Hayes had a taste for the dramatic.

The notion made Trey sick. "I won't ask twice," he said. "Cooperate here, or I'll haul you down to the jail-house."

With a studied toss of her blond mane, Mattie blessed him with a hard glint in her eye. "I've already dealt with one of your kind today. Perhaps tomorrow I'll reconsider. But, for now, if you would please leave me to—"

"It's important." His tone made his point.

Her eyes went flat, the businesswoman gliding into place. "It'll cost you."

"I figured it would."

Mattie Silks might be a well-known madam who peddled the charms of her "girls," but she was also very shrewd. Money spoke louder than a smile, a handsome face or false words.

"Perhaps this will persuade you of the urgency of my task." Trey fit a fifty-dollar bill into her palm.

With a diminutive grin, she closed her hand around the money, excused herself from her companion, then turned her full attention to Trey. With sugar dripping in her voice, she lifted an arched eyebrow. "Perhaps you would like to follow me, Marshal Scott?"

She led the way to her private sitting room.

Once inside, Trey shouldered the door closed behind them.

Mattie slipped the money inside a small compartment in her desk. "You've just purchased a full hour of my time. So what can I do for you, Marshal?"

Trey clenched his jaw. "I want answers, nothing more."

Mattie's gaze swept over him. "I never noticed how handsome you are, Marshal." She leaned forward and trailed a finger up his arm.

Trey didn't bother holding back a shudder of disgust. While he knew many men would be eager to sample Mattie's charms, Trey was not one of them. He suddenly craved Katherine's purity and goodness, to experience relief from the dark emotions that drove him to stand in this brothel and question this madam.

"Like I said before, I want information from you, Mattie. That's all."

Unfazed by his declaration, she looked him up and down, her eyes shifting with curiosity. "I know that glint in your eyes, Marshal. You've got a woman on your mind." She tossed him a pitiful look. "Not one of my girls, of course."

"Mattie, I'm warning you. This is not a conversation you want to have with me."

The madam relaxed into a pose and summoned a faraway look to her eyes. "Now, I know you're friends with that disgustingly noble Marc Dupree. And since Marc is, well, so noble and he's married to Laney—another disgustingly noble creature—it can't be her. So who else is there…"

Trey's head spun with fury, but he held the emotion in check. He could see she was enjoying the sheer drama of her game. He would not give her the satisfaction of knowing how thoroughly she'd hit her mark.

"That leaves…" She held the pause for a long moment. "Kath—"

"Don't finish that sentence, Mattie."

"Ah, but you see, Marshal Scott—" she shook her finger at him "—I've heard all about your shameless behavior with the not-so-proper schoolmarm. It's obvious there's more to the prissy Katherine Taylor than meets the eye."

As soon as the false accusations fled Mattie's lips, Trey's anger exploded—the silvery edge of it tearing away the rational part of him. Unable to speak, he clenched his fists so tightly, his knuckles burned like fire.

"I'll say this once," he managed through his clenched jaw. "Never speak about Kath—*Miss Taylor*—in that ugly tone again."

Hands on her hips, Mattie straightened, her eyes turning frigid. When she spoke, her voice filled with the harder side of the life she'd endured for thirty years—cold and nasty and vicious. "Like mother, like daughter." She waved her hand back and forth.

In one swift movement, Trey captured Mattie's wrist and held her firmly, but not tight enough to cause harm. "I'm through playing it your way."

She held his stare, her gaze as unforgiving as he felt, but Trey saw the flicker of fear just below the surface. He leaned forward, their noses inches apart. Familiar anger surfaced, driving him to reach up and yank the information out of Mattie. Instead, Trey directed the ugly emotion into his hard tone. "Where is Ike Hayes?"

"Changing the subject, are you?" Her voice held none of her fear, only cold contempt.

"I paid you good money, and I want my answers."

Her gaze cleared, then hardened as she slid the successful madam into place, a woman who had seen and done it all. For a price. "You won't find Ike through me."

Though he was revolted, and so angry he could barely see straight, Trey still pulled his lips into a grin. "Make no mistake, Mattie, I will get my answers." He let go of the breath he'd been holding and dropped her hand. "But not like this."

He turned, leaving her breathless and glaring. Opening the small compartment in her desk, he retrieved his money.

"Have you no shame?" she said, rushing toward him.

Stopping her pursuit with a look, he dug into his vest pocket and then tossed a coin onto the bed. "For services rendered."

Her glare spat fire, and her voice dripped with ice. "You've crossed the line, Marshal Scott."

Pivoting on his heel, he threw her one last, disgusted look. "It's not the first time."

He turned his back on her and yanked open the door.

"You don't want to make an enemy of Mattie Silks, Marshal. It's a mistake." Her bitter warning shot through the cold silence that had entered the room.

Trey treated her to one final withering glare. "And *you* don't want to make an enemy of me, Miss Silks. It's a bigger mistake."

Chapter Ten

Hours after leaving Mattie's brothel, Trey couldn't stop thinking about the woman, her lies and the ugly business she ran. His gut twisted in anger as he considered the kind of men who frequented the establishment, violent, immoral men like Ike Hayes, who stole life for the sheer pleasure of it.

Anger surged through him, threatening to consume him, but Trey tamped it down with a hard swallow.

How many of Katherine's childhood years had been spent in a brothel like Mattie's? How many times had she observed women taking money in the place of love and respect? How many lonely nights had she worried her own life would become the same as her mother's—only to have her fears realized when a former customer of Sadie Taylor's stole her innocence?

In that moment, the line between vengeance for Laurette and restitution for Katherine blurred in Trey's mind. He couldn't understand why God would allow such kind-hearted women to suffer brutality. Apparently, there was no mercy in this cruel world.

Leaning back in his chair, Trey propped his feet on the desk in front of him and speared a hand through his hair. Mattie had made it clear that talk had already begun about him and Katherine, just as he knew it would.

Well, Trey might not be able to right the wrong done to Laurette, at least not specifically, but he could correct the mistake he'd made with Katherine. Then maybe, *maybe,* he could alleviate some of his guilt over failing Laurette.

And regardless of Trey's past defeats, Katherine deserved freedom from her fear of all men, including him. If only he understood how she could cling to an invisible God that had abandoned her to a childhood inside a filthy brothel, a childhood that had ultimately led to one night of unspeakable violence. In spite of her personal hardships, she still held strong to her faith.

In that moment, he realized it was that very faith that drew him to her. Before meeting her, he'd been consumed with anger, driven by his hate and blissfully ignorant of the need for peace in his life. Marriage to Katherine Taylor might be just what he needed to start a new life.

But if he did talk the woman into marriage, what would it mean for his love for Laurette? Already, thoughts of his wife were becoming hazier and harder to grasp. In fact, he hadn't even thought of Laurette the past few times he'd been in Katherine's presence. If he found Ike and personally served up justice to the outlaw, perhaps then Trey could come to terms with Laurette's murder at last and move on with his life.

He exhaled a ragged breath. Because of his growing feelings for Katherine, he had not only betrayed the memory of his wife, but he'd inadvertently added further ruin to a fine woman's shaky reputation.

Well, he couldn't change the past, but he could right the

future. It wasn't until after hours of hard thought that an idea finally materialized, one that just might work to convince Katherine to marry him.

Lack of sleep, Trey discovered, made him very smart.

Katherine woke from a fitful, dream-ravaged sleep. Squinting through the shadows, she dragged in a shaky breath and studied the clock on the mantel. Midnight.

Sighing, she tossed to her left, turned to her right, then rolled back to her left again. Unable to find a comfortable position, she huffed, kicked at the sheets, then set to tossing back and forth again.

She turned to prayer, whispering aloud a portion of the thirty-second Psalm. "O Lord, You are my hiding place; You will protect me from trouble and surround me with songs of deliverance. You…"

Unable to remember the rest, she tried another from Matthew. "Come to me, all you who are weary and burdened, and I will give you rest."

No matter how hard she tried to quote Scripture, she couldn't dispel the image of Trey Scott's tender expression as he'd taken her hand into his to show her a moment of comfort. He'd been so kind to her, so gentle, and Katherine never knew she could feel such…confusion.

Before Trey had come along, she'd been completely satisfied with a future dedicated solely to Molly and the other Charity House children. Security, comfort, love— those came from her heavenly Father. There was no point in wondering what other blessings she might find in marriage.

Sleep. She needed the blissful escape of sleep. But even the familiar sounds of the Colorado night couldn't soothe her. The rustling of leaves grated on her nerves; the insects chattering with one another distracted and annoyed. Of course, the fact that Trey's parting words still echoed in her ears didn't help matters, either.

Make no mistake, Miss Taylor, I'll ask...when I'm ready.

Pounding her fist into her pillow, Katherine barely stifled the urge to scream out her frustration. Trey Scott certainly had more than his share of audacity.

There was something alluring about a man who took what he wanted and then guarded it with complete conviction once he had it in his possession. That sort of caring made a woman feel safe, cherished.

With that thought, Katherine threw off the bedcovers and pushed herself out of bed. Gritting her teeth, she began to pace. With each step, she struggled against the awful notion that she'd lost an important battle before it had truly begun. Trey Scott might be a lawman. He might still be in love with his dead wife. And he might carry a driving need for vengeance that could one day destroy him. But he was also handsome and charming and had a way with Molly that truly amazed Katherine.

With a soft thud, something landed at her feet, drawing her attention from her troubled thoughts. She looked down at the object on the floor, leaning over at the exact moment a virtual onslaught of various colors, shapes and sizes rained through her open window.

Reaching to the floor, she picked up one of the...*flowers?* Before she could grasp what was happening, more followed. And more still, accumulating into a soft rainbow of color at her feet. Studying the blossoms, she noted that a scrap of paper hung from each of the flowers' stems. Trying to read one of the scribbled messages, she bent forward. But another batch flew into the window, pelting her gently in the head and shoulders.

As the flower assault continued, a wave of girlish giggles slipped out of her lips. She fumbled to the night-stand and quickly lit a lantern.

Picking up a random stem, she read the scrawled, nearly illegible message aloud. "Marry me."

Half dreading, half hoping to read the same message again, she chose another flower. "Marry me." She picked up three more. "Marry me. Marry me. Oh, and what's this? Marry me."

The protective shield she'd wrapped around her heart started melting.

Another batch of flowers shot through the window, followed by a loud whisper. "Katherine."

With something perilously close to a smile on her lips, she headed toward the window. Only to be hit in the face with a red geranium.

"Katherine, come out here."

Afraid to move, to breathe—and not quite understanding why—she stood frozen in place, staring numbly at the window.

"Katherine."

Realizing Trey's whispers were getting louder with each demand, she dodged another rapid-fire round of blossoms and rushed to the window. Leaning her head into the crisp night air, she locked gazes with her favorite U.S. marshal one floor below.

Whipping off his hat, Trey bowed. "Fair maiden."

When he straightened, his expression looked a bit worried, as though he wasn't completely sure of himself. And for a brief moment, the loneliness Katherine had held at bay all her life disappeared inside a painful hope that Trey Scott would become the man she wanted him to be.

She didn't want to disturb the magnificent picture Trey made with his hat in hand, and his smile flashing, but curiosity got the best of her. "What do you want, Trey?"

He bent down on one knee. "Marry me. Take my name as your own."

Ridiculous as he looked, she'd never been more charmed by a man. "You're going to wake up the rest of the house."

With an uncharacteristic lack of grace, he shifted to a standing position. "Then come out here and let me ask you properly."

She had an insane urge to rush outside and fling herself into his arms. "I don't think that's a good idea."

He lifted on his toes and leaned forward. "Then I'm coming up there."

"You wouldn't. *You can't.*"

He started toward the trellis. "I can, especially when my woman is being unreasonable and stubborn."

My woman? Katherine's pulse picked up speed, but she knew better than to read too much into his words.

Trey Scott had an agenda, coming here at this indecent hour. And it certainly wasn't a godly one.

Looking around to make sure they were still alone, she leaned farther out the window and lowered her voice. "Go home, Trey. We'll talk in the morning."

He wrapped his fingers around the bottom rung in front of him. "Looks like I'm coming up."

"No, you're not. You're going home."

He started to climb, missed his footing then started again.

Panicked that he might follow through with his outrageous threat, she said, "Stop."

He continued, made it halfway up the wall, wobbled a bit
on a faulty slat then fell to the ground, landing flat on his back.

"Trey?"

No response.

"Trey."

Nothing.

"*Trey,* talk to me."

"I'm...all right."

"Can you move?"

He waved a hand in the air.

"Stay there. I'm coming down."

He immediately jumped to his feet. "I knew you'd see
things my way."

"You tricked me, you beast."

"I guess this means I have to come up there, after all."
He had the brass to look pleased.

"Stay there. I'll only be a moment."

Pivoting back to the interior of her room, Katherine
lowered her gaze to the collection of flowers on the floor.
Tears of hope welled in her eyes, mocking her attempt to
remain rational. As hard as she tried to harden her heart,
a wisp of a sigh rose from her soul.

She wasn't accustomed to romantic displays of affection. And, with a woman's instincts, she knew Trey wasn't
accustomed to giving them. Which made his ridiculous
flower shower all the more special.

No. She would not be moved by his calculated attempts
to win her. Trey was a U.S. marshal, a man not only angry
at God, but one who would abandon her and Molly each
time he went to seek vengeance for his dead wife.

With that last thought, renewed determination dug deep. No matter what happened here tonight, Katherine had to get Trey Scott out of their lives.

She jammed her arms into her robe and quickly headed out into the hallway. She padded along the back stairs as quickly as she could without making any noise.

Releasing the lock, she opened the back door leading off the kitchen and collided directly into Trey. "Oh."

With one hand, he reached out, steadied her. "Miss Taylor, always a pleasure."

She glared at him, told herself she was too angry to notice how his gray eyes glinted like silver fire in the moonlight. Or how his hair shone dark as onyx. Nor did she notice how tall and handsome he looked with that devilish grin on his face.

No, she didn't notice any of *that*.

"Are you drunk?" she asked, more out of an attempt to gain equal footing than genuine suspicion.

"I may be a man with my share of sin, but that's one vice you won't pin on me." There was steel, hard and immovable, in his voice.

She'd clearly insulted him.

"Of course. I'm sorry. It's just so late. And you're so…*different* tonight."

He opened his mouth to speak again, but she crooked her finger at him. "Not out here. Come with me to where the neighbors won't see us."

He gave her a two-finger salute.

She ignored his arrogant attitude, squared her shoulders and set out at a clipped pace.

He dutifully followed behind her. Which put her instantly on guard. Trey Scott was anything but accommodating.

Once inside the house, he proved true to form. Shouldering the door shut, he said, "Marry me."

"No."

Angling his head, he spoke in that arrogant tone of his. "Did you like the flowers?"

Her heart flipped in her chest at his eager, almost boyish expression. He really was ridiculous, and a dear, dear man. Her defenses were quickly melting under his sweet attempt to woo her. A bit too quickly.

She had to catch her breath.

"Of course I liked the flowers, you big fool." She motioned to a stool sitting next to the chopping block in the center of the kitchen. "Now sit down and lower your voice."

He reached out and knuckled a lock of hair away from her forehead. "It seems, Miss Taylor, you've driven me to sneaking around in the dark. Don't you think you should try harder at saving my soul?"

She would not laugh. She would not laugh. She would *not* laugh. "I'm not taking responsibility for your tumble from bad to worse." She steered him toward the stool. "Now, sit."

He obeyed, then lifted a single eyebrow at her. "Bet I can change your mind about us."

Fighting the urge to smile at him, she put her best teacher glare in place. "Nothing you say could possibly make a difference to me."

He cocked his head. "Who said anything about talking?"

"You wouldn't dare. Not with the children upstairs. Must I remind you that any one of them could come in here and catch us, like they did this morning?"

"Of course not." He threw his palms in the air. "I came only to talk. Really. You see, I've been thinking—"

"Imagine that."

He talked right over her insult. "I've come up with a brilliant reason why you have to marry me." He tapped his temple. "Got it all figured out."

"I'm running over with anticipation."

"Notice how I'm ignoring your sarcasm?"

Intrigued in spite of herself, she was careful to keep her tone neutral. "Mmm. So what is this brilliant reason of yours?"

"Molly needs a father." He shot her a triumphant grin. "And I think it should be me."

Katherine could only stare at Trey. He wanted to become Molly's father? *That* was the reason for his latest proposal? A strange sense of disappointment hung heavy in her chest, stealing her ability to breathe. Yet, a hidden desire kicked into life.

Oh, to have the opportunity to provide Molly with a complete family, to give her the life Katherine had never had, was tempting. Very tempting.

Needing a moment to gather her thoughts, Katherine started pacing.

"Think about it." Trey scrubbed a hand down his face. "We could provide Molly with two parents, a mother and a father."

She stopped midstride. "Oh, Trey. I—"

His eyes softened. "You'd make a wonderful mother."

For a dreadful moment, as Trey stared at her with that tender expression on his face, Katherine wondered what his child would look like. Black hair, gray eyes—a hidden wild streak.

No. No, no, no. This was the exact kind of thinking that would lead her to make a dreadful mistake. They weren't evenly yoked. And even if Trey mended his anger at God and became a practicing Christian again, he didn't want *her* as a wife. He loved Laurette, sought her killer with such passion, there could be no room in his heart for more.

Yes, he wanted Molly as a daughter. She didn't doubt that for a moment, but on his terms. In the end Trey was a man who would always put revenge for his dead wife's murder ahead of everything else. Katherine would do well to remember that part of the equation.

"I'm predicting we'll have an early snow," she said. "What do you think?"

He rose. "I didn't come here to discuss the weather."

She slid a glance over her shoulder, her breath catching in her throat again. The man looking at her now knew what he wanted. And possibly even why he wanted it.

Which made little sense. As far she could tell, the only thing Trey Scott *wanted* was vengeance. Right?

"I was giving you a chance to get this insane notion out of your head," she said at last.

"Marry me."

"Let's see if I can make this simple enough for you to understand… *No.*"

"But Molly—"

"Is perfectly happy at Charity House. She's not alone here. There are forty other children sharing this home with her."

"You're forgetting the moral implications in the matter." He strode closer. "You're the schoolmarm."

"Yes." She dropped her gaze to her shaking hands. "For abandoned children of prostitutes."

His eyes narrowed, becoming more determined than ever. "All the more reason to keep your reputation clean of any more ugly talk. I find it necessary to remind you that not everyone in this neighborhood wants Charity House to thrive. They could use a scandal of this nature, as unfounded as it may be, to shut your school down."

Her heart skipped only a beat at his words, but the sensation was sharp and fierce. "I have to trust God will protect us from such an occurrence."

His mouth dropped open. "You can't possibly be that naive."

"Believing that God will provide does not make me naive. It makes me—" she poked him in the chest "—faithful."

He simply stared at her, his eyes wide.

"It does," she insisted.

Still staring at her with unblinking eyes, he slowly shook his head. "You were caught cavorting with a man in the supply closet of your school. At best, people will merely talk. At worst, they could try to shut down your school."

"Oh, Trey. Laney and Marc would never let that happen."

His chin lifted at a stubborn angle. "People will say you did things you didn't do. I can't live with that."

Cupping her palm on his cheek, she gave him a patient smile. "I didn't know you were such a prude."

"Having a firm set of ethics and morals when it comes to how people treat you does not make me a prude." He pressed his forehead against hers for a moment, then pulled back and took two steps away from her. "Let me make you a respectable woman. Let me give you the honor you deserve."

The sincerity in his tone nearly had her relenting, but then she remembered his devotion to his dead wife, the passion in which he pursued her killer, and Katherine doubted his words. Besides which, marriage would solve nothing between them. "No."

"Don't you want to be a good example for the children? For Molly?"

"Of course, I do. But, Trey, it's not like we were, well…you know."

"That doesn't matter." He shook his head. "No, actually, it makes it that much more imperative that you do the right thing. You have to lead by example, Katherine, especially in the seemingly small matters."

If only it were that simple. "In case you have forgotten, I'm the daughter of a prostitute." This time she raised her hand to stop him from interrupting. "Though I attend church every Sunday, my faith is always in question. And I will always be Sadie Taylor's daughter."

He winced but continued staring at her for a long moment, measuring. Gauging. "You're afraid."

She swallowed back a gasp, wondered at his meaning for only a moment before denying the absurd accusation. "No, I'm realistic."

He stepped forward, stroked his hand down her hair in an affectionate gesture. "I won't intentionally hurt you, Katherine. Marry me, and let me show you that I know how to treat a woman like you, a woman who deserves nothing but kindness from a man."

"I…I can't. And you know why." She didn't want to bring up his dead wife again—it would hurt them both too much—but she would if he continued pressing the issue of marriage.

As though hearing her thoughts, he placed his finger on her lips. "I won't give you words I don't have, but I promise I will take care of you and Molly."

Be on your guard; stand firm in the faith.... As the Scripture from 1 Corinthians came to her mind, tears threatened. "And if you die? How will you take care of us then?"

He reached out to her, dropped his hand when she shook her head at him.

"It always comes back to that, doesn't it? I might live for vengeance. But you live in fear. Where's your faith?"

"Don't turn this back on me," she said, quickly closing her mind to the possibility that fear, and not logic, fueled her resolve.

"I won't force you to do anything you don't want to do. And I mean anything. We can have a marriage in name only, if that's what you want."

His soft, understanding tone set her on edge. Why was he being so nice, so caring and thoughtful of her fears? Why couldn't she trust in his consideration for her feelings?

Because, deep down, in a place shattered by violence, she didn't believe she was deserving of any man's kindness, especially this man, who only meant to offer her compassion. She was tainted, ruined. And Trey Scott deserved better.

He deserved a woman who wouldn't shy away from his touch.

Without looking at him directly, she turned to go. "Goodbye, Trey."

"We're not through, Katherine," Trey said, his voice barely above a whisper. "Don't leave now that we've come this far. Stay and fight."

She took the coward's way out. "I...*can't.*"

Pivoting, she released a sob and ran from the kitchen.

Chapter Eleven

One week after the incident with Katherine in the Charity House kitchen, Trey stood outside the jailhouse and eyed his surroundings. The buildings lining the street cast long shadows on the pocked mud, indicating the end of another day.

As he pondered his next move with the stubborn Miss Taylor, the only outward signs of Trey's irritation came in the fast, rhythmic ticking of his pulse and the white-knuckled grip he wrapped around the railing in front of him. Otherwise, he stood unmoving as he watched the sun sink into a long finger of reddened clouds in the distance.

A cool breeze whispered across his face but did little to soothe his frustration. The swift spasm in his gut warned him time was running out, and here he stood, contemplating the sun and the sky and the breeze. Yet as hard as he searched for possible options to the problem of Katherine Taylor, not a single solution materialized.

The stubborn, willful schoolmarm had successfully thwarted his efforts to court her this past week. How was he supposed to honor his promise to protect her from the repercussions of ugly gossip when he couldn't even speak to her? He certainly didn't want her to find out from anybody but him that he was leaving town again.

How he dreaded *that* conversation, especially since he knew his departure would work against him in his bid to win her hand in marriage. Why couldn't Katherine accept his need to settle the past in the only language Ike Hayes understood? Violence for violence.

The end was drawing near at last. Trey felt it deep in his bones. And he would rather have Katherine on his side than fighting him every step of the way. Resisting the urge to charge over to Charity House half-cocked, he concentrated on thinking up a new plan.

Unfortunately, nothing came immediately to mind. Going to Marc for help was out of the question. The man was Katherine's friend. And Laurette's brother.

Laurette. Trey sank into a chair behind him and spread his thumb and forefinger across his brow. After knowing what marriage to Katherine would mean to Laurette's memory, he'd been so consumed with devising a plan to get the schoolmarm to marry him, he hadn't thought of his wife nearly often enough.

Even now, when he tried to visualize her in his mind, the image blurred fuzzier than before, wavering further out of his reach.

He didn't want to forget Laurette. As though to torture him further, a vivid memory of her wrapped in his arms and bleeding to death emerged out of the previously foggy images. Would he always be haunted by the memory of the day he'd found her alone, shot and frightened?

Familiar guilt reared. If he could relive that last day,

he'd handle events differently. He would never have left her with only two hired hands to protect her. It was small comfort that he'd balked at leaving her, but she'd been eight months with child. He couldn't have taken her with him, and he couldn't have stayed. The snow was coming, and they'd needed supplies for the winter.

While Trey had been gone, Ike and his brother had come looking for horses or money to steal. They had found neither and had killed for the sport of it.

Blinding rage overwhelmed him. Trey rose and slammed his fist into the railing. Welcoming the shards of pain that spread up his arm, he tried to clear his mind of the painful images of that day four years ago, but the memory wouldn't let him go.

The moment Laurette had died, Trey had vowed to find Ike Hayes and make him pay. Four years had passed, and Trey still hadn't extracted justice. Nothing would change the fact that he had failed to protect his wife. For that, he would never forgive himself. Not until Ike Hayes paid with his life. And whether Katherine understood his quest, whether she married him or not, Trey would hunt the outlaw.

The pounding of footsteps yanked him brutally out of his thoughts. "Marshal Scott, you gotta come quick."

Trey dropped his gaze onto one of the older Charity House orphans. "What?" A dark, ugly fear knotted into a hard ball of panic. "Is it Katherine? Molly?"

"No." Bending at the waist, Johnny slapped his hands on his knees and sucked in gulps of air. "They're fine."

Trey exhaled. However, before he could fully settle into his relief, Johnny's next words sent soul-gripping dread through him. "It's Laney. She's having her baby."

"It's a month too early."

Get 2 Books FREE!

Steeple Hill Books,
publisher of inspirational fiction,
presents

Love Inspired **HISTORICAL**
INSPIRATIONAL HISTORICAL ROMANCE

**A new series of historical love stories that
promise romance, adventure and faith!**

GET 2 BOOKS

IF YOU ENJOY A HISTORICAL ROMANCE STORY that reflects solid, traditional values, then you'll like *Love Inspired® Historical* novels. These are engaging tales filled with romance, adventure and faith set in various historical periods from biblical times to World War II.

We'd like to send you two *Love Inspired Historical* novels absolutely free. Accepting them puts you under no obligation to purchase any more books.

HOW TO GET YOUR
2 FREE BOOKS AND TWO FREE GIFTS

1. Return the reply card today, and we'll send you two *Love Inspired Historical* novels, absolutely free! We'll even pay the postage!
2. Accepting free books places you under no obligation to buy anything, ever. The two books have combined cover prices of $11.00 in the U.S. and $13.00 in Canada, but they're yours to keep, free!
3. We hope that after receiving your free books you'll want to remain a subscriber, but the choice is yours–to continue or cancel, any time at all!

EXTRA BONUS

You'll also get two free mystery gifts! (worth about $10)

FREE!

BUSINESS REPLY MAIL

FIRST-CLASS MAIL   PERMIT NO. 717   BUFFALO, NY

POSTAGE WILL BE PAID BY ADDRESSEE

Steeple Hill Reader Service
3010 WALDEN AVENUE
PO BOX 1867
BUFFALO NY 14240-9952

NO POSTAGE
NECESSARY
IF MAILED
IN THE
UNITED STATES

If offer card is missing, write to Steeple Hill Reader Service, 3010 Walden Ave., P.O. Box 1867, Buffalo, NY 14240-1867

Johnny nodded. "I know. Dr. Shane told me to come get you right away."

"Is she—"

Apprehension filled the kid's expression. "It's Marc. Every time Laney screams, he goes for Doc's throat—" Johnny broke off, took several deep breaths, then stood upright. "We need you to help us hold him off."

Knowing how much Marc loved his wife, Trey could only imagine the battle waging at Charity House. "You were right to come get me."

As Trey started for the stable, Johnny sent him a quick, impatient look. "No time for saddling horses. We gotta go now."

"Right." Trey slammed his hat on his head and broke out in a run for the orphanage.

Johnny followed hard on his heels.

As his feet conquered the distance between the jail and the orphanage, Trey silently prepared himself for chaos at the end of his destination. Rounding the last corner, he nearly barreled over a woman walking her tiny dog. Muttering a quick "Pardon me," Trey rushed up the front steps and burst into the front parlor of Charity House.

The deadly stillness struck him first.

Afraid to consider what the silence meant, he counted almost forty boys and girls of various ages sitting throughout the room. Their unnatural calm knotted a greater sense of dread in his gut.

Was it over then?

Molly broke from the pack and rushed to him. "Mr. Trey, don't let Laney die like my momma did."

Her fear was palpable, glittering in her eyes and throbbing in her voice.

Quiet moans of agreement hummed from the rest of the kids.

Forcing assurance into his voice, Trey picked up Molly, kissed her tearstained cheek, then said, "Nothing's going to happen to her with Dr. Shane here."

"But it's taking too long," said Molly.

Trey hugged Molly tightly against him, then caught Johnny's gaze. "How long?"

"Hours."

The declaration seemed to shake the rest of the kids out of their grim silence. Forty voices rose with questions, their words coming fast and incomprehensible.

Hoisting Molly onto his hip, Trey attempted to speak over their clamor. "Everybody, calm yourselves. She's just having a baby."

One of the orphans poked at him. "But that's how my momma died."

Another one added, "Yeah, mine, too."

Trey wanted to alleviate their fears and tell them they were speaking nonsense, but death in childbirth was a reality even he couldn't deny.

Molly placed a palm on each side of his face and forced him to look at her. "Whattaya gonna do to stop it, Mr. Trey?"

Her unrelenting assurance that he could actually make a difference shook him into action. "Don't worry, kitten. Dr. Shane is the best in town. He'll take good care of our Laney."

A loud crash came from the upstairs, followed by a string of oaths that threatened to blister the wallpaper right off the walls.

Trey set Molly to the floor.

"I think I better make sure the doctor can do his job."
He planted an emphatic smile on his face, then looked at
each of the children. "I'll find out what's happening. Then
I'll be back."

Taking the stairs three at a time, Trey charged toward
the back room where the swearing grew louder, more pronounced. Unsure what he would find, he swallowed his un-
easiness, then rushed into the room without knocking.

The heat hit him first, followed by the smell of sweat
and fear. Concern lay heavy and thick in the air,
wrapping around his throat and squeezing like a noose.
Gasping through a deep breath, Trey circled his gaze
around the room until he found the doctor and Marc in
a contest of wills. The young doctor, Shane Bartlett,
had his sleeves rolled up and was trying to push Marc
away from him.

Marc pushed back, his chest puffed out, his eyes wild
and unfocused. "I'm warning you, Bartlett. Don't let her
suffer anymore."

The doctor's tired, red-rimmed eyes flickered with
frustration. "Then move aside and let me work without
obstruction."

Marc settled into a wide, feet-planted stance. "You leave
my woman alone."

"I'm trying to help her!"

Knowing far too well what that stubborn look on his
friend's face meant, Trey raised his voice. "What can I
do to help?"

Marc answered for them both. "Stay out of this, Trey.
Unless you want a fight, too."

Ignoring the threat, Trey looked around the rest of the
room. Careful to avoid glancing at the bed, he focused on

Katherine as she stood off to one side, turning a wet cloth over and over in her hands.

Her hair had come loose from its braid, cascading in a black curtain around her face. Lines of fatigue rimmed her eyes, but she managed to smile at him. The simple gesture transformed her face, making her look as though she were actually happy to see him. His heart warmed at the thought, but then she angled her head toward Marc and mouthed the words, "Do something."

Trey took a step forward, but then his gaze landed on Laney, lying in the bed. He'd purposely avoided looking at her, and now he knew why. Sweat poured down her face, her eyes glazed over in pain. Instant fear rose in his throat, and he took a quick, reflexive step back.

Was God going to take another woman he loved today?

Until that moment, he hadn't realized how much he cared for Laney. She was like the sister he'd never had, and he didn't want her to die. Yet he knew there was nothing he could do to help her at this point.

He shot her an apologetic grimace.

Laney gave him a watery smile in return, then buckled over. "Give me one of your guns, Trey."

"I don't think that would be a good idea right now," he said, surprised his voice came out as steady as it did.

She panted through what looked like a spasm of pain. Grinding her teeth together, she leaned back into the pillows and growled, "I said give me a gun."

Diverted from his fight with the doctor, Marc rushed to his wife's side and knelt beside the bed. Brushing her hair away from her face, he tried to soothe her with words. "It's gonna be all right, honey."

"Take your hands off me, Dupree." She took a deep

breath, then angled a glare at Trey. "I mean it, Marshal. Give me your weapon. Now."

Marc shared a look with Trey, then turned back to the bed.

"What do you want it for, baby?" Marc's voice wavered with concern.

She sneered at her husband. "To shoot you, of course."

Marc visibly cringed. "I'm sorry, Laney. I'll never touch you again."

Doubling over in agony, she let out a pain-filled holler. "No, you won't."

She ground out more words of condemnation between pants and screeches.

Feeling utterly helpless, Trey turned to Katherine for guidance. But she wasn't looking at him anymore. Her eyes were on her friend as she moved forward, lowered her voice and began whispering instructions into the other woman's ear. "Come on, Laney," she urged. "You have to breathe. Slowly, now."

"Leave me alone," Laney moaned. "I don't want to breathe. *Arr.*"

Katherine shuddered, but her voice came low and even. "That's it. Breathe through the pain."

Laney screamed instead.

Katherine knelt beside the bed and began praying in a soft, convicted voice. Didn't she know her efforts were useless? God couldn't possibly be listening.

But a part of him, the part that still had a shred of hope left, wanted to join Katherine in prayer. Or at least believe her efforts weren't in vain.

Paralyzed into immobility by his conflicting thoughts, Trey could only admire Katherine's calm strength. With each of Laney's pants, she continued to soothe her friend while praying for peace and relief.

"Laney, let me help you," Marc said, his eyes glazed over with a panic Trey felt as well.

"You've done enough already," Laney yelled at him.

Letting out a hiss of frustration, Marc jumped up and gripped the doctor by the neck. "Make it stop, Bartlett."

Dr. Bartlett swung a pleading look to Trey. "Get him out of here, will ya?"

Laney chose that moment to scream again.

Marc released the doctor and whipped back around. But before he made it to the bed, Trey reached for him and physically yanked on his shirt collar. "Let's go, my friend. This isn't a place for either of us."

Dr. Bartlett let out a quick, agitated sigh. "Thanks, Marshal."

Just before Trey turned to go, Katherine looked up and gave him a grateful smile. Within her eyes resided all the words neither had been able to say to one another. He hadn't realized how much he needed this woman's smiles, her softness. How much he needed the comfort he always felt around her. Warming to the notion, he pushed his lips into an answering smile, and a moment of quiet under-standing passed between them.

As though sensing Trey's lack of concentration, Marc twisted and broke free of his grip. He rushed back toward the bed, but Trey moved faster. He grabbed his friend by the arm and clenched him with the force of a man used to dragging unwilling criminals into custody. "You need a break, old man."

"I'm not leaving my wife," Marc growled.

"Yes. You are."

Marc struggled, using his strength against Trey's. Normally, they'd be evenly matched, but Trey was fresher and less emotional. After only a moment of pushes and tugs, Trey won the battle and shoved his friend toward the door. Before he left the room, he caught a glimpse of Katherine and Dr. Bartlett leaning over a basin together. The two worked without speaking, but there was a silent accord between them, a meshing of movements that indicated years of working side by side in a sickroom.

Trey shut his mind to the sudden urge to slug the good doctor and focused on maneuvering Marc out of the room. This was not a time to remember Molly's suggestion—or rather, threat—that she would ask Dr. Bartlett to marry her sister if Trey would not. Nor was it a time for… Was that jealousy he was feeling? Or was it envy for the camaraderie the two shared?

Either way, Trey wasn't going to explore the shocking emotion any further. At least, not while he had an unreasonable, panicked father-to-be literally thrashing in his grip.

By the time he'd wrestled Marc to the bottom of the stairs, the fight had left the other man completely. Satisfied he'd won the war, Trey released his hold. But then Laney let out a scream, and Marc's muscles bunched. He made it up two steps before Trey caught him again and yanked him back down. Tired of the game, Trey slammed his friend against the wall and pinned him there, with a restraining hand against his chest.

"Calm down, Marc. You aren't helping anyone with this behavior. The kids are petrified."

Marc jerked forward, but Trey hurled him back into the wall. Shifting his gaze up the stairs, Marc sighed. "Yeah, well, I know the feeling."

Trey took his friend by the shoulders and shook him. "Get hold of yourself. The children need to see everything's going to be all right."

Marc stared at him with an empty expression but stopped fighting.

Trey blew out a hard breath, then called out over his shoulder. "Hey, Johnny, I need you to come out here."

Johnny sped around the corner, nearly clipping his shoulder on the wall.

"Take Marc into his study. I'll be right behind you."

With his face draining of all color, Johnny looked at Marc, then back to Trey. "Not a chance."

"Don't worry. He'll cooperate. If he doesn't—" Trey glared hard at his friend "—I'll knock him out."

Another scream from the second floor sliced through the air. With the strength of three men, Marc broke out of Trey's grip. Down to his last tactic, Trey wrapped his fingers around his friend's throat. "Take another step and I'll make sure you're out cold for the rest of the day."

Marc glared back at him. Trey kept his feet poised, prepared to stare down his friend for however long it took to communicate his message.

"I think you mean it," Marc grunted.

Curving his lips into a fixed smile, Trey nodded. "I do. And at this point, Laney would congratulate me for it."

Marc glanced up the stairs.

"She's in good hands," Trey reminded him. "Let Katherine and Bartlett take care of your wife."

Trey shut his mind against the fact that Katherine was in that room with the young, handsome doctor, the two working side by side, sharing the miracle of birth…

No, he was being absurd. He had to focus on his

friend, not some petty, selfish jealousy that didn't have any place here.

With his shoulders slumped, Marc bared his teeth. "When this is over, I'm taking you out."

Trey grinned. "You're welcome to try."

Mumbling that it would be his pleasure, Marc stomped off toward his study. With a nudge from Trey, Johnny followed at a good distance behind.

Chapter Twelve

Trey waited until Marc rounded the corner before letting out the breath he'd been holding. After taking several more gulps, he turned in the opposite direction and entered the large parlor. Forty pairs of eyes locked with his. The look of solemn despair he saw staring back at him cut through the thin fabric of his confidence.

These children recognized the yells coming from upstairs for what they were—the sounds of a woman in the grip of a dangerous, perhaps even deadly, situation.

Molly tore herself out of one of the other girls' laps. "Is she gonna live?"

Trey lifted the little girl into his arms. "She's doing just fine. A little tired, but she's tough."

A bloodcurdling scream nearly lifted the roof off its rafters. Molly buried her face in Trey's neck. "She don't sound so very tough."

Trey patted her on the back, smiled at the others. "The hollering is a good sign. Means the baby's healthy."

At least, he hoped so.

Realizing he had to get all of their minds off what was happening upstairs, he looked to the oldest girl. "Megan, why don't you take everyone outside and organize a game of—"

"Baseball. That's Laney's favorite."

"Excellent idea. Choose up teams, and I'll see if I can get Marc to join you outside."

Trey tried to set Molly down, but she wrapped her spindly arms around his neck in a tight grip and sobbed. After a few seconds of prying, he gave up. "I'll just keep Molly with me for now."

One by one, the kids trooped outside, looking as though they were about to face a firing squad instead of heading out to play. Their calm acceptance tore at Trey. Like him, these children had learned that life was unfair, and that loved ones often died before their time.

How could he help anyone have faith when he had so little himself? Doubt filled him, and his breathing picked up speed. Trey knew about hate, he knew about vengeance and anger, but what did he know about being a parent?

As though he could physically protect Molly from the harsher realities of life, he hugged her hard against him, then looked up to find Mrs. Smythe watching him.

"What can I do to help?" she asked. Her voice sounded brave, but Trey knew from the look in her eyes that she was eaten alive with worry.

"Can you keep an eye on the children for us?"

She nodded. "Of course. And I'll make sure they eat something later. So, is Laney—" she cocked her head in the general direction of the stairs "—all right?"

Molly whimpered into his shoulder. Trey gently rubbed the little girl's back as he spoke. "I think so."

Making sure he spoke in generalities—for Molly's

sake—he gave the housekeeper details of what he'd seen in the room upstairs.

"Well, sounds like everything's right on schedule," she said, relief hunching her shoulders forward. "I'll handle the children from here."

Trey nodded, then went in search of Marc.

He found his friend standing by the window in his study, staring at nothing in particular. Johnny stood against the wall on the other side of the room, shifting from foot to foot and looking miserable.

"I've got it from here, kid," said Trey. "The rest are outside, starting up a game of baseball."

Johnny's eyes lit with satisfaction. "I'll be the umpire."

Trey nodded. "Good idea."

Once they were alone, Trey was unsure what to say to alleviate Marc's fears. They lived in a harsh world where good women sometimes died.

Struggling to find words of assurance he didn't have, Trey moved to the center of the room and sat down in one of the two wing-back chairs. He shifted Molly so she could sit more comfortably on his lap, then spoke softly to the little girl. "It's going to be all right, kitten."

Marc turned, focused his gaze on Trey, then dropped it to Molly. Grimacing, he trudged over and ruffled the little girl's hair. "You scared, too?"

Molly's lower lip trembled as tears rolled down her cheeks. "I don't want her to die."

Marc flinched. "Me neither."

Trey lowered a kiss to the top of Molly's head. "She'll be all right." He commanded Marc's stare. "Laney's strong."

Marc spun on his heel and started pacing through the room. "I should *never* have touched her."

Trey recognized the absurdity in his friend's remark. "It's the way of husband and wife. Regret now is useless."

With a sigh, Marc glanced out the window, turned on his heel and tossed his large frame into the chair next to Trey's. He shut his eyes a moment, crossed himself and then looked toward heaven. "Dear merciful God, please protect my wife. Bring her through this safely."

Trey wanted to say his own prayer, but it had been so long. Would God still hear him?

Please, God, don't take Laney, too. Not today. Not yet.

For a prayer, it wasn't much, but it was all he could manage.

Molly patted his hand and then settled back against him. Trey hugged her a little tighter than before.

After a while, the screams slowed, then eventually stopped altogether. Unfortunately, the ensuing silence was far more frightening than the previous confusion and chaos had been. As the time continued to tick forward, with no word from upstairs, Trey's mind drifted to the little girl who sat unmoving in his arms.

So much trauma for one so young. Too much death.

How could he be responsible for adding to her agony? And yet, how could he just walk away now?

Wouldn't that be just as bad?

Molly relaxed her head against his shoulder and eventually dozed off. The moment Trey shut his own eyes, she stirred. With the resilience of youth, she hopped off his lap and grinned. "I think I'll go play now."

Trey waved her on her way. "Have fun, kitten."

Just as Molly left through one door, Katherine burst through the other. She slanted Trey a quick, unreadable look, then turned to Marc.

The other man jumped out of his chair. "How is she?"

"Exhausted, but fine." Katherine glided over to him and patted his cheek with affection. "Now go meet your daughter."

Marc slapped his fist into his palm. "A daughter! Did you hear that, Trey?"

"I certainly did."

Grinning like a little boy, Marc darted out the door. Seconds later his footsteps pounded up the stairs.

Katherine sighed after him. "I never thought I'd see the day when that man panicked like he did this morning."

Trey rested his hand on her shoulder. "He loves his wife."

Katherine turned back to him, tears swimming in her eyes. "And she loves her husband."

Now that he was finally alone with her, Trey had much he wanted to say, but all he could think about was how beautiful she looked in the fading light of the day. A tender feeling clutched his heart as he took in Katherine's disheveled appearance.

Without thinking too hard about what he was doing, he pulled her into his arms and held her tightly against him. "You did good work today."

After a moment of hesitation, she sighed and relaxed into him. "God was in the room, guiding us all."

He didn't know how to respond to that, so he merely stroked her hair, reveling in her warmth, her strength. "You were amazing. So calm."

"Thank you, Trey. But let's not forget, you played an important role as well." She rubbed her cheek against his shoulder. "Confusion ruled until you arrived."

"I'm glad I could help."

She chuckled. "I don't know how you managed to get Marc out of the room."

"Simple." He tightened his grip. "I used brute force."

She let out a long, happy sigh—one of those contented sounds that grabbed a man's heart and twisted. For a second time in a week, she hadn't shied away from him. Was she beginning to trust him?

Stepping back, she stared into his eyes. "Laney asked for you, too."

Knuckling a black, meandering curl off her cheek, he said, "First we should talk. Katherine—"

She pressed her fingertip against his lips. "No, Trey, not yet. Later. We'll talk later. This is Laney's moment, not ours."

He nodded and followed her up the stairs. Once they were back in the room, the tender mood of husband and wife immediately drew Trey's attention. They sat together on the bed, smiling down at the bundle between them.

Marc looked up first and motioned him forward. "Come on in, Trey."

Trey hesitated, struck impassive by the change in his friend. Cradling an armload of squirming blankets, the other man looked as contented as Trey had ever seen him. Marc Dupree had come a long way from the hardened man obsessed with making money, even at the expense of his own happiness.

The startling transformation gave Trey a glimmer of hope that he, too, could change in time.

"Take a look at my daughter, old friend." The pride shining in Marc's eyes was unmistakable.

Trey edged closer, but with each step, a strange feeling of loss and a sense of new beginnings wrestled against one another inside him. With heavy steps, he maneuvered around the side of the bed.

Laney smiled up at him then, her eyes radiating peace and joy. Even in her exhaustion, she looked lovely. It was hard to reconcile this new vision with the desperate woman who had wanted his gun a few hours earlier.

Still grinning, she nudged her husband with her shoulder. "Let Trey hold her."

Marc pulled his arm from behind his wife. Holding his child with both hands, he lifted her toward Trey. "You have to hold her like this."

He demonstrated by cradling the baby in one arm and cupping a palm beneath the impossibly tiny head.

Hands trembling, Trey stepped back. "She's too small. I'll hurt her."

Laney chuckled. "Any creature that can put me through that much torture is not as fragile as she looks."

Reluctantly, he took the child, careful to support her head just as Marc had shown him. At the feel of the gentle weight in his arms, a tangle of emotions locked together in his throat, then sank to his gut and churned.

He'd spent the past four years focusing on death. Now, as he held this perfect little creature, he knew he stared into the beautiful face of life.

"She's perfect," he said, noting the mahogany hair, up-turned nose and long lashes. "Looks just like her mother."

He studied the infant further, taking in the stubborn tilt of the baby's chin. "*And* her father."

Marc peered over Trey's shoulder, placed a hand on the tiny head. "We're naming her Laurette."

Unprepared for the declaration, a pall of bleak silence

trudged across Trey's soul. He couldn't stop the tears from pooling in his eyes, didn't want to stop them.

Blurry-eyed, he looked down into Laney's smiling face. "Are you sure?"

She nodded her head at him, answering tears falling quickly down her cheeks. "God has blessed us with this new life today, and because of His generosity, there's no other name I would want for her."

"Thank you," Trey whispered.

Marc clutched his shoulder. "This is for all of us, my friend. It's time we started looking ahead, instead of behind."

Trey swallowed, unable to wrap his brain around the notion. But then blue, unfocused eyes blinked up at him, and the pain in his chest slowly subsided, as though the grip of grief that had clutched his heart for too many years was finally loosening. Just a little.

The baby gurgled at that moment. Inside that tiny sound, the past separated from the future, leaving only the joy of the moment.

Was it truly time to let go and look ahead?

Drawn by a force he didn't quite understand, he turned and linked gazes with Katherine. She smiled at him, her beauty heightened by the tears and acceptance flickering in her eyes.

In that moment, Trey knew he had to try.

Chapter Thirteen

Katherine didn't belong here. This was a moment for family, and as much as she'd like to think she was part of this tight-knit clan, she didn't have their shared history.

Feeling like an intruder, she shifted her gaze around the room. She caught sight of Dr. Bartlett looking at her, staring at her, really. He quickly broke eye contact, turned to watch Trey holding the baby, and then, just as swiftly, looked back at Katherine with such curious intensity in his eyes she felt a sudden urge to run.

Dr. Bartlett had never made her feel uncomfortable before. She took it as her cue to leave the room.

With careful steps, she silently slipped out of the room and closed the door behind her. Knotted muscles caused her to wince as she staggered down the hallway. Drawing in a shuddering sigh, she stepped into her own room, calmly shut the door, then collapsed against it. Ugly, bleak loneliness dug deep, throbbing in a painful rhythm within her chest.

She knew she was being selfish. She should be helping

Mrs. Smythe with the children, not wallowing in her sadness. Yet her feet wouldn't budge.

Leaning her head against the door, she squeezed her eyes shut. Unfortunately, there was no sanctuary to be found behind her lids.

She shouldn't be disturbed by the emotions she'd seen in Trey's eyes. Loss, acceptance and finally *love*. She'd witnessed a man beginning the process of letting go of the past. But now that he'd taken the first step, she was suddenly terrified about what the end result would mean to her.

Was she holding back from him because of his badge? Or was it a deeper fear? Was she afraid he'd compare her to his dead wife and find her unworthy? Did she fear his rejection more than his abandonment?

Faith is being sure of what we hope for and certain of what we do not see…

Panic climbed into her throat as the Scripture came to mind. Katherine had been lying to herself all these weeks. She wasn't a strong, believing Christian. In truth, she had no faith when it came to her own future.

And just as Trey had accused of her, she *was* afraid. Afraid of his rejection. Afraid one day he'd see her like the rest of the town did, as nothing more than the daughter of a whore, and as a woman forever tainted by one violent act.

No. She countered that absurd notion with a stamp of temper. "Trey doesn't deserve this kind of censure. I will not think like this."

Maybe it was time to walk by faith and not by sight. Maybe it was time to give Trey Scott a chance to be the man she knew he could be in time and with God's healing.

Shoving away from the door, she quickly washed and changed her clothes. Too tired to fool with her hair, she merely brushed out the tangles and let it hang loose down her back.

For a moment, she felt better, stronger, but as she jammed her feet into her boots and went to work on the laces, she thought back over the scene she'd witnessed in Laney's room.

Both Trey and Marc had received the birth of the tiny child as the blessing it was. They were such good men. Each destined to command his family with honor, integrity and deep, abiding love.

Why didn't she feel joy at the revelation?

Because Katherine wasn't convinced Trey would ever love her enough, not the way Marc loved Laney. Not the way Trey still loved his dead wife.

On shaky legs, she rose from the bed and dashed out of the room. Avoiding the other end of the hallway—and the people behind that closed door—she trekked downstairs. Needing to gather her thoughts into some semblance of order, she veered toward the front porch, then slipped out of the house.

And nearly collided into Trey.

She froze, afraid to disturb him, afraid to turn away.

Seemingly unaware of her presence, he stood with his back to her, tense and unmoving. His turmoil was palpable, and she wept inside for him. At the sight of him standing there, looking so alone and sad, a crack in her heart opened, allowing him to fill it for just a moment before she slammed it shut again with a sigh.

He turned at the sound. In one swift movement, he caught her against his chest. Without speaking, he dropped a kiss on the top of her head, the tender gesture breaking her heart a little more. Oh, yes, this man had so much love to give. If only she knew how to trust him with her heart.

She pulled away, then stared up at him. His gaze softened, his eyes communicating something she couldn't quite name—didn't dare name. Out of a perverse need to gain perspective, she lowered her eyes to the tin star on his chest. She tried reminding herself he was a lawman. But, tonight, the dangers of his chosen profession didn't matter so much.

Returning her gaze to his, she raised herself onto the tips of her toes and pressed a kiss to his chin. "Trey—"

"Take a walk with me."

Feeling suddenly vulnerable, she inched backward, shaking her head.

"Please."

The genuine appeal in his eyes called to the part of her that could deny this man nothing. She knew he was hurting, knew he needed her in a way she didn't quite understand. She could no more walk away from him now than cut off one of her limbs. And in that moment, Katherine accepted the truth. She was beginning to care deeply for Trey Scott—a man who would continually come and go from her life, one day never to return.

He would break her heart. And Molly's.

Yet Katherine still yearned for him to find peace above her own selfish fears. She wanted him to experience the freedom in Christ that she had. She wanted him free from pain. And whether he was in her life or not, she wanted him to find true happiness.

Oh, Lord, give me the courage to face these new, frightening feelings. I'm so vulnerable to him right now.

Silently, carefully, she placed her hand in his. Smiling, he drew her down the stairs with him. He smelled of a tangy blend of spice and wood, a scent that would always linger in her mind as his alone.

As they walked side by side, his nearness attacked the doubt clutching at her heart, making her believe—for one small second—that being with Trey was the best thing that would ever happen to her in this life.

Fearful she would blurt out her feelings, Katherine started to turn back, but the gentle touch to her arm stopped her.

"Mrs. Smythe can take care of the children," Trey said. "I need you to walk with me."

His eyes told her he needed much more than that from her.

Katherine's heart rolled around in her chest, pounded violently against her ribs. "I… Yes."

He waited until she drew back alongside him before striding again down the lane. Clasping his hands behind his back, he walked at a leisurely pace. Light from the other mansions illuminated their path. The slender beam of the waning moon glowed small but bright, the stars especially brilliant in the dark fabric of the sky.

They continued to walk in silence, and she reveled in the smooth camaraderie that arose between them. No arguing, no wheedling, just comfortable serenity.

They ambled past the mansions and on to the outskirts of town. Only the stars and moon provided light now, the mountains standing guard, as though protecting them against the fierce enemies of the world.

Trey looked to the heavens, took a deep breath, then turned back to her. "The quiet is nice."

"Quiet?" She chuckled and spread her arms to the sky, sniffing the refreshing, subtle fragrance of the spicy mountain air. "The pine trees are snapping and crackling in the wind. The crickets are singing. I can barely hear myself think."

"You know what I mean."

She turned to him, waited for his eyes to lower to hers again. "Yes, I do."

Pulling a strand of her hair away from her face, he twirled the dark curl around his forefinger. "You've had a long day."

She sighed, barely resisting the urge to lean into him. "It was terrifying, but exciting, too."

Studying her face with the same intensity she'd seen in him when he'd stared at the baby, he released her hair, then dragged a knuckle down her cheek. "You didn't look scared. You looked in complete control."

She let out a self-deprecating laugh. "Oh, I'm a master at exuding confidence when I least feel it. Comes from teaching eager minds with too many questions I can't always answer."

He lifted a brow, amusement replacing the sincerity. "You? At a loss for words?"

"Don't start, Trey. Tomorrow you can scold me several times to make up for it, but not tonight."

"I wasn't going to scold."

She lifted a brow in a gesture identical to his.

A grin played at the corners of his mouth, his white teeth gleaming against his tanned skin speckled with day-old beard. "All right, I was. But you're right. This isn't the time."

The lines around his eyes deepened, while the shadows in his gaze darkened. "I don't understand what happened to me in that room tonight."

He took her hand and pressed her palm against his chest. "It hurts here."

She was content just to stand there, silently counting

each of his heartbeats as they slammed against her hand. But the look in his eyes demanded she respond to his pain.

"You had quite a night," she said. "It's understandable to feel a little shaken."

"It's more than that."

She nodded, dropped her hand. "Yes."

"I don't know much about divine plans or God's will, but the birth of this baby, no—" He broke off, swallowed. "The birth of Lau...*Laurette* seems important. I can't explain why."

His stricken, confused expression had her reaching out and placing her hand on his arm. "Oh, Trey, we can't always know God's ways, or why He puts us through trials. All we can do is believe that good will eventually come to those of us who are in Christ. Even when we suffer unspeakable tragedy."

He didn't argue with her or give her an angry denial, but his mouth curved into a frown. "It always comes down to trust, doesn't it? Blind trust."

"That's what faith is, Trey. Trusting in what we can't see or know for sure. And it's the hardest thing we do as Christians."

He placed a finger under her chin, applying pressure until she looked into his eyes. "Sort of like trusting me to be good to you in our marriage, and trusting that I'll keep my promise to take care of you and Molly."

She stiffened at his words. "We aren't talking about me. We're talking about you and your ongoing struggle with God over the loss of your wife. We're talking about forgiveness."

"Forgiveness. Trust in God. I don't know much of these things anymore." His brows drew together in a heavy frown.

"But you do. *Trust* me, Katherine. Show me how it's done so I can learn how to do it, too."

"Oh, Trey, what a pair we make. You can't trust God, and…and apparently, I can't trust you enough, either."

She heard the disappointment in his unspoken sigh.

"Why do you continue to fight me so?"

He asked a legitimate question. Why *was* she fighting him? She cared for him, and although he didn't care for her in the same way, she knew he did care. She also knew he would eventually find his way back to God, perhaps sooner now with the birth of baby Laurette.

Why not marry him?

Because, ultimately, he would break her heart.

Trey pulled Katherine tight against him, deciding her silence meant she was coming around to his way of thinking. This time he wasn't going to let her walk away from him before they'd settled matters between them.

He didn't know why it was so important to him, only knew his desire to make her his wife had become more than merely accepting responsibility for her reputation.

Maybe this urgency came with the birth of Marc's daughter. Something had happened to him in that room tonight. As he'd held the tiny child, his thinking had shifted. For the first time in years, he wanted a life free of bitterness and anger and vengeance. He wanted a future. And he wanted it with Katherine and Molly.

But he had to settle the past first. He needed to free all three of them from the violence that drove him still. "When I get back," he said, "we're getting married."

She pushed out of his arms. *"When you get back?"*

Shock registered in her eyes, but the pain he saw flickering underneath that stunned expression warned Trey to tread softly. He'd made a mistake waiting until now to tell her. "I'm leaving in the morning."

Her gasp sounded more like an accusation. "You're leaving in the morning."

"I got word—"

"You got word."

In an attempt to lighten the mood, he made a grand show of peering around her. "Did you bring Laney's talking bird with you?"

"You're leaving. Going after a specific criminal, I assume?"

"I have to finish it, Katherine."

A single sob slipped from her lips before she gathered her control. "How long have you known about this…trip?"

"A week," he said, bracing for her reaction.

"A week." The words came out just above a whisper. "And you just tell me now?"

Taking the defense, he puffed out his chest. "It's my job to hunt down outlaws and bring them to justice."

"It's your job."

"I'm getting real tired of you repeating everything I say."

She jammed her hands on her hips and jerked her chin at him. "And I'm getting real tired of having this same conversation over and over with you. God tells us that vengeance is His alone. Quit trying to turn justice into your own personal quest to rid yourself of false guilt."

Trey swallowed back an angry retort and focused solely on winning the argument. "This isn't about guilt, false or real. I've sworn an oath to the president of the United States to uphold justice in this part of the country. *I'm the good guy.*"

She pressed her fingertips to her temples and shook her head. "Right. Of course. How could I forget? You're a lawman, Trey. But you're not a husband. Not *mine* anyway."

"I can be both. One does not preclude the other."

Wanting to soothe her fears, he reached to her. She took a single step back, creating a chasm between them that felt as wide as a continent.

"Are you going after your wife's killer?" she asked in a defeated tone.

He sighed, deciding the truth was the best defense. "Yes. It's time justice was served once and for all."

She gasped. "Justice? This quest of yours isn't about justice. It's about revenge."

"It's the only thing I have left that I can give Laurette."

"It won't change anything."

Hardening his heart to the look of disappointment in her eyes, he shoved a hand through his hair. "Even if Ike Hayes hadn't murdered Laurette, he's killed others. It's my job to find him and bring him to justice. It's what I do. It's who I am."

"And what if you don't come back? What am I supposed to tell Molly? That you were killed seeking revenge?"

With his patience pushed to the snapping point, he glared down at her. "I *always* come back. And when I do, we're getting married. Molly will have the family you want for her. It's no longer up for discussion."

Her only response was a tight-lipped grimace.

"Did you hear me?"

"I heard you."

"Good." He gave her a single nod. "Then it's settled."

"Not by half. Now you hear me, *Marshal*." She poked her finger at his chest. "You better make good on that promise of yours to return. Because if you hurt my little sister, I'll make you sorry you ever chose to mess with a Taylor woman."

With that, she spun on her heel and marched across the open field, her dignity wrapped around her like an iron cloak.

Trey stared at her retreating back, his heart clutching in his chest at her bold threat. "Oh, I don't doubt it, honey," he whispered after her, smiling in spite of himself. "I don't doubt it for a minute."

Chapter Fourteen

One month, two days and six hours after their heated argument, Trey had yet to return home. As the midday sun spread golden fingers of light through the kitchen window, Katherine tried to go about her daily chores as though nothing was bothering her. To little avail.

Sighing, she used her wrist to wipe her forehead and then began pressing freshly kneaded dough into a bread tin.

Perhaps today would be the day Trey returned home.

Did he miss her, she wondered, as much as she missed him? Or was he thinking about their last argument and the ultimatum she'd given him to return unharmed or else she'd make him sorry?

How she regretted those impetuous words. He'd needed her comfort that night, her understanding, as he dealt with the emotions of the past. But she'd offered only accusations and shrewish demands. That wasn't the way she wanted him to remember her while he was gone.

In a matter of seconds, her mind skipped from worry to dread to fear and back to worry again. Furious at herself, she pounded at the dough, kneading with vicious intent.

If only she had some news of him. Was he safe? Had he caught the outlaw? Was he on his way home at last? Or—the worst of them all—was he lying dead in some hidden valley, alone and forgotten?

"I will not give in to this paralyzing fear."

She stopped kneading, closed her eyes and quoted her favorite verse from the Gospel of John. "Jesus said, 'Peace I leave with you; my peace I give you. I do not give to you as the world gives. Do not let your hearts be troubled and do not be afraid.'"

Please, Lord, help me to have faith over my fears. Please, bring Trey home safely to Molly and me.

Her stomach clutched at the thought of never seeing him again. Stifling a moan, she flicked loose flour onto the cutting board and began kneading again.

If this sickening dread was what she had to look forward to every time Trey left to hunt an outlaw, how could she ever expect to survive marriage to him?

She squeezed her eyes shut and prayed, "Lord, give me clarity. Reveal to me what I should do."

A movement just outside the window caught her attention.

Katherine squinted into the sunlight, her eyes focusing on the town sheriff dragging a familiar child in tow. One child. Not three. Not even two. But *one!*

The last time Katherine had seen Molly, the five-year-old had asked to tag along with Johnny and Megan as they headed into town to run an errand for Laney. How on earth had her sister ended up in the lawman's care?

And where were the other children?

In an attempt to gather more information, Katherine studied her heel-scuffing, head-hanging little sister as she made her way toward the back door of the house—with her arm gripped by the sheriff's hand.

Battling a large dose of trepidation, Katherine wiped her hands on her apron, circled around the counter and then opened the door leading into the backyard.

She stood on the top step, waiting for an explanation.

When neither spoke, Katherine bobbed her gaze from her sister to the sheriff and back again. Both held themselves unnaturally stiff, each shifting from foot to foot in an erratic, guilty rhythm.

"What's happened?" When both continued in their silence, Katherine sighed. "Are either of you going to answer me?"

Molly squeaked out an "I'm sorry, Katherine," but kept her head lowered and her arms wrapped around her middle.

"Sorry? For what?" asked Katherine.

Molly dug her toe into the dirt and shrugged.

Katherine turned her attention to the lawman, who seemed surprisingly…contrite?

What on earth was going on here?

"Where are Megan and Johnny?"

Two bushy white eyebrows drew together, and the sheriff shifted his hat to the back of his head. "I don't know about any others. I only found this one in town."

Gasping, Katherine turned her full attention to Molly. "You were in Denver, alone?"

Still gazing at the ground, Molly shrugged again. "I sort of got separated from the others."

Something in the way her little sister refused to lift her head put Katherine on instant alert. "Look at me, Molly. Right now."

The child slowly—very slowly—lifted her head.

"Oh, Molly." A thick, hot blast of air escaped from

Katherine's lungs as she rushed forward and lowered herself to her knees. "Your eye. It's swollen shut."

Molly hunched her shoulders forward. "I kinda fell into Bobby Prescott's fist."

Katherine fought to keep her shock from taking control of her reason. "You *kinda* fell?"

The sheriff cleared his throat. "Don't fret over it, Miss Katherine."

"How can I not?" She shot him an exasperated glare.

His answering gaze turned direct, unwavering. The grizzled lawman was firmly in place now. "Turns out, your little sister has quite a right hook when provoked."

"Molly! You've been fighting?" exclaimed Katherine. Nausea nearly overtook her. What had possessed the child to indulge in fisticuffs?

"At least she gave it to that Prescott boy but good." Lassiter patted her on the head like a faithful pet. "She's a scrappy little thing, your sister."

A strong sense of chagrin left Katherine completely unsettled. "You hit a boy?"

Clearly insulted by Katherine's tone, the five-year-old jerked her chin at an angry angle. "He said you was my mommy. I said, 'Yeah, so?' 'Cause, well, I want you to be my mommy, but then he called you a tramp. He said that you was slinking in closets with men for money. I was just shuttin' him up, but good."

Understanding dawned, and with it came the pain. The humiliation. The bitter reality. The talk had begun, and it had already circled back to Katherine's innocent little sister. "Oh, Molly."

Trey had been right all along. People talked. Reasonable doubt was ignored. Guilt instantly assumed.

And Molly had been the one hurt today.

This was no longer a simple matter of word getting out about a slight indiscretion in the school's supply closet.

It was so much worse.

Katherine took a deep breath and accepted the reality of the situation. It was one thing to hear the whispers directed at her. At least those comments were unfounded. Something had to be done about the new rumors, rumors that were entrenched in a semblance of the truth.

Neither she nor Molly could continue to live in this state of indecision. First, however, Katherine had to attend to Molly's injuries—both the physical and mental ones—and explain the right and wrong way to respond to provocation.

But not in front of a stranger.

Rising to her full height, Katherine turned her attention to the sheriff and gave him a tight smile. "Thank you for bringing my sister home. I can handle matters from here."

Lassiter stabbed a quick glance at Molly; then his lips flattened into a determined line as he returned his stare to Katherine. "Don't you let them town folk and their talk get to you, Miss Katherine. Anyone with sense knows you're a fine Christian woman."

"Thank you, Sheriff," Katherine said, shoving a shaky hand through her hair. "But why defend me? You don't really know me."

"I know what I know. Marshal Scott is the most honorable man in the territory. If he says you're a good woman, well, then I say so, too."

Tears pricked her eyes, but she held them back with sheer force of will. "Trey said that about me?"

He patted her on the arm. "He'll be home soon, and he'll help you sort this all out."

Her heart began to trip at the burden that lay ahead of her. Yet the man's confidence in her was heartening. "Thank you, Sheriff, for everything."

Laney chose that moment to materialize in the door frame. "Sheriff? Is everything all right?"

"I was just leaving. Miss Taylor can give you the sordid details." He rustled Molly's hair. "See ya, kid."

He turned to go but stopped and cocked his head toward Molly. "She's been hiding her right paw under her wing ever since we left town. That Prescott kid's got a hard head. You might want to get the doc to check out her hand."

The words pushed Katherine to action. Ignoring the sheriff now that he was leaving, she dropped to her knees and wrestled Molly's hand out from under her arm. "Let me see what you've done to yourself."

At the sight of the bloody, swollen fingers, Katherine fought back a wave of hysteria. "Oh, Molly."

Laney darted out of the house and knelt down next to Katherine. "You might have broken it, baby," she declared, swiping her fingers across the child's knuckles as she spoke.

Katherine cringed as Molly whimpered. "That hurts, Laney."

"It's what comes of fighting." Laney clicked her tongue. "We'll have to get Dr. Shane."

Fear sprang into the child's eyes, and then the tears started flowing freely.

Katherine smoothed Molly's hair off her forehead. "Don't worry, Molly. We'll get you patched up."

"I'm sorry, Katherine." Sniffling hiccups came out of the little girl, and she wiped her good hand across her nose. "But Bobby was being really, really mean about you. He made it sound like you being my mommy was bad or something."

Even though Katherine wanted to pull Molly in her arms and tell her everything would work out just fine, she also knew she had to set her little sister straight while the incident was fresh in her mind. "You can't hit every boy who says bad things about me, or you, or anyone we care about. You need to turn the other cheek next time."

Two black brows drew together in obvious confusion. "Huh?"

Katherine shared a look with Laney. The other woman nodded encouragingly.

Shifting to her knees, Katherine took the child's face gently into her hands. "What I'm trying to say, Molly, is that when a boy like Bobby says something ugly to you, you have to ignore him and walk away."

"Even when he calls *you* names?" squeaked Molly.

Katherine dropped her hands. "Especially then."

Molly scrunched her face into a scowl and chewed on her lower lip. "That doesn't sound right."

"It is, baby. Forgiving isn't easy, but boys like Bobby need it most from us."

"But he was the one who wronged me."

"Nevertheless—"

Johnny came barreling around the corner, his winded shouts cutting her off. "Katherine, Laney, we lost Mo—" He came to a halt at the sight of Molly. "Oh, you found her. Whoa! That's some shiner, kid."

Laney rose and instantly took charge. Placing her hands on the boy's shoulders, she spun him around toward town. "Johnny, go get Dr. Bartlett. Tell him it's an emergency."

His gaze dropped to her stomach. "Another one?"

"It's for Molly this time." Laney's voice held a stern, unrelenting note. "We think she broke her hand."

"Oh." His eyes widened. *"Oh!"*

Footsteps pelted the ground as Johnny rushed off and descended the hill back toward town.

"Katherine," Laney continued, "get that child inside, and try to wash her up as best you can before the doctor arrives." She raised her voice an entire octave. "And for goodness' sake, everybody try to stay calm."

Swallowing back her rising hysteria, Katherine scooped up her sister and started for the house. At least one good thing had come of the incident. God had given her the clarity she'd prayed for.

In the end, Katherine had a responsibility to her sister. There could be no more waffling on the matter of Trey's proposal, no more worries over her own fears.

Yes, Katherine knew exactly what she would say when she saw Trey again. Of course, the man had to come home in one piece first.

Trey rode at a clipped pace, Logan's horse easily matching the quick gait. With the cool air shrouding them in a watery mist, defeat hung heavy between them. Trey blew into his cupped palms and tried to ignore the condemnation that seemed to brood in every rock.

They'd failed. For over a month, they'd checked out every possible lead but still hadn't come close to finding Ike Hayes. And now, thanks to the wasted time searching for the man who'd turned into a phantom, Trey had to push Drew's trial back another two months.

What was he missing? The instinct that had kept him alive for years kicked in, warning Trey he'd forgotten something important.

Something simple.

Silence clung to the edges of the gray morning, and exhaustion etched across Trey's soul; bitter failure circled around his heart.

He wanted the hunt over, wanted relief from this consuming hatred. He wanted *freedom*.

Katherine had claimed God was the way to Trey's liberty. And with time, both healing and forgiveness would come. All Trey knew was the impossible had happened. Katherine and Molly had inched their way into his heart. And now he needed both in his life, more than he'd thought possible.

Trey scowled, not sure which bothered him more—shoving Drew's trial back or Ike's continued freedom. Every day his nemesis continued to run free, Trey's anger grew more pronounced, rooting deeper into his soul.

Would Trey be able to come back from the violence once the hunt was over? With Ike's death, would Trey find the freedom he now craved?

Or was it too late for him?

As though sensing his edginess, his horse snorted and shifted beneath him. Trey patted the beast's neck until he settled into a rhythmic gait again. Clearing his thoughts, he surveyed the open terrain with a watchful eye. Although the sun was just peeking over the horizon, the day felt crooked to him. Off balance.

"Now what do we do, Marshal?"

Trey's mind cut back to Logan. He was just agitated enough to take out his frustration on his deputy. "First, you're going to refigure last year's expenditures, column by column, month by month. Then you're going to head to Mattie's and find a girl more talkative than the madam. Then—"

Logan cut him off with a snort. "Am I being punished for something?"

With one quick slash of his hand, Trey dismissed Logan's question. "It's time we both got back to our assigned duties."

"But what about Ike?"

As soon as Logan's words were out of his mouth, the solution came to Trey. In truth, he couldn't believe it had taken him this long to realize the obvious.

He'd been so bent on chasing after the outlaw, he'd forgotten the simplest tactic of war—find the enemy's weakness, magnify it, then render it useless and ineffective. "We're going to wait and let him come to us."

"We're going to *what?*"

Trey ignored his deputy's shock and allowed his mind to work through the particulars. He remembered Mattie's evasion when he'd questioned her about Ike, her parting threat when he'd turned his back on her and, lastly, Ike's devotion to his little brother. "I'd stake my life on the fact that Ike Hayes is on his way to Denver, if he's not already there."

Logan's face scrunched into a look of deep concentration; he was obviously trying to work through Trey's logic. "How do you figure that?"

"He's got reasons."

Logan's eyes lit up. "Drew."

"And Mattie."

Logan grinned. "And we plan to be waiting for him."

Trey's lips curled into a smile that didn't reach his eyes. "Exactly."

Soon vengeance would be his to take.

Chapter Fifteen

Regardless of Molly's constant squirming on the kitchen counter, Dr. Bartlett examined her hand without hurting her. Once he finished, he gave Katherine a sad smile.

Apprehension trickled down her spine. "Is it broken?"

"No." He shook his head. "But it's badly bruised."

Relieved, Katherine released a breath and reached out to touch his sleeve. "That's good news."

"I'll say." Molly slid off the counter, and let out a squeal of joy. "Can I go play now?"

With surprising speed, the doctor caught her at the waist and hoisted her back in place. "Not so fast. We need to bandage your hand to keep you from injuring it any further."

With a flick of his wrist, he pulled out a roll of bandages and began wrapping the child's injury. Molly took the opportunity to yank on his hair with her free hand and giggled. "Your hair sticks out kind of funny all over, Dr. Shane."

He smiled at her, obviously used to the declaration. "I know."

"I like it," she declared.

"Well, of course, you do." He winked at her. "All the smart ladies know what's what."

Molly giggled.

Dr. Bartlett grinned.

"Molly's healthy otherwise?" Katherine asked.

"Very," he said, without looking at her. "But I'd like you to come to my office this afternoon, Miss Taylor, so we can discuss her, uh…specific needs."

Katherine's brows drew together. "I think I know what to do. This isn't the first injury at Charity House."

"Nevertheless. I—" He broke off, slanted a quick look at Molly, who was entertaining herself by using her good hand to empty the contents of his medical bag onto the counter beside her.

He lowered his voice to a whisper. "What I have to say is private."

Katherine felt his urgency but had no idea where it was coming from. Had he heard the talk about her, too? Was he going to condemn her for what she'd supposedly done in the school's supply closet? Or would he show her compassion, like he had on the night of her attack, when he'd tended her wounds?

There was one way to find out. And she certainly wasn't going to trek all the way into town when he was standing right next to her in Charity House.

As he continued working on Molly's hand, Katherine said, "I'll be right back."

She stepped into the hallway off the kitchen and motioned Laney to join them. "We're about finished."

"Is it broken?" Laney asked, her eyes filled with concern.

"No."

"Praise the Lord."

"Would you mind taking Molly upstairs to her room while Dr. Bartlett has a word with me about her care?"

Before Laney had a chance to respond, Katherine gripped her friend by the arm and directed her toward the counter. "I'll only be a moment behind you."

Laney's eyes widened; then she looked from Katherine to the doctor and back to Katherine again. With each pass, speculation glittered deeper in her eyes. "I…see."

Katherine waved her off. Her friend was reading signs that simply did not exist. "No, you don't."

Laney lifted an eyebrow but then shook her head and smiled down at Molly instead of pushing further. "Come on, little one. Let's get you settled in the bed."

Molly's expression turned defiant. "I don't want to take a nap."

"You've had a trauma, Molly," Katherine pointed out. "It's best if you rest for a while."

"But I feel fine," Molly whined.

Katherine would not allow the five-year-old to reel her into this argument again. "Then consider it punishment for fighting. If you can't fall asleep, then use the quiet time to think about what you've done and how you will handle Bobby Prescott next time he says something ugly to you."

At that, Molly's head dropped at a wayward angle. "Yes, Katherine. I'm really sorry, you know."

"I know," said Katherine. She swept a braid off Molly's shoulder and clutched her gently. "But you're still going to be punished."

Head hanging, Molly silently followed Laney out of the kitchen.

Once they were alone, Katherine looked at Dr. Bartlett, noting how his features were set and stern, matched only by the severity of his black coat and crisp white shirt.

Prepared for the worst, Katherine lowered herself in a chair near the counter where Molly had been sitting earlier. "What did you want to discuss with me, Dr. Bartlett?"

Unable to meet her gaze, he shifted from foot to foot. He'd seemed so sure of himself earlier, his hands and manner full of confidence when he'd bandaged Molly's injury. But now, it was as if he'd become a different man.

Katherine studied him while he silently struggled to put words together. She'd never really noticed how handsome he was. His rumpled dark brown hair, strong features and gentle hands made a woman feel safe in his presence, even a woman with a horrifying past like hers. He was big, like Trey and Marc, but had been blessed with the soothing touch of a healer.

It was a wonder she hadn't seen any of his finer qualities before now.

"Miss Taylor—" He broke off and set to pacing around the room.

Katherine tapped her foot on the floor, folded her hands in her lap and waited for him to continue.

She watched him move, his grace at odds with his size, his shoulders large enough for a woman to set all her cares upon. Why couldn't her heart have fallen for this man? Shane Bartlett was handsome, compassionate and...*safe*.

The antithesis of Trey Scott.

He stopped pacing, pivoted to face her. Speculation wavered in his gaze. He looked very much like the way he had when he'd watched her in the birthing room with Laney. "Miss Taylor."

A warning twisted in her stomach. "Yes?"

"All this resurgence of talk about you in town, well, I know it's not your fault. Does the man who cornered you in the closet know—"

"I wasn't cornered," she hastened to explain before he accused Trey of something he hadn't done. "Nor was I doing what they say I was doing."

"You weren't—" He broke off, swallowed, then began again. "You weren't…kissing a man in the school's supply closet?"

"Not kissing, no. Or anything else remotely sordid like that. We were just talking. About Molly and her future."

He gave her an odd look. "Well, whatever you were doing, word is all over town that it was a lot more than talk."

Katherine blew out a breath. Although Trey hadn't actually kissed her, in a matter of weeks the gossip had turned decidedly ugly.

"Miss Taylor?" Dr. Bartlett swallowed. "Will the man in question do what is needed to stop the talk?"

She thought of Trey's parting shot when she'd left him gaping at her in the open field. "Yes. As a matter of fact, he's asked me to marry him."

And thanks to the events of today, she'd decided to say yes. That is, if he came back alive, she thought, her heart aching over the terrible prospect.

Oh, Lord, please keep Trey safe. Bring him home so we can sort through this together.

"Well, if he doesn't—" he touched her sleeve "—I'd like to offer to marry you in his stead."

She stared at him in genuine confusion. "You're asking me to marry you?"

His gaze turned solemn. "You can trust that I am sincere."

Although his tired eyes held conviction, she saw none of the tenderness she'd witnessed so often in Trey's gaze when he'd discussed marriage. His motives were clearly not from love and caring. So what urged him forward? "Why would you offer such a thing?"

"Miss Taylor, I see you at church every Sunday, in the same seat each week. In spite of your upbringing and what others say, I *know* you are a good Christian woman."

She smiled at the compliment and then folded her hands in her lap. "What I am, and what others say I am, are obviously at odds with one another."

"You suffer enough shame because of your mother's...profession." He pulled his shoulders forward and broke eye contact as he spoke of her attack. But then he straightened and stared straight into her eyes. "You don't deserve more of the same, no matter the reason."

"You'd marry me simply to stop the talk?"

A sorrowful look flickered in his eyes, only to be replaced with a determination she'd never seen in him before. "If not for you, then let me do this for your sister."

She smiled up at him. "You are a good man."

He shot her a look that had her sitting straighter in her chair. "This isn't about simple kindness," he said. "Or even Christian charity. It's about protecting an *innocent* child from the heat of scandal."

She couldn't help but wonder if there was more underneath Shane Bartlett's calm exterior than she had at first realized. His severe expression told her this was not a man to trifle with, especially on this subject. Which made it imperative that she set him straight. "This is sweet of you, but completely unnecessary."

"No child should bear this kind of shame. Nor should you," he added, almost as an afterthought.

Katherine studied his face for a long, long moment. "You needn't worry about what the good folk of Denver will think of me."

If anything, he set his shoulders at a more determined angle than before. "You're a schoolteacher. Your reputation must be above reproach."

"I will never be considered a decent woman." She ignored his flinch and continued. "Let's not pretend otherwise. I do know what they say behind my back."

Even now, she could hear the words of condemnation echoing in her head. Words whispered within earshot in her own neighborhood.

His gaze hardened. "What do they say?"

She pitched her voice up an octave. "Oh, that's Katherine Taylor, the daughter of that harlot, Sadie. Bet she's just like that no-good mother of hers."

He nodded, a sage look coming into his eyes. "Guilt by association."

Determined to let Dr. Bartlett know she wasn't living in a cocoon, that she knew exactly what was said about her by the "good" citizens of Denver, Katherine continued. "Exactly. They assume I'm just like my mother and all that that implies."

He winced, his face set and stern.

Katherine couldn't help but think there was more to the doctor's strong reaction besides concern for her. But now wasn't the time to ask. "Nevertheless, I'm condemned and shunned."

He paced two steps, then turned to face her, his gaze intense and inflexible. "Perhaps in the eyes of some, you're tainted forever. But if we were to marry, we could leave Denver, go someplace where no one knows you or your infamous connections. You would be the wife of a doctor, and Molly would never have to suffer the…whispers."

Why was he so adamant?

"Leave Denver? But Charity House is our home. Laney took me in when no one else would even look me in the eye. I could never leave—"

"You'd rather Molly suffer the shame of *your* actions instead?" Disapproval glared back at her.

Katherine's hands flew to her heart, knowing the ridicule that was bound to come to her sister if she didn't rectify the situation soon. Regardless of what she and Trey had done in that supply closet, word was out. And it wasn't kind.

The doctor's expression softened as he wrapped her hands in his and knelt before her again. "Will you at least consider my offer?"

"Thank you for asking, but—"

"I'd be a good husband and father."

"Yes. I know you would."

"Does that mean you'll marry me?"

Oh, what a wonderful, wonderful gesture, to *ask* her, instead of ordering her. It was the kind of consideration that deserved complete honesty in return. "I can't."

"But—"

She pulled one of her hands free, pressed it to his lips when he tried to speak again. "Please, don't ask me again. I do appreciate your offer, but I don't love you." She worked her other hand free and clasped his shoulders, ensuring he'd look her straight in the eye. "And you don't love me."

"Love?" He spat out the word. "This has nothing to do with something so trivial. This is about protecting a child from spiteful talk."

His intensity told its own story. Shane Bartlett had very strong beliefs on the matter.

The question, of course, was why.

"This has everything to do with love," she said. "And when you're captured by the emotion yourself, you'll understand why I'm doing both of us a favor by saying no to your offer."

"And I can't change your mind?" Though his tone was mild, his expression was grave.

"No."

He rose, began gathering his things, but stopped and looked at her again. "If the man who threw you into this scandal refuses to marry you, will you reconsider? For Molly, if not for yourself?"

She nodded, hoping for all their sakes it never came to that. "Yes, perhaps I'll reconsider if the situation warrants."

"That's all I ask." He turned his attention to the table once more and began rolling the remaining bandages.

As she watched him prepare to leave, tears pierced through her composure. In little over a month, two men had asked her to marry them. Two *good* men who knew the details of her horrible past, and *still* they wanted to marry her. Her. Katherine Taylor.

Oh, thank You, Lord. Thank You for showing me in such a substantial way that I'm worthy of a man's caring, and that I'm so much more than what happened to me that night two years ago.

Dr. Bartlett made it to the door, stopped, then turned back to her. "Marshal Scott returned late this morning with his deputy. Perhaps you'll want to talk with him right away."

Her hand flew to her mouth. "How did you know? Has talk been that specific'?"

He shrugged. "I don't think so, but I see things."

If Shane Bartlett knew about her and Trey, did others as well? "Did I, I mean, was I…that easy to read?"

"No." He twisted the door handle, his lips descending into a sympathetic grimace. "He was."

Chapter Sixteen

An hour after Dr. Bartlett had proposed to Katherine, she
left the jailhouse dejected and out of sorts. Normally, she
didn't make the trip to town. Although used to the accusing
stares and whispers, she didn't enjoy them. In fact, they
hurt. They hurt a lot. Thus she avoided the experience as
often as possible. Except, of course, on Sundays, when she
went to church.

Today, however, she'd ignored the familiar nervousness as she'd left Charity House and gone in search of Trey
in town. For Molly's sake, as well as her own, it was time
to settle matters between them. But, according to Deputy
Mitchell, she'd missed Trey by less than an hour.

Her first reaction was an excited quiver in the vicinity
of her heart. Trey was home. He was safe. He was no
longer chasing vengeance.

But as she realized that *she* was the one who had sought
him out, trepidation of another sort replaced her joy. Perhaps
he'd changed his mind about her, about them. Perhaps he'd
decided she wasn't worthy enough to become his wife.

No. This false sense of shame, and constant lack of confidence in her own value as a woman, wasn't of God. By allowing the disgrace of her attack to continue festering in her soul, she wasn't living the abundant life promised to her as a child of God.

Well, no longer.

Trey wasn't like the others, who condemned her. It was cowardly and wrong to question Trey's motives, especially after all they'd been through together. She would believe that good came to those who trusted in the Lord.

Nevertheless, a vague sense of doubt still swam through her mind, thundered in her chest.

Scuffing her feet much like she'd seen Molly do, Katherine made her way along the wooden sidewalk. *One, two, three.* She began counting the seams between the planks in an attempt to clear her mind of her foolish uncertainty. A man bumped into her, hard, jerking Katherine's attention from her task and nearly sending her to the ground.

"Oh." Air whooshed out of her, and she flayed her hands in order to find her balance.

The man did nothing to help her. Instead, he scowled, with eyes that had turned gunmetal cold and unforgiving. "Watch where you're going."

A sound of dismay slipped from her lips. "I... Of course, I apologize."

He paused and shot a hard glare at her, looking much like the ladies from church had when she'd encountered them in her neighborhood weeks ago. And just like that last time, her hands started to shake.

"See that it doesn't happen again." He all but snarled the words at her.

Katherine pressed her palms together and tried desperately to keep her rising resentment from taking control of her tongue. They both knew he had bumped into her on purpose. But she was Sadie Taylor's daughter, and that put her firmly in the wrong. Every time. All the time.

Nevertheless, she would rise above this situation and take the godly way out. "Again, I apologize," she said, managing a tight smile.

With a look of disgust on his face, he shoved past her. "Your kind should stay on Market Street, where you belong."

Katherine stood frozen to the spot. Even through the blur of her shocked resentment, her instinct was to turn around and yell after him that she was a good, moral woman, a woman above reproach. A woman deserving of some kindness.

But people saw in her what they wanted to see. They saw a ruined woman whose virtue and innocence were gone. Stolen, yes, but gone all the same.

The pain of her humiliation throbbed thickly in her throat. She wanted to lash out, to scream at the unfairness of it all. In that moment she fully understood why Molly had answered Bobby Prescott's accusations with her fists.

Although the encounters were never easy, Katherine had come to terms with this type of prejudice. But Molly was still a child, and for Katherine's innocent little sister, the guilt by association ended today.

Of course, respectability would come at a price. Marriage to Trey could be the worst decision she ever made. Or the best. At that last thought, a tiny whisper of hope threaded through her doubts.

Trust. Where she and Trey were concerned, it all came

down to trust. And just as Sheriff Lassiter had said when he'd brought Molly home this morning, Trey would come to her, and they would work everything out.

With renewed determination, Katherine made the trip home in record time. As she crossed the threshold, her senses were assaulted with the fresh smell of furniture polish and the sound of familiar voices.

Katherine stopped and listened.

Molly's excited chatter came from the vicinity of Marc's study. "Whattaya think of my new bandage, Mr. Trey? It's really big, huh?"

Katherine's breath hitched in her throat when she heard Trey's deep voice respond to the question. "Very impressive," he said.

A long pause followed, and the breath she'd been holding escaped past Katherine's lips. She stabbed a quick glance to her left and then her right, discovering she was alone in the hallway.

Perhaps she would listen a moment longer.

Trey cleared his throat. "Tell me again how you hurt your hand."

An even longer pause followed the question. A vague sense of hope filled Katherine, and she moved another step closer to Marc's study.

"Kitten?" he urged softly.

Knowing it was wrong to eavesdrop, Katherine couldn't find the courage to make her presence known just yet.

"Well," Molly began, clearly reluctant to tell the full tale. Katherine could almost hear her sister shifting from one foot to another, her young mind sorting through the various explanations. "Like I said, Bobby Prescott's head kinda ran into my hand."

"Just like your eye ran into his fist?" Trey's voice sounded more than a little ironic.

"Right. Just like that. I think he got it but good for saying those bad things about my sister, but Katherine says I'm supposed to forgive him anyway."

Katherine held her breath, waiting to see if Trey would contradict her efforts at teaching Molly good Christian values.

The silence seemed to stretch out, but then Trey let out a grim, impatient snort. "Your sister is right, kitten."

"But, Mr. Trey—"

"Don't argue, Molly. No good ever comes from fighting."

Relief flowed through Katherine, and she decided she'd heard enough. Whether or not Trey truly agreed with her didn't matter at this point. He'd backed her up with her little sister. Perhaps he was finally coming around to her way of thinking.

Oh, Lord, please let it be so.

Placing what she hoped was a confident expression on her face, she entered the study. "Molly was valiantly defending my good name," she began. "Even if we all agree she didn't choose the best avenue to do so."

Trey rose from his crouched position in front of the child. His gaze slammed into hers and held firm. "Hello, Katherine."

At the sight of his intense expression, she had to fight for air, nearly gulping the next breath into her lungs. How she wished she'd prepared herself better for this first glimpse of Trey after his month-long absence.

She cleared her throat. Sighed. Forced a smile. "Hello, Trey."

A muscle shifted in his jaw.

Her heart skipped a beat.

He took a step forward.

She took a small step back.

He stopped, blew out a breath, took another tentative step forward.

This time she held her ground.

"It's good to see you," he said at last.

Unable to find the words, she gave no response. In truth, they'd left off on such bad terms, she didn't know where to begin their conversation.

"Katherine?" Molly angled her head. "Are you feeling all right?"

"She's fine, kitten," Trey said, grinning like a fool as he spoke. "She's just so happy to see me, she's struck speechless."

At that remark, Katherine found her tongue. "Molly, would you mind leaving us alone for a moment?"

The child fixed Trey with a questioning stare.

"Go on, kitten," he said. "You can tell me the rest of your story after I have a word with your sister."

Looking unhappy, Molly nodded obediently and left the room without a word of protest.

Shocked, Katherine stared after the skipping child. "What did you do to my sister?"

"Let's just say we understand one another." His gaze turned concerned. "Now, about her fight with the Prescott boy. We need to discuss what we should do next."

The genuine worry in his eyes took her breath away all over again. Trey's obvious concern for Molly ran deep. As deep as her own caring was growing for him, a caring that was quickly turning into...

Oh, please, Lord, not...not...love.

Frightened of her own emotions, she focused on her little sister. "It's actually very simple," she said a bit too quickly. "We settle things between us and stop the talk for good. That's why I went looking for you at the jailhouse."

"You went looking for me?" The happy note in his voice made her heart beat harder in her chest. She didn't tell him about the confrontation on the sidewalk. He'd only go in search of the man and settle matters in the Old Testament way.

And because of that, knowing Trey would protect her against something as small as a snub in town, she fell a little harder for him.

"I did," she said. "But you had already left."

He closed the distance between them, drew her hand into his and smiled into her eyes. "It's embarrassing, truth be told, how much that pleases me."

The declaration was swift, uncalculated. And powerful.

In spite of her every effort to remain unmoved, her eyes drank in the sight of him. He was big and healthy and *safe*. "I see you made it back in one piece."

He dragged her farther into the study and shut the door behind them. "Is that your way of saying you missed me?"

She had to remember her little sister and the reason for Molly's fight with Bobby Prescott this morning. Or she'd blurt out her feelings for him too quickly, too completely. "*Molly* certainly missed you."

"But did you?" he persisted.

She looked away from him, unsure how to answer without revealing everything in her heart.

He arranged his face into a pitiful frown, the gesture making him appear more boy than man. "You're going to make me work for this, aren't you?"

She sniffed. "I don't know what you mean."

"Right." He sank into a nearby chair. Lifting his arms into the air, he clasped his hands behind his head and relaxed into his palms. "Go ahead. Proceed with your best scolding."

"Of all the… You are a mannerless brute, Trey Scott."

In response, he proceeded to look at her with lazy tolerance. And then he raised a single eyebrow.

"Oh, honestly." She threw her hands up. "Yes, I missed you. *Terribly.* There, I said it. Satisfied?"

"Completely." The smile he gave her made her think of love and futures and possibilities.

A feeling of doom buckled her knees. She reached out to the desk for support. "I think you should know what started Molly's fight."

"The kitten told me."

"And?"

"Let's just say I am resisting the urge to tell you 'I told you so.'"

"Yet you said it anyway."

He rose. "Katherine. I *hate* that I wasn't here to defend you and Molly against the vicious talk in town." His tone turned serious, heartfelt. "I should have known it would come to this. Because of me, and what happened in that supply closet, Molly suffered today. It's time the nasty town gossip moved away from my women. It's time I made it right for both of you, before matters get any worse."

Tears slipped around in her eyes. She blinked rapidly, hanging on to her emotions as best she could. But how could she not be touched by Trey's words? He understood. The big, gorgeous, heroic brute. He might still be locked in the past, but for now—today—he was right here with her. And in spite of her very real fears for his physical and spiritual safety, Katherine would trust that God would provide for them all.

Walk by faith, not by sight...

In that moment, Katherine was filled with certainty.

Trey narrowed his eyes. "You're not going to get all weepy and female on me?"

She hitched her chin high. "Maybe."

"I've a better idea." He pulled her carefully toward him. When she didn't resist, he wrapped his arms around her shoulders.

It quickly sank in that she was being held in the shelter of Trey Scott's arms, and there was no panic, no shuddering fear racing through her. Slowly, she roped her arms around his waist and rested her cheek against his chest.

"Quit battling me, Katherine," he said softly. "I may not be your first choice, or even your second. Marry me anyway, and make me a better man. I promise I'll defend your honor *and* Molly's with my life."

Of course, he would. "Oh, Trey. That's a much better proposal than before."

He tightened his hold. Just a little. And all she felt in response was comfort. Safety. A warm sense of homecoming.

Was she finally healed of her fear?

"I've missed you, Katherine." He sounded more amazed than shocked by the declaration.

"I missed you, too." She sighed against him, wanting only to focus on what she could control. "Dreadfully."

As the silence lengthened into a comfortable calm, Trey kissed the top of her head and then took several steps away from her. "Now that we've settled that, I have a gift for you."

"You bought a gift for me?" Her heart gave a happy twist at the notion.

"Don't sound so surprised." He tapped her on the nose. "I am capable of considering someone other than myself."

She closed her eyes, remembering all the times she'd watched him playing with Molly and the other Charity House children. For months, she'd refused to see Trey as he really was—a man who cared deeply for his own.

For better or worse, she and Molly were his now. She just had to tell him so.

Smiling down at her, he placed a black velvet box in her hand. "I found this in Colorado Springs and thought immediately of you."

An enchanting, albeit uncharacteristic, nervousness flickered in his eyes. "Take this as a token of my affection," he said. "And a promise of my loyalty to you and Molly forever."

Katherine found she could only stare at the tiny box. Other than Laney and Marc, no one had ever given her a gift.

"Go ahead. Open it."

Her fingers shook as she pulled back the lid. A gasp flew out of her lips the moment her gaze fell on the sparkling sapphire ring.

Trey edged toward her, with a tentative smile on his lips. "I picked the stone to match the color of your eyes."

The thoughtful way he'd chosen this gift sent her heart aching for the man Trey could become if he allowed himself to let go of the guilt of his past and his drive for vengeance.

She knew he was on the right path, but would she truly be at the end of it?

Yes. She had to believe in him, and in God's power to heal his heart.

"I…I don't know what to say," she said softly.

"Say you'll marry me. Let me make you a respectable woman, for all our sakes."

He plucked the ring out of its case, his eyes clouding over with a new emotion. He had a look about him that she'd seen once before, in the birthing room with Laney and Marc. Hope overwhelmed her as he slid the band onto her finger and commanded her gaze.

Something had changed in him. She wasn't fool enough to question the what or the why at this point. "Oh, Trey."

She lowered her gaze to the ring, rotated her wrist so the gem caught the light. As she stared into the sparkling stone, her decision became remarkably clear. Somewhere between Molly's need for a family and her own need for security, Katherine had lost hold of all the reasons why she had to refuse this man.

Trey fiddled with the hair that fell across her cheek. "We can make it work."

She sighed and thought of a verse from Ephesians. *Be completely humble and gentle; be patient, bearing with one another in love.*

She and Trey might not be evenly yoked spiritually. Yet. But Katherine knew he'd once believed in God. Surely he could again.

Oh, Lord, soften his heart, she prayed. *Help him find his way back to You. And if it's in Your will, use me as Your vessel along that path.*

With one last swallow, the fight finally let her go. "Let's find out."

Trey's mouth hung open. He clamped his lips together,

narrowed his eyes, then started sputtering. "What… What did you say?"

She lifted her gaze to his, discovering that she liked this man flustered, especially when she was the one doing the flustering. "I said, let's get married."

His eyes narrowed, suspicion coloring over his shock. "Are you doing this for Molly?"

Refusing to lie, she nodded. "And for other reasons."

His lips pulled into a lopsided grin. "That's enough for now."

She smiled at him in return.

With a careful tug he pulled her into his arms. Eyes full of intent, he lowered his head slowly. Very, very slowly.

He was going to kiss her. Right here. Anyone could walk into the study. But instead of feeling scared or even nervous, Katherine felt…excited.

Sighing, she settled deeper into his embrace and lifted her face to accept his kiss. Their first kiss.

"My sweet, sweet Katherine," he whispered.

And then he pressed his lips to hers at last. The connection was so soft, so gentle she wasn't sure whether to be relieved or disappointed. Before she could decide which, he set her away from him.

Spinning in a circle, he stabbed impatient fingers through his hair, then looked back to her. "I have to go."

"Go?" she asked. "Go where?"

"To make plans for our wedding, of course."

They laughed in unison, the sound linking them together in their own private world of understanding. Oh, how handsome Trey was when he laughed.

Katherine vowed to give him many reasons throughout the ensuing years to laugh more often.

* * *

Trey watched several emotions flit across Katherine's face. Thankfully, he didn't see any regret. "I'll be quick," he said. "I don't want to—"

A loud, insistent knocking interrupted the rest of his speech.

"Trey Scott," bellowed an angry voice from the other side of the door. "Open up. I know you're in there."

At the sound of Marc's voice, a sigh of dismay slipped from Katherine's lips. "What is he so upset about?"

Trey made a face. "He's obviously heard the talk."

"Oh, dear."

Wanting to protect Katherine from an ugly confrontation, Trey went to the door to head off his friend. But with a hard shove, Marc pushed into the room and grabbed Trey by the lapels.

"Is it true?" He shook Trey hard. "Did you and Katherine do what they—"

"*Calm down,* Marc." Trey yanked away from his friend. "You're out of control."

"Me? How can you say that after what you've done to Katherine!"

Trey shook his head. He should have known it would come to this. "No matter what you think you've heard, it's misinformation."

Marc looked wildly around the study, his gaze seeking and finding Katherine with phenomenal speed. "Talk is all over town about you two. And it's ugly. I'm told some of the neighbors are already drawing up a formal complaint against you."

Katherine lifted her chin, but her eyes were filled with trepidation.

"Leave her alone, Marc." Trey would not allow his friend to accuse Katherine of something she hadn't done. "She didn't do anything wrong."

"Maybe *she* didn't." Spinning back to glare at Trey, Marc continued, "You, on the other hand, had no right to corner her in the school's supply closet."

Trey bristled as renewed guilt knotted around his heart. "I didn't even kiss her," he defended.

But he knew he'd wronged her simply by seeking her out when she was alone and unprotected.

"It doesn't matter what you did or didn't do, Trey. You *knew* her past. You also knew how the town treats her because of it. This time they have real ammunition against her. Charity House will weather the storm. We always do. But you shouldn't have put Katherine in a position to suffer again."

Trey froze at the accusation. Marc was right, of course. Although Trey had tried to rectify the situation since that auspicious day at the Charity House School, he'd been more consumed with finding Ike than pushing the matter with Katherine. In truth, Trey hadn't tried hard enough to set matters right.

"I've trusted you like a brother," Marc said, waving his hand in an angry slash toward Katherine. "And this is what you do with that trust?"

Trey heard the unspoken words as loudly as the ones his friend said aloud. "You got something to say to me, say it plainly."

"All right. For four years, your quest for vengeance has consumed you. I've watched, helplessly, as the soothing of your own misplaced guilt turned you greedy and selfish. It didn't matter so much before, because you were only hurting yourself, but now you're hurting Katherine and Molly. You're going to make it right."

Trey scowled. Until Marc's outburst, he'd considered the other man a friend, a brother, the only one who understood his burning need to hunt down Ike Hayes and avenge Laurette's senseless murder.

Trey inched his gaze across Marc's features, arranging his own face into a look designed to start a fight. "And you're going to dole out the consequences if I don't, is that it?"

Marc nodded. "If it comes to that, yes. But, first, I want the facts so I can prepare for an official attack." As he glanced to Katherine, his expression softened with genuine concern. "Did Trey force you to do anything against your will?"

She looked at Trey as she answered the question. "No. Of course not."

Marc's eyes narrowed. "Did he tell you to say that?"

Friend or not, Trey wasn't about to let this man question Katherine's integrity. "You want a fight? You bring it to me. But I'm warning you now. Leave. Her. Alone."

Marc's lips formed into a sneer, disfiguring his features into a tangle of raw emotion. "A not-so-friendly threat. Is that it, Trey? Well, here's one of my own. You better be planning to marry her."

Trey's fists rose in response.

Katherine swiftly moved in front of Trey, placed her hands over his and pushed until he lowered them to his sides.

"Marc," she said, turning to look at him directly. In the process she shifted in front of Trey, as though she were shielding him. "I appreciate your gallant effort on my behalf, but it's already settled. Trey and I are getting married as soon as he can take care of the details."

Marc stared at her, with a look of disbelief on his face. "Are you telling me the truth, and or are you trying to protect him?"

"Oh, honestly. As if he needs my protection. Maybe this will make my point." She flashed her ring at him.

Marc looked at her hand, up to Katherine's face, then back to her hand. "When did all this happen?"

Trey gave his friend the kind of self-righteous sneer that was meant to make him see red. "That's none of your business. All you need to know is that we're getting married by the end of the week. You can either congratulate me on my good fortune or move aside."

A grin slipped onto Marc's lips. "Well, it's about time you came to your senses, old man." He reached out and smacked Trey on the back. "I couldn't be happier for either of you."

Trey nodded. "You're invited to the wedding, of course."

Looking nearly as happy as he had at the birth of his daughter, Marc's grin widened. "Oh, I'll be there. I plan to bring my shotgun, in case you get any ideas about begging off."

"Won't happen," said Trey.

Trey turned to Katherine, stared at her for a long, thoughtful moment. She was so beautiful. So kind.

And soon she would be his wife. His future.

His heart jumped in his chest at the possibility of real freedom. All along he'd told himself his desire to marry Katherine was to protect her from town gossip, and from the legal implications if a complaint was filed against the Charity House School. But he now realized, as he stared into her guileless eyes, there had been more motivating his offer of marriage. A desire for a fresh start, a chance to right a wrong for one woman when he'd failed another so miserably.

It was time to start taking action. And the sooner he married Katherine, the better. "Come to think of it, I should make the arrangements before *she* changes *her* mind."

A promise filled Katherine's eyes as she repeated his words back to him. "Won't happen."

Thank You, Lord, was his only clear thought after that.

Chapter Seventeen

A week later, Katherine lingered at the back of the church, shifting restlessly. Now that the time had come to pledge her life to Trey's, nerves threatened to consume her. With her agitation barely under control, she studied the group assembled around her. Marc stood like a sentry by her side. Laney and Molly were poised at the ready in front of her.

A riot of emotion tangled in her chest. Needing an encouraging word from a man who understood the situation better than the rest, she turned to Marc. But at the sight of his concentrated intensity, her heart dropped to her toes and stuck. This man wasn't going to let her walk out of the church until the nuptials were complete.

His fatherly concern of the past week would have been sweet if his fingerprints weren't all over the wedding. He'd been involved in every aspect of the planning, rushing decisions as though time was of the essence. Worse, he hadn't allowed her and Trey any time alone, claiming they might change their minds if they actually talked to one another.

If Katherine didn't know better, she'd think Marc truly wanted this marriage to happen. And not just for Molly's sake.

She only wished she understood why.

The moment Mrs. Smythe began playing the music on the out-of-tune organ, Katherine shook away her confusion and inched forward. The pews were full of forty grinning faces. She caught sight of Sheriff Lassiter sitting next to a solemn Shane Bartlett. There was no one else from town.

She didn't need anyone else.

"Ready?" she whispered to her sister.

Molly lifted the basket in her good hand and gave a quick, solid nod. "Ready."

Katherine couldn't help but notice how lovely the little girl looked with her long black hair hanging loose down her back, flowers sprinkled throughout. Thankfully, her eye had healed. The only sign of her fight with Bobby Prescott was the bandage on her right hand.

"You look beautiful, Molly."

Molly's answering smile was as radiant as Katherine had ever seen it. "So do you."

Reveling in her sister's joy, she squeezed Molly's shoulder. Angling her head toward the other end of the aisle, she said, "Okay, you can start walking now. Laney will follow behind you, just like we practiced this morning."

"Let's go get married."

Her heart filled with Molly's contagious enthusiasm, and Katherine nodded. "Let's."

Molly started down the aisle, stopped in midstep, then swerved back. Lurching forward, she threw her arms around Katherine's waist and buried her face in the flowing skirts. "Thank you for marrying Mr. Trey."

Swiping the back of her wrist across her eyes, Katherine swallowed a shuddering sigh; then she eased Molly's chin up. She stared into eyes identical to those of the mother they'd shared and lost. A tug on her heart hitched her voice up an octave. "I love you, Molly. The best thing that ever happened to me was getting that letter from the mine's foreman."

"Me, too."

With a two-finger salute exactly like the one Trey always gave them, Molly started back down the aisle. Katherine's heart clutched in her chest as she watched her little sister tossing rose petals on the church floor. She couldn't remember ever seeing the little girl as contented as she had been these past few days. Trey's presence in Molly's life had turned her into a vivacious, happy child. Nothing like the silent, frightened creature Katherine had rescued from the mining camp.

Through championing the child, Trey Scott had worked a near miracle in Molly's life. For that alone, Katherine would adore him until the end of her days. She would trust him to care for her as well.

And though the issue of his vow to avenge his wife's murder wasn't settled, Katherine had confidence in God's providence and healing power. When the time came to seek vengeance—*if* the time came—she prayed God would lead Trey to make the right decision.

Molly skipped the last five steps, then vaulted into Trey's arms. Trey spun her around, kissed her on top of the head, then set her down next to him. He whispered something in the little girl's ear that had her giggling, then scooted her to his right.

As Katherine watched the two interact, the sincerity of

their affection for one another spoke louder than any declaration. Trey had taken on the role of father. And it suited him.

Laney always said that God was a God of new beginnings and second chances. Well, Trey was Katherine's second chance, and she was his.

For a moment, just one, everything seemed to slow down and stop. Even her breathing. She loved Trey, really, truly loved him. It was that simple. And that complicated.

Laney cleared her throat, bringing Katherine's attention to the back of the church once more. "Are you sure this is what you want?"

Katherine glanced over her friend's shoulder, her gaze uniting with Trey's. His eyes were filled with promises, and an eternal vow. If she'd had any doubts before, they disappeared under his silent appeal.

There were no guarantees, but with God's help, Trey would heal in time, just as Katherine had. For now, Katherine would take what happiness she could while she had him with her. "Yes, I'm sure."

Laney tilted her head to the side and regarded her with a searching look.

"Truly," Katherine said.

Laney nodded, relief flickering along the edges of her eyes. "Then I wish you the same happiness I have with Marc."

She winked at her husband, then began her stroll toward the front of the church.

Watching Laney's willowy descent down the aisle, Katherine suddenly remembered what her mother used to say when times were rough. "Where there is life, my dear, there is still hope."

Yes. While Trey was alive, Katherine would concentrate

on each day as it came. She would no longer chose loneliness simply because she was afraid of being left alone.
She would become the sort of wife a man like Trey would
hate to leave, one to whom he couldn't wait to return time
and time again.

A still, small voice whispered through her mind. *My
power is made perfect in your weakness.*

Resolved, she lifted her foot to begin the march into her
future, but Marc held her back. "You're sure this is what
you want to do?"

Katherine winced. "What is it with you and Laney? A
person would think you weren't sure of the wisdom of
this marriage."

"A person would be right."

She opened her mouth to argue, to remind him of his
heavy-handed machinations in the planning of every detail,
but didn't know where to begin.

Surveying his concerned expression, she lifted her eyebrows. When he merely returned her look with a questioning glare of his own, she sighed in frustration. "Marc, I can
tell by your expression, you have more to say to me. Just
say it and let's be done."

He shifted his gaze to the other end of the church, then
back to her. "Katherine, I know I've pushed you this week,
but I don't want to force you into something you don't want
to do."

"This? From you? The man who brought his shotgun
to my wedding?"

He slid her a sheepish grin. "It was a jest."

"Ha-ha."

Glancing to the heavens, he shook his head. "Marriage
is permanent."

"So is raising a sister."

Failure flashed in his gaze before it turned hard and un-wavering. "All the more reason to make sure. Your past makes no difference to Laney and me. Never has. You and Molly will always have a home at Charity House. No censure, no condemnation. Nothing would have to change."

"That's sweet, but—"

"Say the word and we walk out of this church. Charity House will face whatever scandal comes from this to-gether, as a family."

"Oh, Marc—"

"I mean it."

"I know you do, and that's what makes it all the more special. But I *want* to marry Trey."

He gave her a sad smile. "You don't have to pretend with me. I know how you really feel about him."

"You do?"

Could Marc see how much she loved his brother-in-law? Did he pity her because he knew Trey would never love her the way he'd always loved Laurette?

The concerned parent slid into place as Marc gestured toward the opposite end of the church. "I know you're afraid of him."

A strange disappointment etched across her soul. Ap-parently, Marc didn't understand as much as she'd hoped he would. "I admit there was a time that was true, but not anymore. I trust him completely." She smiled, then decided to tell Marc the rest. "I love him."

"Oh, Katherine."

"Yes." She sighed. *"Oh, Katherine."*

"He… I don't want to build any false hope for you, not

now, not ever. Although I don't doubt he'll try, Trey may not make you a good husband."

"I know that."

"I'm confident he won't hurt you physically, but he's stuck in his anger and drive for vengeance."

"I know that, too. But with help from our heavenly Father, I believe Trey will find peace and forgiveness one day."

"If that never happens—" Marc rested his hand on her shoulder "—would you still be willing to go through with this?"

"Yes."

Squeezing her hand gently, he studied her face for what felt like an eternity. "You really do love him, then."

She patted his sleeve, and he dropped his hand to his side. "I know what you're trying to say, Marc. You don't want me to foolishly build a hope for something that may never occur."

"Don't misunderstand me. I love Trey. He's my brother, and he needs you, Katherine. He might never be able to tell you that, but he does. That doesn't mean he'll make you happy. He isn't an easy man."

"You forget, I've seen him at his worst." *And his best.* The sudden thought washed through her, cleansing her fears, solidifying her resolve. "Let's stop this disturbing talk, shall we? I want to get married."

Marc nodded, but the concern only increased in his eyes. "All right then, if that's what you really want."

"It is."

He jutted his elbow toward her, and she settled her hand in the crook of his arm. As he started down the aisle, she fell into step beside him. "If he hurts you, Katherine, I'll kill him."

Now that did it. Katherine had had more than enough of Marc casting his "brother" in the role of outlaw.

"And what if *I* hurt him?" She didn't bother hiding the righteous anger in her tone.

Obviously shocked, Marc stopped walking. He turned his head to study her with a look suspiciously close to respect. "Then you answer to me."

"Good. Because it goes both ways. It's just like you said, Marc, Trey needs me. And *I* need him."

"Then make him happy."

"I will."

With his heart choking in his throat, Trey watched Katherine and Marc walking arm in arm down the aisle. As though hearing his silent call, Katherine lifted her eyes to his. Captured by her beauty, he felt an unfamiliar sense of peace fill him.

They *would* make a good life together.

He liked how she studied him in return, her gaze skimming along his face, down his nose, along the contour of his jaw, each sweep a soft caress.

This woman would soon be his wife.

Trey braced his shoulders for the guilt to assault him. But none came. His throat convulsed with a heavy swallow, his head no longer full of reminders of the woman he had lost but of the woman he'd found.

With one final blink, he shifted his mind to Katherine and let Laurette fade into the past. He knew that a part of his dead wife would always live in his heart, but Katherine was his today, his tomorrow—his future.

And he couldn't be more pleased.

Gliding toward him, she looked fragile, beautiful, the

blue dress matching her eyes. She'd pulled her hair into a fancy hairstyle, sprinkling flowers identical to the ones in Molly's hair throughout her own. Compelled to compare the two, he looked down at the kid. She grinned up at him, her smile so much like the one her sister had just flashed— minus a front tooth or two—his heart clutched in his chest. In the past few months, this child had become more daughter than friend.

It felt right.

Returning his gaze back to Katherine, his throat convulsed through a heavy swallow. She looked like spring. New love. Forever. His breath tensed in his lungs, held firm. He knew his bitter soul didn't deserve this woman, but now that he'd received her caring, her generous spirit and her unbending devotion, he couldn't give her up.

He wondered what Marc had said to her before they'd started down the aisle. He was probably trying to talk her out of the marriage. Trey couldn't much blame his friend. Katherine had that way about her, made a man want to protect her.

Well, Trey might not be filled with youthful optimism. His heart might hold more bitterness than most. But he would do his best to keep her safe and honor her and never harm her. He would do everything in his power to make life for Katherine—and Molly—secure.

Marc drew to a stop and gave Trey a warning glare. Just to be ornery, Trey grinned at him, then planted a kiss on Katherine's mouth.

"You look beautiful," he told her, his voice quivering with emotions he couldn't name.

"Thank you."

"Are you ready to do this?"

She nodded, her eyes filling with tears.

He cupped her cheek. She leaned into his touch and gave him a watery smile filled with…love.

The truth sent blinding shards of pain and excitement through him. Katherine Taylor loved him.

His heart cracked opened, and with one final wave to the past, he allowed her inside. This woman was his future. He took a step forward, roped his arms around her and kissed her lips again. "I'll give you the best of me."

The minister began the ceremony. "We are here to join Ethan Wendell Scott III and Katherine Monica Taylor together in holy matrimony. Katherine has chosen the first Scripture to be read from Ecclesiastes.

"Two are better than one, because they have a good return for their work. If one falls down, his friend can help him up. But pity the man who falls and has no one to help him up…"

In that moment, with his eyes burning, Trey silently vowed to become the man he saw shining in Katherine's gaze.

Chapter Eighteen

"You did good today, Mr. Trey."

Trey smiled at the little girl sauntering toward him, the flowers in her hair bouncing with each step she took. Watching her approach, he felt his heart burst with the need to protect, to love. "Thank you, kitten. I couldn't have done it without you."

She looked over her shoulder, giggled. Trey sent his gaze in the same direction, caught sight of his wife in deep conversation with Laney. Emotion squeezed his chest. Would he ever tire of looking at Katherine? She was so beautiful, and not merely on the outside, where everyone could see. Sometimes it hurt, deep in his soul, to look at her.

She'd suffered so much torment in her young life. How he wanted to do right by her now, as he hadn't been able to do for Laurette.

"I can't believe you did it," Molly said, still looking at her sister, obviously unaware of his turbulent thoughts. "You really married Katherine."

"I did. She's officially my wife now. And as far as I'm concerned, that makes you my daughter."

Wife. Daughter. It felt good to know they were both pledged to him forever now.

With a swish and fancy, little-girl swaying, Molly turned back around. A look of deep concentration marred her brow. "Did you know, Mr. Trey, Katherine hasn't yelled at you all day? I think that's the only time ever."

He tried to keep his features blank, his mood as serious as the little girl's. "I know."

"That's really good."

Unable to hold back any longer, he let go of his grin and chuckled. How easy life was in the eyes of a five-year-old. For the rest of the day, he vowed to let Molly's world prevail over his.

"Want to know a secret?" He leaned over, lowered his voice to a whisper. "Although it's sometimes fun to fight with your sister, I really like it when she doesn't yell at me."

Molly gave him one solemn nod. "Me, too."

Raising her arms to him, she waited. Understanding her silent command, he lifted her into his embrace, settled her on his hip, then offered his cheek. She planted a big, wet kiss on the same spot as always. "I love you, Mr. Trey."

His response was immediate. "I love you, too, kitten."

Suddenly shy, she cocked her head at him. "So do I get to call you daddy now?"

She might as well have gripped his heart and squeezed. "Absolutely."

Flattening a palm against his cheek, she nodded again. *"Daddy."*

Trey's heart stopped beating completely, then kicked wildly back to life. "Promise me something, Molly."

"Sure, okay," she said, her expression serious, her eyes never leaving his face. "Anything, *Daddy*."

He was sure his heart was going to explode from the affection he felt for this child, his daughter. He had to blink to stop the burning in his eyes. "Be good tonight while your sister and I are at the hotel."

She hitched her chin at him, mutiny blazing in her eyes. "I'm always good."

He lowered her to the ground, dropped a kiss on her head. "Right. I forgot."

Shaking her head at him, she planted her left fist on her hip and swung her bandaged hand back and forth. "Daddy. Daddy. Daddy."

"I know. I forgot. How about you go run over there and tell your sister goodbye. We're leaving soon."

She angled her head, considered him for a moment. "Be nice to Katherine tonight."

He hitched his chin at her in a similar show of stubbornness. "I'm always nice."

Obviously unconvinced, she stared at him a while longer, then stamped her foot. "Promise," she demanded.

He looked past Molly, fixed his gaze on his wife. As though hearing his silent appeal, Katherine looked up and molded her lips into a ready smile. "All right, kitten, I promise I'll be nice to your sister tonight."

That was one vow he knew he'd have no trouble keeping.

Katherine allowed Trey to lead her away from the church, the guests following them to the carriage hired to take them to the Palace Hotel. The plush interior of the coach was finer than any Katherine had known. Another detail Marc had insisted he settle for them. She had no idea where he had found such an elaborate conveyance. But, as she slid across the seat and allowed the sheer luxury to wash over her, she decided not to ask questions.

Today was a day for joy.

She splayed her fingers along the red velvet cushions, which stood in stark relief against the dark mahogany of the inlaid ceiling. Sitting in so regal a carriage, Katherine felt like a queen—with a very attentive king by her side.

Trey's gaze hadn't left her face since she'd joined him at the altar, making her feel cherished, special. The ceremony had been short, lovely, sweeping her away into a world of hope and possibility. Not wanting her senses to return and ruin the moment, she shut her eyes and pressed her head against the plush cushions behind her.

Trey climbed inside, his weight slightly tilting the carriage toward him. He issued the order to the driver, then shut the door behind him.

As he settled in next to her, his voice drifted over her like a soft whisper. "Look at me."

She opened her eyes, and her heart hammered against her ribs at what she saw in his gaze. Trey Scott had the look of love in his eyes.

As he leaned closer, his lips curved into a beautiful smile. "No regrets?" he asked, with something oddly hesitant in his manner.

"Not yet." She'd thought to tease him, but her words came out stilted, earnest.

He sighed. "Not a very hopeful answer, but an honest one, I suppose."

He stroked her cheek, her jaw, and a low rumble sounded in his chest. "I'll be gentle with you tonight, my love. We'll go at your pace, and I'll do only what you want me to do."

Sudden fear clogged her throat. "What if…what if I can't go through with it?"

"Then we spend the night talking. Get to know each other better."

Her heart turned troubled, unsure. She knew enough about men from her mother's business to know what he offered was unusual. Heroic, even. "That would be enough for you?"

Trey leaned forward and kissed her lightly on the nose. "I can be a very patient man, Mrs. Scott. Resourceful, too. Even if it takes a lifetime, I plan to give you every reason to trust me to take care of you in our marriage bed."

"A lifetime?"

"Yes."

"Well, then." Her eyes glittered back at him, and his heart hitched in his chest. "Let's hope it doesn't take *that* long."

Trey laughed, the sound chasing away the remaining tension between them. "Beautiful Katherine, I'll do everything in my power to be a good husband to you."

She covered his mouth with her fingers. "I know, Trey. I believe you."

"Good." He took her hand and pressed her palm against his heart. *"Good."*

He closed his eyes a moment and just breathed in her clean, fresh scent. His stomach felt a little funny all of a sudden, and then the sensation spread up to his chest. Once he could breathe again, he decided he liked the feeling.

Liked it very much.

Chapter Nineteen

The next morning Trey woke first. Settled comfortably in an overstuffed chair, he drank a second cup of coffee while his bride continued sleeping in the other room. At the sound of her soft, feminine snoring, a wave of contentment rippled through him.

He couldn't help but think God had blessed him with this new marriage. And for the first time in four years, the thought of the Lord's hand in any part of his life didn't bring anger and bitterness.

Only awe. And a large dose of gratitude.

The evening had been filled with firsts for them both. And as their wedding night had progressed, Trey had been able to show Katherine just how patient he could be with her. Together, they'd overcome the obstacle of her fear of physical intimacy.

With a large dose of satisfaction, Trey kicked his feet onto the ottoman and wondered if they'd made a baby when they'd consummated their marriage.

But as soon as the thought came, painful memories of

what had happened to Laurette and their unborn child broke through his pleasure. Heart-pounding fear gripped him, nearly paralyzing his ability to breathe. He'd failed Laurette. Violence had won that round.

Could he keep his new family safe? Or would he fail them as well?

No, he would not. This time he would do what was necessary to protect what was his.

Until he found Ike, there were going to have to be rules, nonnegotiable rules. When he had to leave town, Katherine, Molly and any children that came along would stay with Marc and Laney at Charity House. Once the school year began, he'd appoint a deputy to watch the premises.

A muscle shifted in his jaw as gripping anxiety clogged his throat and stole his breath. The drive to finish the business of the past was suddenly obscene, like a sharp, fiery stake stabbing into his heart.

He heard Katherine stir. Shaking away his ugly thoughts, he set his cup on the table next to him and went to the doorway that led into the bedroom. Leaning against the jamb, he studied his wife as her eyes blinked slowly open.

With her gaze unfocused, sleepy, she looked youthful, beautiful. His momentary concern for the future faded, and Katherine Taylor Scott filled his world. "Good morning, Mrs. Scott."

A smile played at the tips of her mouth. "Good morning, Mr. Scott."

"Sleep well?"

She stretched, yawned. "Lovely."

Trey's heart dipped in his chest. "Hungry?"

"Ravenous."

Laughing, he shoved away from the door. "Me, too."

In the same moment he leaned down to kiss her lips, a pounding came at the door.

"Marshal, you in there?"

Logan. For a lawman, the deputy had rotten timing.

Katherine blew her hair out of her face and sighed. "Looks like breakfast will have to wait."

"If we don't answer," he whispered, "he'll go away."

Three more raps. "Marshal. It's important."

Katherine sat up, wrapped the covers around her and then slid him an annoyed look, as though she was as disappointed as he was by the interruption. Unfortunately, the underlying dread in her expression was impossible to miss.

They both knew Logan would interrupt them for only one reason.

"Answer the door," she said at last.

He wished he knew what to say to alleviate her worry, but his mind wrestled with two thoughts—it was time to serve up justice, and it was too soon to leave his wife.

Logan's plea turned urgent. *"Marshal."*

"I'm coming," Trey shouted back. "Give me a moment."

He waited until Katherine snuggled deeper under the covers before moving back into the sitting room. He gave her one last look over his shoulder, then padded barefoot through the room.

Yanking the door open, he growled at the other man. "This better be good."

Logan tried to enter the room, but Trey barred entrance with his body. "Well?"

Shrugging, Logan stepped back. "A telegraph came in from the marshal in Nebraska territory. He caught Ike Hayes."

He caught Ike Hayes.

The need for justice knotted in Trey's gut, and all he could do was stare at Logan as the news slowly sank in.

This was it, then. After all these years of searching, retribution was within his grasp. Laurette would receive justice at last. She would not have died in vain.

"Marshal Roberts wants us to meet him in Cheyenne," Logan continued, "so he can turn over the prisoner to you personally."

"I'll be ready to leave in an hour," Trey said. "Meet me at the stables."

Trey shut the door behind Logan's nod of agreement. No time for thought. Only action. With deliberate movements, he gathered his belongings. Against his best efforts to remain calm, his head filled with memories, and his heart exploded with anger and frustration.

Ike Hayes had preyed on the innocent and killed for sport for too long. Trey would not miss this opportunity to bring the man who'd killed his wife to trial.

If for no other reason, he owed it to Laurette.

So consumed with ending the violence, he'd nearly forgotten about Katherine until his glance fell on the bed. She sat there, unmoving, her knees wrapped in the covers and pulled to her chest. She didn't say anything, just quietly watched him.

Her eyes were big and round and worried, and in that moment, she looked only a few years older than Molly.

"I have to go," he said.

She nodded, her eyes never leaving his face. He understood the fear settling over her. Just as he recognized the strength it took her to hold the emotion at bay.

"I have to do this," he said, his tone more desperate than firm. "He's the man who killed my wife."

She jerked at his declaration, sighed and then dropped her gaze to her knees. "Of course."

"Try to understand, Katherine. Justice must be served."

He wanted to repeat the words over and over, until he made her accept how important this was to him. To them and their future together.

She lifted her gaze and simply stared at him. After a long, dead silence her eyes filled with a deep sadness, but she continued to hold his gaze, with an unwavering conviction that belied her emotions.

"You have to do what you think is best, Trey."

"I *have* to finish this." Even to his own ears, his voice sounded hesitant, uneasy. "Then I—*we*—can move on with our lives."

She simply nodded. "Of course."

Katherine's patient acceptance shattered him. Where was the fight in her? The yelling? The accusations? A battle he could handle? This calm understanding—it nearly broke him.

"I—"

"No. Don't say anything else." She rushed to him, reached for his hand and clutched it to her heart. "Godspeed, my love. May you have the peace of Christ and the conviction of the Holy Spirit in your heart as you go."

He dropped his belongings and pulled her into his arms. "Once I... Once justice is finally served, we can start our new life together, Katherine. We'll be free from the past. I promise."

And as with every promise he'd made to her in the past, he would keep his word.

* * *

As weeks turned into months, and still no direct word from Trey, Katherine's worry increased, putting her on edge.

Oh, Lord, please bring him safely home to me, she prayed. *Let this capture of Ike Hayes be the end of Trey's need for revenge. Give him the freedom only You can give.*

But no matter how hard she focused on her husband, Trey's safety wasn't Katherine's only concern. A few weeks ago, her body had started changing, no longer feeling like her own. The morning the vomiting had begun, she'd realized she was carrying Trey's child. One night together—their beautiful, all-too-short wedding night— had been enough to create a baby.

Out of her healing, and Trey's gentleness, had come this new life. She couldn't have asked for a richer blessing.

Unfortunately, the morning sickness had gotten worse these past two days, throbbing with the tenacity of sharp little rat's teeth. She lay in her bed just as dawn broke, trying her best to control the spasms of pain gripping her stomach.

She prayed softly for strength.

Lifting her Bible off the nightstand, she flipped to the thirty-first chapter of Deuteronomy. "Be strong and courageous. Do not be afraid or terrified—"

Another spasm cut through her. Leaning over the chamber pot, she spilled the last of the contents of her stomach. She hadn't been able to keep food down for two days now. She was so tired, uncharacteristically weak, and her stomach ached miserably. Even now, the energy to get out of bed eluded her.

Her throat clutched again. Unable to bear another bout of nausea, she willed the pain away and began reading where she'd left off. "For the Lord your God goes with you; He will never leave you nor forsake you."

In spite of the chill in the room, she started sweating. Her legs ached through to the bones, and her heart swelled with fear. Something was wrong. This pain couldn't be normal.

But she'd wasted too much time in bed already. Attempting to lift her head, she collapsed back against the pillow, conquered by the rush of agony. The terror, both thick and huge, ripped a single moan from her lips.

Another spasm of pain clutched her stomach, and she dropped the Bible to the floor. Rolling herself into a ball, she prepared for the inevitable nausea, but instead another pain followed the first. The third one made her cry out.

She expelled three more shaky breaths, then managed to stand. A hot, sticky liquid slid along the inside of her legs. Looking to the floor, she saw the red stain on her nightgown, the blood creating a small puddle at her feet.

"Oh, Lord, no. *Please,* not this. Trey doesn't even know he's going to be a father."

Just as she cried out for Laney, the room spun, and Katherine's head filled with dizzying, life-altering fear.

"Trey," she whispered just before her vision turned black.

Katherine opened her eyes to find Dr. Bartlett standing over her, a concerned expression on his face. The pounding in her head made her squint against the sharp light piercing the room.

She tried to lift her head off the pillow—someone had obviously moved her to the bed—but the effort wore her out. "What happened?"

The fast clicking of heels to wood accompanied Laney's soft cry. "Praise God, you're awake."

Katherine opened her eyes just as her friend knelt beside the bed, placed her cool palm against her forehead.

"We've been so worried about you." The terror was there in the other woman's eyes, in her shaking fingers, her stilted voice.

Katherine tried to close her mind to what Laney's fear meant and focus only on the words spoken. "We?"

"Me, Molly, Marc, the Charity House children."

Giving up the fight, Katherine allowed her mind to concentrate on a memory, one that refused to let her go but wouldn't fully materialize. Her head pounded out a series of sketchy details, then went blank. But then one painful, heart-wrenching image came into focus—the blood at her feet. "My baby?"

Tears filled Laney's eyes. "I'm sorry, Katherine. You lost it."

Why couldn't she make her head understand what Laney was saying? Why did the terror embrace her heart?

Dr. Bartlett's melodious, soothing voice drifted over her. "I'm sorry I didn't get here soon enough."

What sort of cruel twist was this? She and Trey had made a baby together, but it was dead. How would he accept this new loss? How would she?

Overwhelmed by too many fierce emotions, she simply stared at Laney and Dr. Bartlett.

Oh, Trey, why aren't you home yet?

She needed his strength, his arms around her. She needed him to tell her it wasn't true. But it was true; she saw it in the concerned eyes that watched her. Her baby was dead, and Trey hadn't even known of its existence.

For weeks, she'd spent her days worrying about Trey,

about the harm that could come to him both physically and spiritually if he didn't let go of his drive for vengeance.

It hadn't occurred to her that she might be the one in danger. Had her ignorance killed her baby? Had she neglected some detail? Had she been so consumed with worry that she'd killed her child?

Laney sighed, the sound cutting through Katherine's terrifying thoughts. "I'm so sorry."

Although she heard the words, knew them to be true, Katherine couldn't make her mind focus on the fact that she'd lost her child.

The doctor moved slowly into view. "We nearly lost you as well."

Laney gripped her hand and squeezed. "You've been very ill, unconscious for four days now. We've all been praying for you."

"Four days?" The headache gripping the inside of her brain twisted to her eyes. She reached up to rub her temple, shocked at the shake in her hands. "The last thing I remember is calling for you."

"I found you in a heap on the floor. Marc carried you to the bed, then sent Johnny for the doctor."

Making prayers out of her wordless sighs, Katherine tried to call up the details of the past few days. She got nothing. "I never woke?"

Dr. Bartlett shook his head.

Laney squeezed her hand again. "Katherine, I know you're weak right now, but Molly has been…in a state."

Molly. Oh, her poor little sister must have been petrified. "Go get her, Laney. *Hurry.*"

Laney looked to the doctor.

Dr. Bartlett nodded. "Go ahead."

Once she was alone with the doctor, Katherine's fears twined inside her sorrow and guilt. "What did I do wrong?"

Shaking his head, he looked more tired than usual, as though he'd lost a lot of sleep. Over her? Had she truly been that ill? "This wasn't your fault," Dr. Bartlett said.

Words backed up in her throat. "Then why did my baby die?"

"Sometimes these things happen." He brought a cup of water to her lips and lifted her head. As she drank, he continued. "I know that doesn't bring much comfort to you, but there are mysteries of the human body we just don't understand. As the Lord says, 'My ways aren't your ways.' But Jesus will give you comfort if you turn to Him."

Katherine shut her eyes. She was aware that Dr. Bartlett was watching her reaction to his words, but she ignored him. Comfort, it seemed, wouldn't come with a few well-placed prayers this time.

She spread her hand across her stomach, not quite able to believe that her baby—the one she'd only just started to get to know and love—was no longer living inside her.

Oh, how she'd wanted this baby, more than she'd understood until now. She couldn't help but feel that she'd lost a part of Trey with their child.

Would this loss haunt her always? Would she never be free of the ache?

Guilt ate at her. Was this the sort of pain Trey had suffered these past four years? She finally understood a part of what drove him, but at a far too painful cost.

The door swung open, and Molly inched into the room. The terror on the little girl's face forced Katherine to push her own grief aside.

Reaching out a hand to her sister, she said, "Come here, Molly."

Molly tiptoed forward, looking once more like the little girl Katherine had met in the mining camp, instead of the vivacious child of the past few months. Where was the childlike energy, the infectious laughter Katherine had come to associate with the five-year-old?

Katherine swallowed past the pain in her head, the aching in her bones. "It's all right. You can come closer."

Molly's eyes widened, and she took a step backward.

Katherine called on every scrap of her strength, sat up and forced a smile on her lips. "See? I'm fine."

A sob burst from Molly's lips, and she vaulted across the divide between them, then halted abruptly at the foot of the bed. "You look so sick," she said, her voice barely more than a squeak.

Katherine wanted to soothe her sister's fears, but she couldn't lie to her. "I am sick. But I'm not going to die."

Molly's face scrunched into a frown. "But, Katherine, sick people die."

"Not always."

Blinking back tears, Molly scuffled around to the side of the bed. When she got closer, tears started spilling.

"I'm sorry I worried you." Katherine patted a spot on the bed. "Come. Sit with me."

Molly shook her head, her gaze darting to the doctor, over to Laney, to the doctor again, then finally back to Katherine.

"It's all right. You won't hurt me."

"Really?"

Katherine lifted her arms. "Absolutely."

Leading with a knee, Molly edged one leg onto the bed. Ignoring her own pain, Katherine wrapped the little girl in her arms and tugged her tightly against her. "See? I'm completely alive."

Molly wiped her cheek on Katherine's shoulder. "You scared me, Katherine."

"I scared myself."

Sniffing, the little girl pushed away. "Promise you won't get sick again."

If only she could make such a vow. "I'll certainly try not to."

"I would have been a good big sister."

For a shocking moment, Katherine feared she was going to break down and sob, unable to stop for days. She hated that her innocent little sister had been subjected to the cruelty of another loss, hated that the loss had occurred. But she couldn't give in to the weakness of her grief now. With her chin trembling, she forced a bright smile on her face. "I know, Molly. The best."

"I miss Mr. Trey. I mean…*Daddy*." Molly's crestfallen expression mirrored the emotions in Katherine's heart.

Katherine dragged her little sister back into her arms. "Oh, Molly, me, too." She allowed a single tear to fall before she blinked the rest into submission. "Me, too."

Chapter Twenty

Trey arrived in Denver hungry for blood. With leaden feet, he trudged up the back stairwell of Miss Martha's boarding house. The cracked paint on the barren walls did nothing to improve his mood. He'd intentionally chosen this place to live because it left him cold. At the time he'd only needed somewhere to rest his head at night. In truth, it had felt wrong to commit time and money to a house when Laurette could no longer help him turn the brick and mortar into a home.

Thoughts of his dead wife still plagued him, heightened by his recent defeat. Thus, when he reached the top step, white-hot anger swirled up so fast, so completely it clogged the air in his lungs.

He forced the emotion down, took a deep breath and entered his room. Deadly silence slammed into him. The space felt foreign. Unwelcoming.

Empty.

He hadn't realized how solitary and lonely his life had become in the years since Laurette's murder. All his goals, all his dreams had been reduced to the sole quest for revenge.

He was tired of the pain. Tired of the burning hatred.

Trey suddenly wanted Katherine and Molly. Just seeing them would lift his mood and make him forget, for a time, the defeat he felt so strongly now. But first he needed to clean off weeks of trail dust and defeat.

While he washed, his mind kept running through the infuriating events of the past two months. By the time he and Logan had arrived in Cheyenne, Ike Hayes had escaped custody. Although Marshal Roberts had wounded Ike in the scuffle, the outlaw still lived.

Trey's jaw clenched with the effort to hold back his fury.

Ike. Still. Lived.

Those three words had driven Trey in his ruthless pursuit of the outlaw. He'd tracked Ike all the way from Cheyenne to Nebraska City. At each town, Trey had been no more than a day or two behind the killer. A week ago, the trail had dried up completely. Trey had been forced to return to Denver and to his original plan of waiting for Ike to come to him.

Looking out the window, Trey noticed the bustling activity on the street below. How could everyone act so normal?

Absently, he mixed shaving cream in the bowl he cupped in his palm. Ticking off the past weeks, one by one, his mind returned to the morning after his wedding night. The last time he'd seen Katherine.

Until the moment when he'd stared into her frightened, dejected eyes, Trey hadn't truly understood how much his quest for vengeance hurt her. By allowing grief to rule his every move, he'd kept Laurette's memory alive in his heart—and prevented Katherine from truly becoming his wife.

But after four years of seeking vengeance, he'd become comfortable in his bitterness. He didn't know how else to live. Nevertheless, he couldn't continue on the same angry path. He owed it to Katherine and Molly to break the cycle of pain and hurt.

Trey swallowed. Hard. If he never brought Ike to justice, if he never took revenge, could he truly commit his life, his heart and his future to Katherine and Molly?

How could he just let go of Laurette without finishing the quest to avenge her murder? How could he continue hurting Katherine and Molly?

He hadn't counted on finding love again. Katherine, with her goodness, and Molly, with her childlike devotion, had broken through his defenses. And the more they took over his heart, the less he hated.

Trey didn't believe God's plan for his life had included losing Laurette and their unborn baby, but he couldn't deny that their deaths made finding Katherine and Molly that much more precious to him.

He had the strongest urge to take both woman and child into his arms and tell them how much he cared.

He'd figure out the rest later.

Impatient to get to Charity House, he quickly shaved and finished dressing. But the moment he slammed his hat on his head, a sick feeling of dread navigated along his spine.

Something wasn't right.

He knew it in his gut.

Trey left his room in a haze and rushed down the street, toward Charity House.

As he drew up to the front of the house, the lack of

activity struck him first, convincing him to stand on his guard. At this hour, the children were usually at their loudest, with an adult voice or two raised over the chatter.

Looking around him, a dark premonition shot through him, sending a shiver across his soul. The deadly stillness enveloped him. In response, an ache started in his gut, wrapped around his heart and then turned into the same twisting agony he'd endured when he'd ridden onto the ranch four years ago and found Laurette dying.

Pushing through the front door, he tossed his hat to the nearest chair. He only had time for impressions as he searched for human life. The ticking of the clock. The lemon oil Laney used on the furniture. The candles and lanterns blazing, casting their light into the room.

Where was everyone?

Trey raised his voice, surprised at the shake in it. "Hello. Anyone here?" He glanced around him, then swallowed several times. *"Anyone?"*

Mrs. Smythe shuffled into the hallway. The look on her face confirmed his worst fears. "Oh, Marshal Scott, I'm so sorry. She just didn't have the strength."

"What do you mean?"

A myriad of emotions flickered across the woman's face. "It's Katherine."

A gut-wrenching fear twined into guilt and finally settled into self-recrimination for leaving his wife alone for so long.

"What about Katherine?" Trey didn't realize he'd shouted until he saw Mrs. Smythe step away from him.

She pointed over his shoulder. "Upstairs."

The way she said the word sent a shiver of terror racing along the back of his neck.

"The doctor is with her."

Doctor? Stifling the panic that rose in his throat, Trey spun around and took the stairs three at a time. Katherine was in trouble, and just like with Laurette, he hadn't been here for her.

Guilt mingled with panic pushed him faster as he headed straight for her room and burst through the door.

His gaze sought and found his wife. Pale and small in her bed, she looked like a woman who had given up on life. Molly sat next to her, gripping her hands in hers while tears ran down her face.

Katherine was dying. And he was too late to save her. *Just like Laurette.*

He sensed others in the room, but Katherine and Molly were all that mattered to him now. Molly sprang from the bed and vaulted into his arms. "Daddy, you came home."

Trey hugged her tight against him, his eyes never leaving Katherine's blank stare.

"I always come back, kitten." *Just never in time.*

No, he wouldn't allow death to defeat him, not this time. This time he would fight harder.

He settled Molly on his hip and then made his way across the room. He kept his gaze centered on Katherine, forcing his own fears aside as he recognized the loss of will in her. He'd always thought of Katherine as a woman full of sparkle. But now she looked dull, lifeless.

Every part of his body went on alert.

"Katherine," he whispered.

She shut her eyes, swallowed. A shudder wracked through her body before she looked at him again. The blank stare she gave him confirmed his doubts. Whatever had happened to her, she'd allowed it to defeat her spirit.

A hand touched his shoulder. He turned, his gaze landing on Laney's worried expression. "Don't worry, Trey. She's going to live."

He defied one of his own rules and allowed fear to overtake logic. "What…what happened?"

Molly tapped him on the shoulder. "She lost the baby," she whispered.

She lost the baby. Pain suffocated his ability to take a breath. Hoping he had misunderstood Molly, he looked to Laney. She nodded slowly, sadly, and then Shane Bartlett moved within his line of vision. "It's true."

"I didn't know," Trey said softly.

"She found out only a few weeks ago," Dr. Bartlett replied.

Katherine had learned of their child while Trey had been hunting Ike Hayes. As his new wife had started preparing for their future, Trey had been clinging to the past, instead of remaining home with his family, where he belonged. *Where. He. Belonged.* The realization hit him hard.

Molly's lower lip trembled. "I would have had a sister or brother."

He patted Molly's back, turned to look at Dr. Bartlett.

"Katherine? Is she going to—" He broke off, unable to say the words, afraid if he did, they would come true.

Dr. Bartlett sighed. "She's fine, healthwise. But…" He lifted a shoulder in helplessness. "She's been like this since yesterday."

Trey turned back to his wife. She looked only half-alive, and then he knew what Dr. Bartlett was trying to tell him. Katherine was in shock, caught inside her pain and unable to release herself from the grief…the guilt.

He knew about those feelings, had felt them for months—no, years—after Laurette had died in his arms. For the first time since that fateful day, his quest for vengeance seemed secondary, less significant. All that mattered now was helping Katherine come back from the black world in which she hid.

If anyone knew what she was suffering, it was Trey.

He lowered Molly to the ground and then knelt in front of the little girl. "I need to be with your sister, alone."

"I think that's a good idea," Laney said as she took Molly by the hand and led her out of the room.

Dr. Bartlett left as well, shutting the door behind him with a click. The silence hung thick and heavy in the room as Trey strode toward his wife. *His wife.* He knelt beside the bed, touched her cheek. He was home. He'd finally come home. But was he too late? Was he bound to fail his women when they needed him most?

Familiar guilt ripped through him all over again. This time the feeling was stronger, more real, than ever before. Katherine hadn't wanted him to go, but he'd put vengeance ahead of her and her fears.

And now her soul was dying.

He shut his eyes and prayed a second time since Katherine had come into his life.

Oh, Lord, give me the strength to help Katherine break free from her grief. Give me another chance to do right by her.

He brushed the hair away from her face.

She blinked but didn't respond to him otherwise.

"Come back to me, Katherine."

As though his request finally lifted the veil cloaking her soul, her eyes cleared, and she slowly, hesitantly, lifted her arms to him.

The invitation was unmistakable.

With a moan of sorrow, he pulled her into his embrace,

cradled her against his chest. There could be no more holding back, no more pretending this woman didn't mean the world to him. "My Katherine. I love you."

He just hoped he hadn't waited too long to speak his heart aloud.

A huge shudder worked through her, followed by a giant gasp.

"Let it out, honey."

Her sobs came then, spiraling on top of one another. Big, heart-wrenching sobs that ripped through his body as sure as if he'd been the one crying instead of her.

He rocked her as her whimpers grew louder, more painful to bear. But for her sake, he accepted them as her due. He knew she needed to grieve, needed to cry over her loss, but with each of her gasps, his heart broke a little more.

"I wanted our baby," she said through tight, short breaths.

The silent sobs in his heart screamed for release, but he buried them. There would be time enough later for his own grieving. "Me, too."

She raised her guilt-ridden gaze. "It's all my fault, Trey."

How many times had he said those same words? How many times had friends told him they weren't true? In that moment, he finally understood what so many had tried to tell him. No man, or woman, could control life and death. That was God's territory alone. Why hadn't he seen the truth sooner?

Forgive me, Lord.

"No, baby, no. You aren't to blame. These things happen."

Pain flickered in her gaze, but she nodded. "Dr. Bartlett said that the Lord, in His infinite wisdom, has a plan bigger than me. Bigger than my understanding. Bigger than this tragedy."

"Shane is right." And Trey knew—he *finally* knew—the same was true for him.

She fell silent, her sobs turning to an occasional sigh of distress. Eventually, she turned limp in his arms, and he laid her gently back on the bed, pulled the sheet up to her chin.

"I want you to do something for me, my love," he said.

She blinked up at him, her gaze clear but unreadable.

"Concentrate on getting well."

"There's too much to do. Charity House, chores…the school."

He cupped her cheek. "Laney is a very resourceful woman. She'll manage until you're well again."

"Molly—"

"I'll take care of her. She's my family now, too." Katherine opened her mouth; he placed a finger over her lips. "Do this, please. For me."

Tears welled in her eyes. "I don't know how to be sick."

How he loved her strength, her independence, but not enough to relent on such an important matter. "Then now is as good a time as any to learn."

She shook her head, clearly preparing to argue with him.

He dropped a gentle kiss to her lips. "You're not going to be sensible about this, are you?"

An echo of a smile quivered at the corners of her mouth. "Those lessons in patience never took."

Relieved by the small glimpse of the Katherine he'd left weeks ago, Trey pressed his lips to her forehead. "Concentrate on getting some sleep."

He rose from the bed, but her hand shot out to still his progress. "Don't leave me."

"Never. I just have to take care of a few things. Then I'll come and sit with you."

She nodded. "I'd like that."

He kissed the top of her head, then caressed her cheek, stunned he could feel both joy and fear at the same time. "I'll be right back."

"Trey, I have a question for you," she said, her voice stopping him as he tried to turn and leave.

He strode back to the bed, knelt beside her and waited.

Shifting her gaze around the room, she sighed. "What…what happened with Ike Hayes?"

She spoke in a deceptively mild tone, but her eyes reflected her concern for him.

Even when she needed to focus on her own healing, she fretted over him. Part of Trey admired her ability to think of others before herself, but part of him wanted to shake her and order her to concentrate on Katherine for a change.

Nevertheless, he owed her the truth. "He escaped."

"You didn't kill him or bring him back with you?"

"No."

"Will you go back—"

"No." He pulled her hand to his lips, pressed a kiss to her palm. "I don't know whether I'll ever get the chance to serve up justice, or whether Ike will run free forever, but I'm going to let God handle the particulars from here on out."

He wanted to believe his own words—for Katherine's sake as well as his own—but Trey didn't know if he could hand over the control to God completely.

As much as he wanted to start his new life, he couldn't abandon the notion that until Ike Hayes was caught and brought to trial, Trey would stand poised between two women—one gone forever, the other within reach, yet still so far away.

Both women pulled at him, each with her own power over his future. And because he wasn't sure he could fully release one for the other, his heart broke for them all.

Chapter Twenty-One

A week later, Katherine stood in her room, staring out the window at the activity in the yard below. As she watched the children play, the sound of their laughter skipped through her heart and tugged a happy smile onto her lips. Ready to join the healthy again, she pivoted on her heel, picked up her skirt and finished dressing, making sure she moved slowly, patiently.

If she were honest with herself, she would admit that some good had come out of her loss and subsequent illness. Confined to her bed, she'd had a lot of time to pray, to mourn and to reassess what she wanted and needed from her husband.

As fearful as she'd been of falling in love with a lawman, her heart had defied her good sense. And now the prospect of a future with Trey Scott by her side didn't seem so terrifying.

All her life she'd felt like she was on the outside looking in, never truly belonging anywhere. She'd been judged and found lacking so many times, she'd lost hope that she would ever find genuine love and acceptance beyond the Lord's unshakable love. Craving certainty, she'd built her own orderly life in a world that didn't want *her kind*.

Then Trey had come along and had beaten down her defenses with his arrogance, masculine pride and mule-headed persistence.

In the end, he'd shown her trust, commitment. And love. He'd helped heal her shame. Now she wanted to help him find his way back to God.

If only she'd tried harder to protect the seed of their new love. Clutching her stomach, she resisted the urge to cry yet again. It still hurt to think of their child, their mutual loss. Perhaps with time, a lot of prayer and Trey's love, healing would come here as well. With that thought in mind, she went in search of her husband.

She found him in the parlor. He stood looking out the window, silently watching the children at play in the yard, as she had done in her room moments before. A heady blend of spices and wood filled her senses as she moved closer.

From his clenched jaw and rigid stance, she knew something was wrong. A storm was brewing in him, and he looked ready to do battle. Fear surged up in a primal haze, gripping her heart and twisting. On shaky legs, she moved closer, and immediately recognized the hint of longing in his unfocused gaze.

"Trey?"

He turned to her, his expression grave and serious. She waited, afraid to move. He didn't respond, just clenched his jaw harder and stared at her as though he were looking straight through her.

Angling her head, she ignored the panic gnawing at

her and focused only on his silent turmoil. "What is it? What's happened?"

As he continued to stare at her, despair coursed through her blood. But then his expression cleared, and with one swoop, he tugged her against him, bending his head until his lips landed lightly against hers.

It felt so good to be in his arms again. So right. And when he deepened their kiss, Katherine relaxed against him. In that moment, she knew they could have a true marriage. A happy marriage. If only they both tried a little harder.

But as he drew his head away from her, she had a sudden urge to cling. Something wasn't right.

"How are you feeling?" He whispered the question, as though he was afraid if he raised his voice, he would cause her irreversible harm.

"Weak," she admitted as she toyed with the hair falling over the back of his collar. Dropping her hand, she sighed. "But stronger than yesterday."

He nodded. "Good."

Tucking her under his arm, he dropped a kiss on her forehead. The unpracticed intimacy of the gesture rendered her hopeful, in spite of the foreboding that filled her.

She knew with a woman's instinct that this man loved her deeply. The kind of love she'd given up hope of ever winning in this lifetime because of the taint of her past. If only it was enough to conquer the apprehension tripping along her spine now.

Oh, Lord, give me the strength to hear what he doesn't want to tell me.

"What's on your mind?" she asked.

He turned toward the window, pulling her with him.

"Molly. I was thinking how much she's changed over the past few months. She's a different child than the one I first met."

Gratitude overcame her, nearly buckling her knees. "You had a lot to do with that."

He didn't answer right away. The echo of a smile wisped across his lips. "I love her like my own."

The declaration warmed her heart, but the weary resignation in his voice put her on guard. "What's wrong, Trey?"

Straightening to his full height, he lowered his gaze to hers. "We have to talk."

A burning sensation knotted behind her eyes, and she was suddenly so very cold. She could tell by his concerned expression that he wanted to alleviate her worries, but they both knew he wasn't enough of a liar to pull it off.

Sensing what was about to come, and hoping against hope she was wrong, Katherine kept her eyes locked with Trey's.

He brushed her hair away from her face. "I have to leave you again."

Air caught in her lungs, clogging just below her throat until she was gulping for it. Not trusting herself to speak without begging him to stay just a little longer, she swallowed her words behind a sniff.

"I don't know how long this will take."

She folded her arms across her chest, but she couldn't still the wave of doom surging through her soul. Her heart ached for him. For her. For them both.

Although he moved restlessly under her unwavering scrutiny, he regarded her with severe gray eyes. "I'll come back to you."

"Don't make promises."

With the turmoil of decisions already made mixing with the regret swimming in his eyes, he sighed, "Maybe I need to make promises. Maybe this time *I* need the words."

He shifted his gaze to a spot over her shoulder, shuddered, then squeezed her tightly against his chest. "Katherine, I almost lost you while I was away. I don't want to leave you again. Not even for a few hours."

"Then why go?"

His frustration seeped into her. "I have to."

"What aren't you telling me?"

"Ike Hayes was spotted in Colorado Springs yesterday. I believe he's heading for Denver. I have to get to him before he gets here."

Katherine pressed her cheek against his shoulder, stilling the cry of despair rising from her soul. "How do you know he's coming here?" She was only half-aware that her words came out shrill.

He stood with the posture of a man who refused to bend. Ever. "I know."

A shiver started at her knees, moved through her stomach and ended in a vicious tremble that rattled her pounding head. "I suppose asking you not to go is a waste of breath?"

The determination in his eyes seared her to the bone. "He killed my wife and child."

Katherine staggered out of his embrace. Pain exploded in her head, making her dizzy and knocking her off balance. Regardless of all he'd said, Trey still hadn't let go of the past. He hadn't let go of his love for his dead wife.

Just as she'd always feared, he would continually leave her to avenge Laurette's death, even if he said otherwise.

And yet, Katherine still wanted him in her life. Enough to take whatever part of himself he could give her. She knew that made her pathetic, but there was no reasoning with a heart bound by love. "You have to do what you think is best."

He flinched as though she'd slapped him. "Katherine, don't do this."

"Do what?"

"Meekly accept what I have to tell you. Where's the fighter I married? The woman who challenged me at every turn?"

A bitter wind blew through her soul. "Is that what you want? Do you want me to tell you what a fool you are? Tell you your quest for justice has turned into a selfish drive to ease your own guilt?"

"No. Yes." He waved a hand between them. "I don't know. Is that what you really think?"

"Does it matter?"

"Yes. You're my wife. What you say is important to me."

"Then tell me what you want to hear, Trey, and I'll say it."

"I want to hear honesty."

"All right. Vengeance isn't ours to take. It's God's. Life is all about loss, Trey. No matter how many times you go after Ike, and even if you kill him with your own hands, you won't bring your wife back."

"Katherine, *you're* my wife."

She shook her head at him. "Not as long as you continue this self-appointed, one-man quest to avenge Laurette's murder. What happened to letting God have the control? Why can't you at least try to show mercy?"

"Mercy?" He spat the word. "Ike Hayes kills without conscience. I can't and won't give mercy to a monster like that."

"Oh, Trey. None of us deserve mercy. That's the point of the cross. God sacrificed His Son for us, not because we deserved it, but out of His grace."

"It's not that simple." She could see the emotions waging a bitter battle in his eyes.

"Yes. Yes, it is."

"I have to do this for us, for our future together," he said, with a frustrated hiss. "I have to finish it."

"Don't lie to me, or to yourself, Trey. This isn't about us. Going after Ike Hayes is for you, only you."

His jaw flexed, but he didn't deny her words. "I can't change what I am."

She would not cry. Not this time, not in front of him. "You think I don't know that? No matter what I say, you're going after that man. You say you want honesty from me? Well, here it is."

She ignored the foreboding that refused to let her go, the feeling that if he left now, he'd never come back. "Part of you will always be locked in the grave with your wife. If going after Ike Hayes is what it takes to set you free, then go."

His expression hardened to an unforgiving glint. "Why can't you understand? This isn't about Laurette. Or even Ike Hayes. It's about justice."

"*Your* justice."

"A threat to justice anywhere is a threat to justice everywhere." The fury in his eyes cut deeper than his words. "I made a vow when I took this badge. I left ranching because this is what I'm supposed to do."

"God calls us to love our enemies."

His eyes hardened. "That's an impossible command."

She felt the blood drain from her face as the truth struck like a fist. Trey wasn't just a man who wore a badge. He was the badge. "Go catch the bad guy."

He wrenched her into his arms. "Katherine, stop worrying. I will come back to you. No matter how many times I leave, I'll *always* come back. One day you'll understand that."

She held herself rigid in his arms, daring not to relax into him for fear she'd start begging. "You seem to think highly of yourself. Didn't you tell me I couldn't control life and death when I wept over our baby's death? Since when did you become immortal, the master of destiny itself?"

He stepped back, glaring at her. "Katherine, I need you to understand."

Katherine dropped her gaze to the floor. "Just go."

"I want—"

She clapped her hands over her ears, blocking the rest of his declaration. "I said, *go.*"

He stalked to the door, tossed her one final frustrated glower, then turned and walked out of the house.

Nursing her fears, Katherine couldn't shake the notion that this was the last time she'd ever see her husband whole again.

Oh, Lord, how will I survive without him?

Chapter Twenty-Two

Trey charged down the front steps of Charity House, saddened that Katherine didn't understand why he had to stop Ike Hayes, personally—with his own hands if necessary. No matter how much he craved the freedom she spoke of, Trey couldn't turn vengeance over to God that easily.

How could offering mercy to the man who'd killed Laurette erase the bitterness and guilt that had driven Trey these past four years?

"Daddy. Daddy." Molly rushed across the yard, screaming his name repeatedly. Skidding to a stop, she favored him with a little-girl glare. "*Daddy*, didn't you hear me calling you?"

Trey forced aside thoughts of Ike Hayes, grinned down at Molly, then ruffled her hair. "Sorry, kitten. Guess I have a lot on my mind."

"You wanna come play baseball with me?"

At the eager look in her eyes, regret split Trey's heart. He hated to disappoint the child, but he needed to confront Ike, face-to-face. "I have to go to work today."

Her eyes widened. *"Oh."*

Although he'd expected this reaction, Trey felt trapped by Molly's accusing stare. The worry trembling on her lips didn't help, either. This agony was what came from caring again.

He hadn't wanted to love this little girl, or her sister, hadn't wanted to start a family. But what he'd wanted and what had happened were two different matters. This child had become his daughter. Her sister had become his wife. Both were now a part of him, in his heart forever.

For that alone, he had to serve up justice to Ike and finally put the past in the past.

As the silence lengthened, Molly's lips dropped into a frown. "You're heading out again, aren't you?"

Unwilling to leave on an unpleasant note, Trey pushed his growing impatience aside and crouched in front of her, knuckled a braid off her shoulder. "Yes, I am."

The look on her face made him sick. It was somewhere between accusation and acceptance. Why was he destined to hurt and disappoint the women he loved most? "Kitten, don't worry. I'll be back soon."

She nodded, her lower lip quivering harder. "I know."

"Do me a favor while I'm gone?"

Her eyes turned wary, and wisdom far exceeding her five years flickered into life. "Sure. I guess so."

Concerned he had to leave like this—without time to make the necessary preparations—he tugged her into a tight hug. "Be especially nice to your sister."

Squirming, she pushed against him. "You are holding me too tight."

Tiny fists beat against his shoulders.

He loosened his grip, blinked back the emotion threatening to pull tears from his eyes. "It's 'cause I love you so much."

She sighed, patted him on the back. "Me, too. But I'm still angry at you for leaving again so soon."

"I know, baby." Kissing the top of her head, he eased her back to arm's length and faced the situation head-on. "But I have to catch the bad guy."

She stepped farther out of his reach, then slapped a hand against her chest. "The one you hate? The one that killed your wife?"

Trey hadn't realized Molly knew so much about his past. "Yes."

She looked at him with a confused expression on her face. "But Katherine says we have to forgive those who hurt us, even the mean ones we hate most."

A part of his soul shattered at the grown-up look on her face, the childlike stubbornness in her stance. But he'd tried Katherine's way already. For her sake, he'd really tried to let God administer justice to Ike Hayes, only to have the snake slither back into his life. Right here in Denver, where his new family lived.

"Say you'll come back soon," she said.

He forced a smile onto his lips. "I will."

"Okay." She bounced toward him again, kissed his cheek. "Bye, Daddy. Stay safe."

"Bye, Molly. I'll try."

In the next second, she was gone, back to her world of carefree play. Her desertion left Trey with an empty feeling in the pit of his stomach. Why couldn't he shake the notion that he was making a mistake by leaving this time?

Because he knew, in his heart, that Katherine was right. He *was* seeking vengeance for selfish reasons, reasons that kept him from making Katherine and her little sister a real part of his life.

But he also knew he'd be stuck in the grave with Laurette forever if he didn't follow through with this perfect opportunity to dole out retribution at last.

Either way, someone would end up hurt today. He prayed it was Ike Hayes.

With that thought, he left the orphanage on full alert.

When Trey arrived at the jailhouse, Logan was waiting for him outside. Relief fell across the deputy's face. "I was just on my way to Charity House to get you."

The premonition he'd been trying to ignore all day settled over Trey. "You got news of Ike."

Logan nodded. "He's at Mattie's. I'm sure of it."

Trey's first instinct was to charge over to the brothel and shoot the man in cold blood. But too much was at stake, and there were too many unknowns yet. He had to deal only in the givens. Or risk making a mistake.

Swallowing his impatience, he focused on gathering the information he needed in order to make the smart move. "Did you see him?"

"No."

"So you're not sure." Relief warred with disappointment, making his temper flare, but he held his reaction under tight control.

"Oh, I'm sure. You see, I was doing what you told me, uh, that is, I was, uh—" He broke off, swallowed, shook his head. "Well, I was getting friendly with one of Mattie's girls, just like you told me…"

Trey didn't see the need to remark on unnecessary details. "Go on."

"Anyway, I heard a commotion in the parlor. By the time I got there, the room was empty."

"Then how do you know—"

"Because Mattie was missing, and so were all the other customers. Usually at this time of day, the brothel's real busy, and Mattie's in the parlor, surveying her domain like she's the reigning queen of the world."

"What does this have to do with Ike?" Trey barked.

The deputy scowled at him. "I was getting to that. From what Lizzie says, only three men can get Mattie alone in her room. And only one can clear out the entire brothel."

"Ike."

"Right." Logan gave him one solid nod. "At first, I thought I'd take him out myself, but then I remembered what you've always told me. 'Never go into an unknown situation alone.' So I was heading to get you, after I checked to make sure Drew was still behind bars."

Trey was impressed. The young deputy had acted on logic instead of emotion. He'd make a fine marshal one day. "You made the right decision," he said, then cocked his head toward the jail. "Is Lassiter keeping watch over our prisoner?"

"Yeah."

Satisfied he had all the information he needed, Trey said, "Let's go."

Tamping down the desire to let emotion rule, he untied his horse, mounted and rode off, barely giving Logan time to get out of his way.

The thundering of hooves followed hard behind him.

Trey pushed his horse faster.

Logan matched the pace.

Side by side, they made short work of the distance between the jailhouse and Mattie's brothel. Turning onto Market Street, Trey slowed his horse to an easy walk. Logan did the same.

With a sweeping gaze, Trey studied the fringes of the district, then turned and focused on the center of the street. Shouts echoed across the street. A man called out to a woman waving from a window in one of the brothels. A horse whinnied in the distance. The smell of cheap perfume, trail dust and stale whiskey wafted together in the air, nearly choking him.

Resisting the urge to cover his nose, Trey counted eleven men on foot, moving in groups of various sizes along the sidewalks. A lone horse and rider meandered down the middle of the street. Trey waited, watched. Patience was his ally now.

A group of three men entered a brothel on Trey's right while two men spilled out of another one on his left. Slapping one another on the back, the new arrivals staggered past a horse and carriage and then entered a well-marked saloon three doors down. Five more men followed them in.

That left three men on foot, one man on horseback.

"We do this right," Trey said to his deputy while keeping his eyes on the horse and rider trotting out of sight.

"I'll follow your lead, Marshal."

"Good." Once the street was clear of the three remaining men, Trey turned his full attention back to Logan. "No heroics today. Shoot in self-defense only."

Logan nodded, his gaze centered on Mattie's brothel, ahead of them.

Trey dismounted, drew his gun and then checked the

load. "I'll go through the front door. You come in from the back. We'll work as a team."

Logan climbed off his own horse. "You can count on me."

While Logan moved into position, Trey focused his thoughts on Ike Hayes and what he'd done to Laurette and their unborn child.

Trey tested the handle on the front door, huffed out a breath when it wouldn't budge. The wood was too sturdy for an easy entry. Stepping back, he unloaded two shots into the lock. He gave the door a hard kick, and it flew inward. The force of the blow dragged Trey and a cold stream of air through the opening.

Charging forward, gun poised at the ready, Trey took quick inventory of his surroundings. The foyer and main parlor were full of flickering candlelight but empty of human activity.

The hurried footsteps and slamming of doors on the upper landing told Trey that Mattie's girls knew trouble was coming.

They were wrong.

It was already here.

As Trey slipped around the perimeter of the parlor, his eyes gauged, searched. Step by step, he inched in the direction of Mattie's room. White-hot rage heightened his senses.

The terror Ike Hayes had spread around the territory ended today.

Trey's breathing came fast and hard, in short, painful gasps. Creeping closer to his destination, he twisted the knob, then eased the door open a crack.

The sick smell of death hit him hard. But before he

could enter the room, Mattie Silks materialized from the other side of the door. With a hard shove, she pushed Trey back into the hallway and pulled the door closed behind her, leaving a small slit.

"I'm busy with a customer, Marshal. You'll have to come back another time."

"I'm here to arrest Ike Hayes. Turn him over to me now and I'll ignore the fact that you are harboring a wanted criminal."

"Well, it ain't Ike in there." Mattie looked at Trey with disgust. "So you can just be on your way, now."

"Right." He began to walk away, then turned back and pushed past her.

"Now see here." She yanked on his arm hard enough to stop his pursuit.

Keeping his eyes locked with hers, Trey shrugged her off and slowly, very slowly, pointed his gun toward the doorway.

"You won't need that." Mattie sighed in defeat as she glanced at his drawn weapon. "He's too ill to fight back."

Ignoring her, Trey shoved into the room. And stopped dead in his tracks.

The pale, sickly man that lay propped in Mattie's bed was obviously fighting for his life. Unable to reconcile his mental image of Laurette's killer and the man before him now, Trey could only stare.

"Are you Ike Hayes?" he asked, aiming his gun at the center of the outlaw's chest.

The man's eyes remained closed, his breathing ragged.

Mattie rushed to the end of the bed, then turned back to glare at Trey.

"Move aside, Mattie."

She spread her arms out as though to shield the outlaw from Trey's wrath. "Can't you see this man is nearly dead from a gunshot wound already? It won't do you any good to shoot him again."

Even a madam was lecturing him now. "Just how close to death is he?"

Mattie took a step forward but kept her arms outstretched. "I don't know."

"Then go fetch Shane Bartlett, and he'll tell us for sure."

Mattie didn't respond, just stood rooted to the spot as she looked around the room, like she was searching for an answer out of the empty air.

Trey hissed out a warning. "I suggest you go now, before I lose my patience entirely."

Mattie's eyes widened at the threat. She dropped a quick glance to his gun, then whipped her gaze back to him. "Maybe I will go see if I can find the doctor."

"You do that."

"Right." She kept her unblinking stare locked on Trey's weapon as she edged out of the room.

Alone at last with his prey, Trey watched Ike struggle for every wheezing breath.

How could this sickly, thin shell of a man be the murdering criminal Trey had hunted for four long years?

Of course, evil came in many forms. Trey refused to be fooled by the pathetic picture the outlaw made.

"Wake up, Ike. It's judgment time."

Red-rimmed, faded blue eyes blinked slowly open.

Trey was instantly struck by the oddity of the gaze staring back at him. Had Laurette looked into the same wicked, empty eyes? Had she felt terror rather than the rage racing though Trey?

"Ike Hayes?" he asked, surprised his voice came out as steady as it did.

"Who wants to know?" The man had the stupidity to shift toward the bedside table, where a six-shooter lay just out of his reach.

Trey cocked his pistol. "Go for that gun and you're dead."

Ike froze, his hand hovering near the weapon. Trey could see the outlaw's mind working, eyes shifting, hand trembling as he calculated the time it would take him to reach his gun and shoot.

"We both know you won't make it. Not with my weapon already cocked and aimed."

"Maybe I want to go down fighting."

Trey disabused him of the notion with a single shot. The bullet hit the lamp on the bedside table and shattered glass over Ike's entire forearm.

Ike's gaze turned wild, frantic, but eventually he raised his hand in the air, palm facing forward.

"Wise decision," Trey said. "Now let me see your other hand." Before Ike could move, he added, "Nice and slow."

"You ain't got the guts to shoot me," Ike snorted, his chest rising and falling with every ragged breath he took.

The need to kill rode him hard, but Trey forced cool indifference into his heart. He had precious little time before Logan joined them. Trey could shoot the outlaw now, for Laurette and all the other innocent victims the man had killed. No one would doubt the why behind Trey's actions.

Liking the idea, he felt his finger quiver on the trigger, but he staved off the hunger for blood. Barely.

Poised between past and future, Trey narrowed his choices down to two: offer mercy or administer vigilante justice.

Which would bring freedom fastest? Which would bring the longest-lasting relief?

As though sensing Trey's predicament, Ike snarled, "Are you going to stand there pondering what you *want* to do, or you gonna have the guts to do it?"

Trey's hand began to shake from the control it took to remain impassive.

What was taking Logan so long?

Ike's hand shifted an inch closer to the table where his gun lay. Trey stepped toward the bed. The driving need for justice overwhelmed all other thought. This man had killed Laurette. Killed her with ruthless intent, uncaring of the shattered lives he'd left in the wake of her death.

"This situation presents an unparalleled opportunity." Trey lifted his gun, his vision going black from hatred. "I can end both of our pain with a single shot."

"I must say, there's not much to criticize about your performance." Lacking any signs of fear, Ike laughed, then broke into a fit of hacking coughs.

Once the coughing was under control, Trey aimed dead center of the man's head. As he stared into Ike's evil eyes, all hope of offering forgiveness and "turning the other cheek" washed out of Trey, leaving behind only the cold, hard need to seek vengeance with his own hands. For Laurette. For their unborn child.

For himself.

"I'm sending you straight to Satan's playground," Trey said.

"No need to rush things." A smile slid onto his lips as he focused on the gun pointed at his head. "I'll be there soon enough."

Trey began to pull the trigger, but a soft, willowy thought of Katherine tugged his finger away from the metal.

Trey shut his eyes and tried to concentrate on his bride. But, still, his hand itched to finish the deed he'd waited four long years to accomplish.

It won't bring Laurette back....

Katherine's words echoed through his head, knifing through his white-hot anger.

Vengeance is mine, the Lord said...

The command stopped Trey cold. What was he doing? He was about to kill in the same manner as had the man lying in the bed before him.

In that moment Trey knew he'd *never* be free if he killed Ike in cold blood.

Freedom would only come from letting go of his hatred.

Trey finally understood the healing power of giving mercy where it wasn't deserved. And from now on, he would leave final justice up to God. But just as he lowered his weapon, a shot rang out.

A burning sting spread through Trey's right arm.

Pain exploded in his head.

He paused. Staggered backward. Lifted his gun.

Another shot rang out.

Trey's hand went limp, and his gun slipped from his fingers. Instinct had him dropping to the floor as another shot blew toward him.

This one hit Trey high on the shoulder.

Ike's laughter rang shrill and cold-blooded, and was the first thing Trey heard as he swam out of the vicious black pain in his head.

Trey reached for his gun again, just as Logan burst into

the room. With a split-second sweep, the deputy took in the situation, shifted left and jumped on Ike.

Before Trey could scold his deputy for rushing into open fire, a numbing blackness consumed him. This was it, then.

The end of the fight.

But was God taking him to heaven? Or sending him to hell?

Chapter Twenty-Three

From the moment Trey left Charity House, Katherine hadn't been able to shake the notion that he was in trouble. And this time it was more than a selfish fear based on lack of faith.

It was a certainty.

So when the news came that her husband had been shot in the process of capturing Ike Hayes, her greatest concern was that she wouldn't get to him in time. That she wouldn't be able to tell him how much she loved him, and how sorry she was that she'd sent him away angry.

Oh, Lord, I pray Trey's wounds aren't serious. Forgive me my insecurities and lack of faith in Your will for our lives together. Please, please, give me another chance to show Trey how much I love him.

As she waited on the front lawn of Charity House for Marc to bring the wagon around, she continued praying, silently, fervently, asking the Holy Spirit for the words when her mind went blank from her overwhelming fear.

Finally, the sound of horse hooves broke through her

prayers, and Marc pulled to a stop right in front of her. His set expression showed the same concern and apprehension she felt in her own heart.

"Don't worry, Katherine." He hopped down and came around to her side. "Logan said it was just his arm."

Katherine nodded, petrified the deputy had skipped over the details of Trey's injury for fear she wouldn't be able to handle the truth. What if his injury was life threatening?

No. The Lord commanded her to "Fear Not." For Molly's sake, as well as her own, she put on a brave face and pretended all was well.

Kneeling in front of her little sister, she swept the hair away from a tearstained cheek. "Don't worry, Molly, I'll bring Trey home. We'll get him well, just like you two helped me."

Molly's face collapsed into a mutinous expression. "Don't want to stay," she whined, taking a shuddering breath after she spoke. "I want to go with you."

"We've been through this already. You have to stay with Laney."

"*No.*" Molly stomped her foot, becoming the unruly child she'd been the day they'd argued over a bath. "I want to go with you."

Katherine held on to her temper. Barely. "Mattie's isn't a place for little girls. Marc and I are going to bring him home, as soon as Dr. Shane finishes stitching up his wounds."

Molly's face turned red with rage, and she opened her mouth and screamed. At the top of her lungs. Loudly. Uncontrollably. Barely taking breaths in between.

Katherine had seen her share of tantrums, but nothing

quite like this one. She looked helplessly to Laney, then to Marc.

Laney sighed, lifted her shoulders. "I don't know what to tell you."

Molly raised her voice even louder. "I want to see my daddy."

Marc touched Katherine's sleeve. "You might as well let her come. She'll just make herself sick. And that won't do anybody any good, especially not Trey."

Realizing this was not a time to play the stern parent, Katherine nodded. "All right, Molly. You can come with us."

It took a moment for Katherine's words to sink in, but once they did, Molly sucked in a deep gulp of air. Blinked. Then grinned through her tears. "I get to see my daddy first."

"That, young lady, is out of the question," replied Katherine.

Molly opened her mouth to start screaming again, but Katherine wouldn't have it. "If you so much as make a squeak of protest again, you're not coming with us."

Molly's mouth gaped open, but mutiny soon rose in her gaze.

Little sister eyed big sister. "No," Katherine said.

Molly's eyes darted to Laney.

Laney shook her head. "Don't do it, Molly."

Molly shot a silent appeal to Marc.

"You're on your own if you scream again," he said.

Pursing her lips, Molly said, "I'll be second, after Katherine."

Katherine lifted the little girl into her arms, kissed her on the cheek. "Good choice, Molly." She hugged her tightly against her. "Now let's go get our Trey back."

* * *

Trey sank into the blessed softness of the pillow beneath his head, gritting his teeth as Dr. Bartlett sewed up the last wound on his shoulder.

"I'm almost done, Marshal."

Trey nodded through the agony, taking each sliver of pain as his due. Considering the situation, he was fortunate to be alive. According to the doctor, he'd been unconscious for over an hour. During that time Logan had dealt with Ike Hayes's arrest and subsequent journey to his new residence in the Denver jail. In the meantime, Dr. Bartlett had orchestrated Trey's transfer to this room in the back of the brothel.

Trey knew he owed his deputy his life. No amount of thanks would be enough. And no amount of apologizing could erase the agony he'd put Katherine and Molly through in his quest for vengeance.

Katherine had warned him that vengeance was God's alone. He'd even agreed with her, in theory. But when he'd had an opportunity to confront Hayes face-to-face, he'd taken it.

In the end, Katherine had been right to worry. Trey had been so consumed with hate, he hadn't taken the precautions to protect himself.

Now, as pain screamed through his body, he realized his mistake. He wasn't in charge of his own life. He'd never been. God was the only one who controlled a man's destiny. Trey just hoped it wasn't too late for atonement.

Lord, forgive my pride and arrogance. I've lived with a hard heart these past four years. Help me to change.

Dr. Bartlett tied off the last stitch. "Okay, Marshal, that should do it."

"Thanks."

"It's going to hurt like the dickens for the next week or two."

"Nothing I don't deserve."

Dr. Bartlett didn't respond. Instead, he gathered his things, dropped various instruments into a black leather bag. "Just make sure you keep the wounds clean and free of infection."

He turned, then pinned Trey with a glare.

"What?" Trey asked, knowing he didn't really want the answer.

Shaking his head, Dr. Bartlett sighed. "Just get well."

Trey squeezed his eyes shut a moment, flinching at the underlying warning. "I will. For Katherine and Molly."

Dr. Bartlett nodded, his eyes holding a solemn expression. "They deserve nothing less from you."

Before Trey could comment on *that* remark, Katherine rushed into the room, looking wildly around her. She appeared frantic, out of breath. And he'd done that to her.

Her gaze finally connected with his. *"Trey."*

She seemed to put all her love, worry, anger and affection in that one word.

Trey lifted his head to greet her, but in his hurry, he shifted his arm at the wrong angle, and pain exploded through him. Gulping through the agony, he collapsed back onto the bed. "I'm sorry, Katherine."

She hurried to his bedside, her eyes filling with tears. "Oh, Trey." She looked at his torn shirt and gasped. "There's so much blood."

"It's not as bad as it looks," said Trey.

Dr. Bartlett, brutally honest man that he was, had the audacity to offer his professional opinion. "Actually, it *is* as bad as it looks. If he gets an infection, he'll lose the whole arm. Maybe even his life."

Worry flickered in her eyes but was instantly replaced with steely determination. She knelt beside Trey and brushed her fingers along his cheek, the tender gesture belying her heated tone. "I'll nurse him back to health myself."

As Trey touched her lips with his good hand, she captured his wrist and sighed. "I love you, Trey."

Pleased with her declaration, he gave her one of his rare smiles. "I love you back, Katherine."

Dr. Bartlett cleared his throat. "I'll just leave you two alone."

Trey waited until they were alone before speaking his heart. "Once I'm well, I want us to buy our own house and start our new life together. You, Molly and me."

A spark of hope welled into an inferno in her eyes. "I like that idea."

With his good arm, he pulled her onto the bed with him, winced, swallowed hard, then smoothed his fingers through her hair. "Walk in faith with me, Katherine. Let's take life day by day. Revel in what we have, and don't worry about what we could lose."

She shifted off the bed, knelt before him and took his hand in hers. "First, help me to understand why you went after Ike Hayes. And I won't ever bring it up again."

After all they'd been through, he needed to tell his wife the truth. Only then could they move forward. "You were right, Katherine. By seeking vengeance, I kept Laurette alive in my heart."

He saw how painful this was for her to hear, but she urged him on anyway. "Go on."

Katherine Taylor Scott was the bravest person he knew. He wanted to follow her lead. "Because I wasn't able to save her, I thought if I avenged her death, I could make it right."

Her warm fingers rubbed his palm. "Oh, Trey, what happened on your ranch wasn't your fault."

He blew out a long breath. "I thought God had abandoned me that day. I still don't think I've completely forgiven Him, or myself, for what happened. Change that drastic doesn't come quickly. But I want to find my way again."

Her gasp of hope tore through four years of well-laid defenses.

"I had the chance to shoot Ike, but I walked away."

"Oh, Trey. You gave him mercy, only to be shot for your efforts." Her eyes were glazed with worry.

"I got careless. If I had been less driven by my hunger for blood, I wouldn't have let my guard down."

She gave him a soft smile. "That's one mistake I'd like to ask you not to make again."

She looked so flustered and beautiful and full of love for him. How could he not love her with all his heart? He inhaled, exhaled slowly, until his breath became normal again.

"From this point forward, I'll leave vengeance to God," he said. "Even though I'm still an Old Testament man at heart, I'm working on the rest."

"Through Christ, all things are possible, my love."

"Yes. *Yes.*" He lifted her chin, commanded her gaze. What he had to say was too important for her to miss. "Every time I face a gun, I know I risk my life. More importantly, I now realize just how much my death would hurt you."

Her eyes filled with tenderness and love. "Yes, Trey, your death would hurt me, as much as Laurette's has hurt you."

Why had it taken him so long to see the truth? "I'm sorry, Katherine."

The sheen of tears in her eyes spoke of acceptance, forgiveness…trust.

Certainty filled him.

They'd come so far. But the next step was his alone. "I'm giving up my position as a U.S. marshal."

Her eyes widened. "You're what?"

He shifted uncomfortably under her glare. "You heard me. I won't risk dying and leaving you and Molly alone."

She smiled at him, but the silent accusation in her eyes told a different story. "So you would quit for Molly and me?"

How could he find the words to tell her she made him want to be a better man? The man he'd thought he'd buried with Laurette. "By resigning my position as marshal of this territory, I let go of Laurette. And I commit to you and Molly, once and for all."

She angled her head at him, blinking back tears. "You'd do that for us?"

Trey had no more defenses left. "Yes, and for our future together as a family."

She dragged in an uneven breath, swallowed and then gave him a nod. *"No."*

"You— What did you say?" He shot up in the bed, ignored the pain shooting through his arm. "But I… We…"

"Stop sputtering, Trey. As much as I appreciate the gesture, you can't resign. The territory needs you, and when you offered Ike mercy, you let the past go at last."

He released a short hiss. "What if I die?"

She threw his own words back at him, the ones he'd used on her that first time, in Marc's study. "One day, we all die."

"That's not what I meant."

"I know what you meant. And, if that awful event happens, then I'll mourn you for the rest of my life. But until that time, we must live every moment together. Fully. Completely. As a family. For however long our forever turns out to be. We must put our future in God's hands and live one day at a time."

"You're sure?"

"You wouldn't be the man I love if you weren't also a federal marshal."

He hooked a tendril of her hair around his finger. In spite of his sins, God had blessed him with a woman to love not once, but twice. The first had been the delight of youth and dreams, while the second was a strong, mature love that would last the rest of his life.

"I'm still an insufferable, mule-headed pig," he said, unwilling to leave anything unsaid.

"I love you anyway, *Marshal* Scott."

With his good arm, he pulled her into his embrace, then smiled into her hair. "You've made me a happy man, Mrs. Scott."

Molly sprinted into the room, skidded to a stop when her eyes landed on Trey. "Daddy?"

Trey kept Katherine clutched against his chest, but he gave Molly a huge smile. "Hi, kitten."

Molly tore around the side of the bed and peered at her sister. "What's Katherine doing to you?"

Trey chuckled, then turned his expression serious. "She's hugging me."

Two little eyebrows lifted over wide eyes. "Do you want her to hug you?"

"Oh, yes. Means she loves me."

Molly shifted from foot to foot, then peered around Katherine again. "You know, Daddy, I love you, too."

Trey opened his arm wider, his heart filling with joy. "Then you better join us in this hug."

Molly bounced into his embrace, wrapping her arms around him and her sister.

With a big smile on his face, Trey pulled his women close and accepted the first in a lifetime of hugs.

Epilogue

❦

Six years later

Ethan Wendell Scott IV pressed his compact little body closer to his big sister. "You gotta save me, Moll. I don't wanna take no stinkin' bath again this week."

Those big round eyes and trembling lower lip reminded Molly of her own predicament six years ago. "Don't worry. I have a plan."

"That's what you said the last time."

"Well, this time it's a good one."

He nodded in satisfaction, grinning up at her with little-brother devotion. "I knew I could count on you."

Molly grinned back. Ethan was her favorite little brother, even if he was her only little brother.

But, really, what's not to love? she thought. The little boy could spit as far as any of the Charity House orphans and twice as far as she could. In her book, that made him pretty special.

Trying her best to look stern, she glowered at the big

man looming closer and closer. She couldn't help but think her dad got bigger and handsomer and kinder every year. One day she wanted to marry a man exactly like Trey Scott.

Not that she'd admit it now, when he'd turned into the stinkin' enemy. She scooted her brother behind her, mutiny twisting in her heart. No one would stand in her way as she protected the boy.

"You can't have him," she warned. "I mean it."

Stopping inches in front of them, Trey widened his stance, then settled into the standoff as though he had all the time in the world. "Hand him over."

"Never."

As they continued to stare at one another, Molly allowed a rebellious smile to lift the corners of her lips. A swift glimpse to her left revealed an opening in the hedge. Mentally, she measured the dimensions. The hole was the perfect size for a forty-pound boy and his eleven-year-old big sister.

"We're getting out of here, Ethan," she whispered from the corner of her mouth. "Just follow me."

Inching across the grass, Molly tugged her little brother toward freedom.

The enemy matched them step for step.

Bending forward, Molly lowered her voice. "Looks like I'm going to have to take out Dad. You make a run for it on your own. 'Kay?"

"But what if Momma catches me?"

Molly winked at him. "Don't worry about her. Her belly is too big, what with the baby almost here. She'll never keep up with you if you pump your legs real fast."

Chuckling, Trey pulled around to the left, effectively closing off their escape. "Don't even think about it."

"Stay back," Molly ordered, pressing Ethan tighter against her. "I'm warning you…"

Trey glanced to his right, then let out what sounded like a regretful sigh. "Now you're in for it. Here she comes."

Molly threw her own gaze in the direction of their house. Her sister was bearing down fast.

Determined to remain focused, Molly leveled a look on Trey that she'd practiced in the mirror for nearly a year now. It was the same one Katherine gave the students at school when they wouldn't listen to her. Molly just hoped it worked on U.S. marshals turned dads.

"I'm taking Ethan to the Charity House baseball game, and that's the end of it," Molly declared.

"Oh, no, it's not," Katherine said, drawing to a stop next to her husband.

Shifting her attention, Molly snarled at the woman who had become the best mother a girl could have—when she wasn't trying to force the bath issue, of course. "I promise we'll be home before dark."

Katherine sighed, then shared a look with Trey.

He lifted a shoulder. "I tried to warn her," he said, as though that was the end of his responsibility in the matter.

Molly grinned. Sometimes her dad could be such a man.

Shaking her head, Katherine turned back to Molly. "You two can go to Charity House after his bath. Not before."

Ethan chose that moment to voice his opinion, by stomping his foot and declaring, "But I want to go now."

Katherine snorted and then turned to Trey. "This is your fault, you know."

He glanced to the heavens and sighed dramatically. "I

know, I know." Wrapping his wife in his embrace, he shifted so the baby didn't get in the way, then smiled down at her, affection glittering in his eyes. "It's *all* my fault."

Katherine smiled in return. "You know I can't resist a man who admits when he's wrong."

"Oh, I was wrong." He dipped his head toward hers. "I was *very* wrong."

Molly snorted. "You two aren't going to kiss, are you?"

They answered in tandem. "We certainly are."

"Oh, honestly," said Molly.

Ethan mimicked her, adding five-year-old enthusiasm to the words. *"Oh, honestly."*

Molly ruffled his hair. "Our parents are so strange."

"Yeah, strange," echoed Ethan.

Katherine pulled out of her husband's arms and settled back into the fight. "Surrender, you two."

Cornered and nearly out of ideas, Molly appealed to the man who'd defied her sister six years ago on her behalf. "Do something, will ya?"

Trey gave her a pitiful look. "Sorry, kitten, I'm going to have to agree with my wife this time."

So be it.

"All right, Ethan," Molly whispered in the little boy's ear. "We're going to make a run for it."

A low whimper slipped from his lips. "But, Moll, they'll catch us. They always do."

Molly looked to the heavens, sighed. Little brothers were so unforgiving of a few big-sister mistakes. "Hold on tight, kid. I'll show you what I mean."

Balancing on the balls of her feet, Molly tucked Ethan firmly in the crook of her arm. Leading with her shoulder, she charged forward. With the element of surprise on her side, she made it five whole steps without incident. But then she slipped and fell to her knees.

Next thing Molly knew, both she and Ethan were lying flat on their backs, a parent holding each of them down.

"Should we attack?" Trey asked Katherine, a look of sheer joy on his face.

Katherine's answering chuckle floated through the afternoon breeze. *"Absolutely."* She grinned down at Molly. "And this time we're finishing them off."

In a blur, fingers poised, then went swiftly to work. Ethan squealed in delight, enjoying their defeat entirely too much—the little traitor.

Molly Taylor Scott was made of sterner stuff. She clamped her lips shut, controlling the urge to laugh. "How many times have I told you," she gritted through her teeth, "I'm not ticklish?"

Undaunted, hands worked quicker, fingers searched and jabbed unmercifully. And then, just like every other time, Ethan did the unthinkable. He joined the enemy.

"Surrender, Moll," he said and started tickling her feet.

Molly bit down on her lower lip, but then someone went for her bottom left rib, and she couldn't control herself any longer. Letting out a hoot of laughter, she said, "You got me. I surrender."

Ethan jumped up, bounced around the yard, with his hands waving in the air. "We won, we won."

Molly shook her head at him. "You are such a turncoat."

Her voice belied the harshness of her words, holding all the affection she felt for her little brother. Even if he didn't know the difference between the good guys and the bad guys, he was still a pretty good kid. Most of the time.

Just like Katherine always said, God had blessed them

all. But especially Molly. Her heavenly Father had given her the perfect family for her—a loving sister-turned-mother, a devoted, hardworking father and a feisty little brother, with another sibling on the way.

A day didn't go by when she didn't offer up thanks. *Thank You, Lord. Oh, thank You!*

Her dad helped her stand, hugged her to him. "Cheer up, kitten. Even the best warriors lose a battle or two."

Joining the embrace, Katherine squeezed in from behind. Little Ethan wasn't to be left out. He hopped on his dad's back, then grinned down at Molly over his shoulder. "You know, Moll, you were right about what you said this mornin'."

Molly twisted so she could look into little-boy eyes. "I was?"

"Yeah." He eyed his mother, then his father, then turned back to her. "We have the best parents in the whole world."

She tightened her hold, secure in the midst of her family's love. "We do, baby brother. Oh, we do."

* * * * *

Dear Reader,

Thank you so much for choosing *The Marshal Takes a Bride*, the first book in my Charity House series. I hope you were inspired by the story of two people becoming one in God's eyes and the healing power of family.

Speaking of family, I have a confession to make. I'm a daddy's girl. I adore my father and couldn't imagine my life without him in it. That's why, when I realized how deeply wounded Trey had become and how far he'd wandered from his faith, I knew I had to give him a little girl of his own to love. After all, what better way for a hardened, vengeful lawman to learn about childlike faith than through the example of a child?

But that's not all Trey needed to learn. He needed to learn how to accept the love of a godly woman before he could accept his Savior's unconditional love for him.

I hope you enjoyed reading about these three wounded souls and their journey toward becoming a devoted, loving, albeit untraditional family.

I have one more confession to make. I love hearing from readers. If you wish, please contact me through my Web site, www.reneeryan.com, where you can also read about my upcoming releases in the Charity House series.

Blessings,

Renee Ryan

QUESTIONS FOR DISCUSSION

1. In the opening scene, Trey battles Katherine over Molly. Why do you think he fights so hard to protect the little girl from a seemingly harmless event in her life? Why do you think Katherine fights back just as fiercely?

2. For all intents and purposes, Katherine is a single mother. Why is she working so diligently to create a safe home for Molly and herself? Has she achieved her goal? Why or why not?

3. Why do you think Molly gravitates toward Trey and not the other adults in her life? Why do you think Trey gravitates toward Molly and Katherine?

4. Why do you think Katherine brings out Trey's protective instincts? Why do you think he feels guilty over the fact that he is drawn to Katherine, even though his wife and unborn child have been dead for four years?

5. Katherine is afraid of Trey because of what happened to her two years ago. How does Trey add to her fear? How does he help her eventually overcome her fear?

6. Charity House provides a home for children the more respectable orphanages in the territory have turned away. As a result, do you believe it is easier or harder for the children to believe in the redemptive power of God? What impact do you think the Charity House adults have on the orphans' faith?

7. Trey originally proposes to Katherine in order to protect her virtue. What does this reveal about his character? What does Katherine's refusal reveal about her feelings over her own difficult past?

8. Trey accuses Katherine of using her Christianity as a shield. Is he right? Why do you think Katherine is afraid to take a chance on Trey? Are her reasons valid? Why or why not?

9. Trey has refused to walk inside a church ever since well-meaning Christians told him his wife's death was part of God's will for his life. Is that an understandable reaction on Trey's part? What would you have said to him? How would you have said it?

10. Jesus calls Christians to a childlike faith. How does Molly exemplify such a trait? What is her impact on Trey and Katherine's faith? In terms of your own faith, what have you learned from the children around you?

11. What is Katherine's role in helping Trey let go of his drive for vengeance? How does she inspire him to show mercy to his enemy? What impact does that act of forgiveness have on them both?

12. What do you think Trey, Katherine and Molly have learned about love and family by the end of the book?

Turn the page for a sneak peek
of RITA® Award-winner
Linda Goodnight's heartwarming story,
HOME TO CROSSROADS RANCH.
On sale in March 2009
from Steeple Hill Love Inspired®.

Chapter One

Nate Del Rio heard screams the minute he stepped out of his Ford F-150 SuperCrew and started up the flower-lined sidewalk leading to Rainy Jernagen's house. He doubled-checked the address scribbled on the back of a bill for horse feed. Sure enough, this was the place.

Adjusting his Stetson against a gust of March wind, he rang the doorbell, expecting the noise to subside. It didn't.

Somewhere inside the modest, tidy-looking brick house, at least two kids were screaming their heads off in what sounded to his experienced ears like fits of temper. A television blasted out Saturday-morning cartoons—SpongeBob, he thought, though he was no expert on kids' television programs.

He punched the doorbell again. Instead of the expected *ding-dong,* a raucous alternative Christian rock band added a few more decibels to the noise level.

Nate shifted the toolbox to his opposite hand and considered running for his life while he had the chance.

Too late. The bright red door whipped open. Nate's mouth fell open with it.

When the men's ministry coordinator from Bible Fellowship had called him, he'd somehow gotten the impression that he was coming to help a little old schoolteacher. You know, the kind that only drives to school and church and has a big, fat cat.

Not so. The woman standing before him with taffy-blond hair sprouting out from a disheveled ponytail couldn't possibly be any older than his own thirty-one years. A big blotch of something purple stained the front of her white sweatshirt and she was barefooted. Plus, she had a crying baby on each hip and a little red-haired girl hanging on one leg, bawling like a sick calf. And there wasn't a cat in sight.

What had he gotten himself into?

"May I help you?" she asked over the racket. Her blue-gray eyes were a little too unfocused and bewildered for his comfort.

Raising his voice, he asked, "Are you Ms. Jernagen?"

"Yes," she said cautiously. "I'm Rainy Jernagen. And you are…?"

"Nate Del Rio."

She blinked, uncomprehending, all the while jiggling both babies up and down. One grabbed a hank of her hair. She flinched, her head angling to one side as she said, still cautiously, "Okaaay."

Nate reached out and untwined the baby's sticky fingers.

A relieved smile rewarded him. "Thanks. Is there something I can help you with?"

He hefted the red toolbox to chest level so she could see it. "From the Handy Man Ministry. Jack Martin called. Said you had a washer problem."

Understanding dawned. "Oh, my goodness. Yes. I'm so sorry. You aren't what I expected. Please forgive me."

She wasn't what he expected either. Not in the least. Young and with a houseful of kids. He suppressed a shiver. No wonder she looked like the north end of a southbound cow. Kids, even grown ones, could drive a person to distraction. He should know. His adult sister and brother were, at this moment, making his life as miserable as possible. The worst part was they did it all the time. Only this morning his sister, Janine, had finally packed up and gone back to Sal, giving Nate a few days' reprieve.

"Come in, come in," the woman was saying. "It's been a crazy morning what with the babies showing up at 3:00 a.m. and Katie having a sick stomach. Then while I was doing the laundry, the washing machine went crazy. Water everywhere." She jerked her chin toward the inside of the house. "You're truly a godsend."

He wasn't so sure about that, but he'd signed up for his church's ministry to help single women and the elderly with those pesky little handyman chores like oil changes and leaky faucets. Most of his visits had been to older ladies who plied him with sweet tea and jars of homemade jam and talked about the good old days while he replaced a fuse or unstopped the sink. And their houses had been quiet. Real quiet.

Rainy Jernagen stepped back, motioned him in, and Nate very cautiously entered a room that should have had flashing red lights and a *danger zone* sign.

Toys littered the living room like Christmas morning. An overturned cereal bowl flowed milk onto a coffee table. Next to a playpen crowding one wall, a green package belched out disposable diapers. Similarly, baby clothes were strewn, along with a couple of kids, on the couch and floor. In a word, the place was a wreck.

"The washer is back this way behind the kitchen. Watch your step. It's slippery."

More than slippery. Nate kicked his way through the living room and the kitchen area beyond, though the kitchen actually appeared much tidier than the rest, other than the slow seepage of water coming from somewhere beyond. The shine of liquid glistening on beige tile led them straight to the utility room.

"I turned the faucets off behind the washer when this first started, but a tubful still managed to pump out onto the floor." She hoisted the babies higher on her hip and spoke to a young boy sitting in the floor. "Joshua, get out of those suds."

"But they're pretty, Miss Rainy." The brown-haired boy with bright-blue eyes grinned up at her, extending a handful of bubbles. Light reflected off each droplet. "See the rainbows? There's always a rainbow, like you said. A rainbow behind the rain."

Miss Rainy smiled at the child. "Yes, there is. But right now, Mr. Del Rio needs in here to fix the washer. It's a little crowded for all of us." She was right about that. The space was no bigger than a small bathroom. "Can I get you to take the babies to the playpen while I show him around?"

"I'll take them, Miss Rainy." An older boy with a serious face and brown plastic glasses entered the room. Treading carefully, he came forward and took both babies, holding them against his slight chest. Another child appeared behind him. This one a girl with very blond hair and eyes the exact blue of the boy's, the one she'd called Joshua. How many children did this woman have anyway? Six?

A heavy, smothery feeling pressed against his airway. Six kids?

Before he could dwell on that disturbing thought, a scream of sonic proportions rent the soap-fragrant air. He whipped around ready to protect and defend.

The little blond girl and the redhead were going at it.

"It's mine." Blondie tugged hard on a Barbie doll.

"It's mine. Will said so." To add emphasis to her demand, the redhead screamed bloody murder. "Miss Rainy."

About that time, Joshua decided to skate across the suds, and then slammed into the far wall next to a door that probably opened into the garage. He grabbed his big toe and set up a howl. Water sloshed as Rainy rushed forward and gathered him into her arms.

"Rainy!" Blondie screamed again.

"Rainy!" the redhead yelled.

Nate cast a glance at the garage exit and considered a fast escape.

Lord, I'm here to do a good thing. Can you help me out a little?

Rainy, her clothes now wet, somehow managed to take the doll from the fighting girls while snuggling Joshua against her side. The serious-looking boy stood in the doorway, a baby on each hip, taking in the chaos.

"Come on, Emma," the boy said to Blondie. "I'll make you some chocolate milk." So they went, slip-sliding out of the flooded room.

Four down, two to go.

Nate clunked his toolbox onto the washer and tried to ignore the chaos. Not an easy task, but one he'd learned to deal with as a boy. As an adult, he did everything possible to avoid this kind of madness. The Lord had a sense of humor sending him to this particular house.

"I apologize, Mr. Del Rio," Rainy said, shoving at the wads of hair that hung around her face like Spanish moss.

"Call me Nate. I'm not that much older than you." At thirty-one and the long-time patriarch of his family, he might feel seventy, but he wasn't.

"Okay, Nate. And I'm Rainy. Really, it's not usually this bad. I can't thank you enough for coming over. I tried to get a plumber, but being Saturday…" She shrugged, letting the obvious go unsaid. No one could get a plumber on the weekend.

"No problem." He removed his white Stetson and placed it next to the toolbox. What was he supposed to say? That he loved wading in dirty soapsuds and listening to kids scream and cry? Not likely.

Rainy stood with an arm around each of the remaining children—the rainbow boy and the redhead. Her look of embarrassment had him feeling sorry for her. All these kids and no man around to help. With this many, she'd never find another husband, he was sure of that. Who would willingly take on a boatload of kids?

After a minute, Rainy and the remaining pair left the room and he got to work. Wiggling the machine away from the wall wasn't easy. Even with all the water on the floor, a significant amount remained in the tub. This left-over liquid sloshed and gushed at regular intervals. In minutes, his boots were dark with moisture. No problem there. As a rancher, his boots were often dark with lots of things, the best of which was water.

On his haunches, he surveyed the back of the machine, where hoses and cords and metal parts twined together like a nest of water moccasins.

As he investigated each hose in turn, he once more felt a presence in the room. Pivoting on his heels, he discovered the two boys squatted beside him, attention glued to the back of the washer.

"A busted hose?" the oldest one asked, pushing up his glasses.

"Most likely."

"I coulda fixed it but Rainy wouldn't let me."

"That so?"

"Yeah. Maybe. If someone would show me."

Nate suppressed a smile. "What's your name?"

"Will. This here's my brother, Joshua." He yanked a thumb at the younger one. "He's nine. I'm eleven. You go to Miss Rainy's church?"

"I do, but it's a big church. I don't think we've met before."

"She's nice. Most of the time. She never hits us or anything, and we've been here for six months."

It occurred to Nate then that these were not Rainy's children. The kids called her Miss Rainy, not Mom, and according to Will they had not been here forever. But what was a young, single woman doing with all these kids?

* * * * *

Look for
HOME TO CROSSROADS RANCH
by Linda Goodnight,
on sale March 2009 only from
Steeple Hill Love Inspired®,
available wherever books are sold.

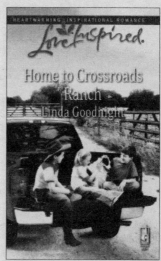

Love Inspired
HISTORICAL
INSPIRATIONAL HISTORICAL ROMANCE

After years of a quiet existence, young widow Jocelyn Tremayne is suddenly embroiled in a maze of deception, trickery and counterfeiting. With no one to turn to for help, Jocelyn seeks out old friend and government agent Micah Mackenzie. As they work together to uncover the truth, Micah is determined to restore Jocelyn's faith and win her trust—along with her heart.

Look for

The Widow's Secret

by

SARA MITCHELL

Available March wherever books are sold.

Steeple
Hill®

LIH82807

REQUEST YOUR FREE BOOKS!

2 FREE INSPIRATIONAL NOVELS
PLUS 2
FREE
MYSTERY GIFTS

Love Inspired
HISTORICAL
INSPIRATIONAL HISTORICAL ROMANCE

YES! Please send me 2 FREE Love Inspired® Historical novels and my 2 FREE mystery gifts (gifts are worth about $10). After receiving them, if I don't wish to receive any more books, I can return the shipping statement marked "cancel". If I don't cancel, I will receive 4 brand-new novels every other month and be billed just $4.24 per book in the U.S. or $4.74 per book in Canada, plus 25¢ shipping and handling per book and applicable taxes, if any*. That's a savings of over 20% off the cover price! I understand that accepting the 2 free books and gifts places me under no obligation to buy anything. I can always return a shipment and cancel at any time. Even if I never buy another book, the two free books and gifts are mine to keep forever. 102 IDN ERYA 302 IDN ERYM

Name	(PLEASE PRINT)	
Address		Apt. #
City	State/Prov.	Zip/Postal Code

Signature (if under 18, a parent or guardian must sign)

Mail to Steeple Hill Reader Service:
IN U.S.A.: P.O. Box 1867, Buffalo, NY 14240-1867
IN CANADA: P.O. Box 609, Fort Erie, Ontario L2A 5X3

Not valid to current subscribers of Love Inspired Historical books.

Want to try two free books from another series?
Call 1-800-873-8635 or visit www.morefreebooks.com

* Terms and prices subject to change without notice. N.Y. residents add applicable sales tax. Canadian residents will be charged applicable provincial taxes and GST. Offer not valid in Quebec. This offer is limited to one order per household. All orders subject to approval. Credit or debit balances in a customer's account(s) may be offset by any other outstanding balance owed by or to the customer. Please allow 4 to 6 weeks for delivery. Offer available while quantities last.

Your Privacy: Steeple Hill Books is committed to protecting your privacy. Our Privacy Policy is available online at www.SteepleHill.com or upon request from the Reader Service. From time to time we make our lists of customers available to reputable third parties who may have a product or service of interest to you. If you would prefer we not share your name and address, please check here. ☐

LIH08R

Love Inspired.
HISTORICAL

TITLES AVAILABLE NEXT MONTH

Available March 10, 2009

THE WIDOW'S SECRET by Sara Mitchell

After years of a quiet existence, young widow
Jocelyn Tremayne is suddenly embroiled in a maze
of deception, trickery and counterfeiting. With no one to
turn to for help, Jocelyn seeks out old friend and government
agent Micah Mackenzie. As they work together to uncover
the truth, Micah is determined to restore her faith and win
her trust—along with her heart.

THE HAND-ME-DOWN FAMILY by Winnie Griggs

Eager to get married, Callie Gray agrees to become
a mail-order bride. But before she even meets her husband,
he leaves her a widow. For the sake of three orphaned
children, her husband's brother, Jack Tyler, offers her
a marriage of convenience. Can she break through his
hardened heart and show him that love, faith and family
are all he truly needs?

LIHCNMBPA0209